RISE OF THE DRAGON MOON

RISE OF THE
DRAGON
MOON

GABRIELLE K. BYRNE

WITHDRAWN

{Imprint}
MAKE YOUR MARK

NEW YORK

[Imprint]
MAKE YOUR MARK

A part of Macmillan Publishing Group, LLC
120 Broadway, New York, NY 10271

Printed in the United States of America by
LSC Communications, Harrisonburg, Virginia.

Library of Congress Cataloging-in-Publication Data is available.

ISBN 978-1-250-19555-5 (hardcover) /
ISBN 978-1-250-19556-2 (ebook)

Our books may be purchased in bulk for promotional, educational,
or business use. Please contact your local bookseller or the Macmillan
Corporate and Premium Sales Department at (800) 221-7945 ext. 5442
or by email at MacmillanSpecialMarkets@macmillan.com.

Book design by Rebecca Syracuse
Imprint logo designed by Amanda Spielman

First edition, 2019

10 9 8 7 6 5 4 3 2 1

mackids.com

To dragons, the tales of their great deeds and misdeeds are the
foundation of their reputations. While humans are meager, bony-bites—
steal this book, and a dragon will undoubtedly hunt down its
treasured tale and eat you.

FOR ALTHEA AND ROWAN—

MY STORIES, MY HEART

STONETREE
FOREST

THE GREAT HALL

HUNTING
GROUNDS

N

W   E

S

ICE BARRENS

THE QUEENDOM
OF GALL

HOUSE OF
REMEMBRANCE

HUNTER'S
SHRINE

NECROPOLIS

ICE BEETLES

SINGING ICE

THE PASS →

FROM THE TALES OF NYA-DREAM-SOWER

The stars are our dreams. Nya, the larger moon, swollen fat with our hidden hopes, casts them out across the bowl of the sky as she travels. If she finds our dreams worthy, they may grow heavy and fall, taking root in the ice to become something more.

Then the Dragon Moon, Nya's father—so small and mean— will make his yearly climb up the edge of the distant mountains. When he does, we must all hide our dreams well, for the dragons will soon rise, and be hungry.

CHAPTER ONE

A year had passed, but the nightmare began the same way it always did. Princess Anatolia crouched, hidden in the icy shadow of the Southern Wall, panting through waves of fear that threatened to cloud her vision. A hundred yards out from the wall, the hunters stood in a line, their backs turned to their homes, as the two dragons swept down, wind rippling across their feathered wings. None of the hunters had fought a dragon. Not ever—yet every thump of Toli's heart told her the hunters would give their last breath to defend the Queendom of Gall.

Her father stood in the front, lifting his sword. Her blood raced as she ran, not away as she should have, but toward him, with a blade in her hand.

The memory—for that's what it was—played out in hazy flashes, as dreams do. His face as he turned to look. The whites of his eyes as he saw her coming. The sound of her fur-wrapped feet pounding the snow. The dragon's scales glinting in Father Moon's green light as it tipped its wing and dived toward her father. The creature's amused voice, like the deep knocking of the ice, as it called out to its partner, then changed course, turning toward her with deadly grace. Her father's shout.

A single talon was half as tall as her, and just as it had happened in life, she saw the dragon's tail coming, too fast, too huge. She took the impact in her gut and ribs, flying backward to smash into the cold, hard wall.

Then—waking, at the foot of the wall, so cold, in a pile of snow and broken ice, her heart still beating like the heels of a hare, and knowing with the certainty of the ice that her father was dead. Gone forever, because of her.

A fissure opened in the ground to swallow her.

She woke.

Sometimes she would lie frozen in bed, willing her lungs to breathe and her heart to beat. The helplessness sometimes stayed with her for days, even weeks.

Not this time. This time, she woke restless, and late for the hunt.

Anatolia's body hugged the ice, the cold biting against her skin despite the layers of fur and leatherleaf. Her numb face hovered just over the surface, her auburn braids like ropes holding down her gloved hands. Though her fingers ached to move, she didn't dare. To be a true child of the ice—a daughter of Ire and a princess of Gall—she must be still, indistinguishable from the miles of frozen wasteland around her.

She resolved to be as silent as the sky.

Toli squinted against the glare of Nya-Daughter Moon's light, gleaming against patches of ice. Far away, and very high up, she made out the dim dot of the almost useless sun. At her side, Sigrid Spar, the Queendom's hunting master, was so motionless she might have been carved from the ice itself. Toli had the fleeting thought that Spar's heart could stop, and there would be no sign. Everything about her mentor was powerful, from her above-average height to the way her heels hit the ice when she walked—as if she had already reached her destination the moment she took her first step, and crossing the space in between was just an inconvenience. Every movement Spar made was a required one. Every word was efficient.

Toli's stomach growled. She flicked her eyes toward her mentor, a sigh escaping before she could stop it.

"Be still," the huntress breathed.

"What if they don't come?"

"They'll come. And if you want your Queendom to have fresh food for the table tonight, we must stay low to the ice no matter how cold you become."

"I'll only let the palest thread of air across my lips," Toli whispered, allowing herself the teasing echo of her stern mentor's teachings.

Spar's mouth hardened, the burn scars that covered half her face darkening. "You are too young for this."

A warm flush raced to Toli's cheeks despite the cold. She should have known it was the wrong time for teasing. There was no right time to tease Spar.

"When does the ice forgive?"

Toli didn't hesitate, answering with the certainness of experience. "The ice never forgives."

"When does the ice forget?"

"The ice never forgets."

"Will you bend the ice's will?"

"It cannot bend. You will break trying."

"Correct. A child of Gall is a child of the ice. You must be centered and certain before taking any action—even a breath. We stalk a herd of thousand-pound creatures. At this time of year, with the dragon-waking so close, their instinct is to run. To get a kill, you must be sure and swift, but sureness in every movement must come before speed. Think before every motion— before each breath."

"I'm sorry. I know. The bison are—"

Spar's dark eyes flashed. "Fast. And sure. And skittish."

Toli fell quiet, fighting the wave of shivers that gathered at her back. It would only prove her mentor right.

The dragons' yearly tithe—usually the last kill of the year— lay frozen in a storage outbuilding. It was a blessing from Nya herself that the bison herd was passing the Queendom again before the dragons woke and the herds went to ground for three months, hiding themselves away deep in the stonetree forest. Food was scarce, and they would need all they could get, so Spar had gathered them for one last hunt.

Beyond the need for food, and beyond the hope that she could grow to walk her father's path as a hunter, Toli had more important reason to hunt. It moved through her like wind howling. She must be ready to defend her little sister, Petal, and the rest of the Queendom against dragon attack, and to train for that, she had to earn Spar's respect. She would never let them take someone she loved again.

Toli let her eyes rise toward Nya, glaring as if she could will the Daughter Moon to stay up awhile longer. In this season she would cast her light for only about six hours a day, rising late and setting early, and she was halfway through her rise. *Hailfire.* If the herd didn't show up soon, they'd be out of time. Once Nya set, the wind would rise, and the cold would be too intense to hunt, even for Spar.

The sudden imagined scent of meat roasting on the hearth, the fat dripping and sizzling on the fire, was so strong it made Toli's mouth water. She squinted against the glare of moonlight on ice and wondered if Wix and the other hunters were having better luck, hunkering somewhere to the east.

A smirk played at the corner of her mouth. Wix had even more trouble holding still than she did. He *was* a better shot though. She stared across the ice to where the fog billowed, rolling like steam across the surface of a stewpot. If the others spotted the herd first, Wix might get a chance to try his hand—if Pendar was feeling generous, that is. Then again, Pendar didn't like to take any chances when it came to putting food on his plate.

Pendar's wide bulk and steady gaze might intimidate a

stranger, but in truth he wasn't just one of the best hunters in Gall, he was also one of the most tenderhearted. He had a contagious laugh and crinkles at the corners of his eyes that were so deep you could fall into them.

Still, if it wasn't Spar who spotted the herd of bison in the fog, it was more likely to be Luca. She had the sharpest eyes—almost as sharp as her tongue—and if Wix did anything to ruin the hunt, the sinewy blonde would be furious.

Toli cringed inside, remembering how just that morning she and Wix had begged to come along on the hunt.

"Twelve is old enough," Pendar had said, wiping ice root from his wiry black beard and clapping Spar on the back. "She's a Strongarm, after all." His eyes twinkled against his warm brown skin.

Spar crossed her arms and scowled. "And if the princess—heir to the throne—is killed?"

Toli twisted the end of one of her braids in a freckled hand as she and Wix waited for the verdict.

"That'd go over well," Luca snorted, whipping her long blond braid over her shoulder.

Pendar shrugged. "You know the princess is hail-bent on fighting dragons ever since her father died. Should the need arise," he hastened to add. "Hunting bison is a baby step. We just need to be sure nothing goes wrong." He met Spar's amber eyes. "You know the queen wants more trained. We need all the dragon-blasted hunters we can get."

Spar stilled.

Pendar was hungry, or distracted, or both, she thought.

People didn't often forget that Sigrid Spar was the only person in the Queendom to survive an actual dragon blast. The burns covering half the hunt master's face, neck, and right arm all the way down to the tips of her fingers didn't let them.

Pendar sputtered, his eyes flicking to Spar's face. "Sorry," Pendar mumbled. "It's true though."

A moment more passed before Spar cleared her throat to acknowledge his words. "I know it, but *you* know that however badly we might need more hunters trained, the queen's feelings about training *her daughter* are complicated."

A gust of biting wind hurtled past, tearing Toli from her memories. Below her feet, the ice spoke its mind in groans and knocks like a living thing, full of complaints and opinions. From the corner of her eye, she saw Spar's attention sharpen. Low fog drifted over the surface of the ice, glowing in Nya's light.

Then she saw them, and her mouth ran dry.

They were about five hundred yards away, and as the herd of gray-white bison appeared, the steam of their breath gusted into the swirling fog, covering their faces. They moved slowly, dipping their jaw-horns to scratch out the green mats of maka within just the top layer of the ice. Toli's mouth puckered just thinking of the bitter taste. For people, maka was starvation food, nutritious but impossible to make taste good.

The bisons' bodies might be mistaken for chunks of ice, or stone, if stone weren't so rare, and if it weren't for the gleam of Nya's light against their white horns as they shifted their weight.

Toli's heart pounded like hooves. She held her breath, trying to calm her pulse. If she gave them away, Spar would never forgive her, and everyone would have to eat dried meat and mushrooms for the next six weeks and hope it was enough.

In front of her, Spar slid forward across the ice, just under the layer of fog. Tiny swirls in the air were all that marked her passage. Luca appeared, sliding up next to Toli. She tipped her chin, her eyes widening, as if to say, "What are you waiting for?"

The bison had poor vision, but an excellent sense of smell. A bull might stand five feet tall, and their first instinct, if they sensed anything was off, would be to run to the forest's edge—straight through anything in their way, including a team of hunters. One well-placed kick could crush bone, and at this time of year, if even one startled, the whole herd would follow. They were always skittish before the dragons woke.

Worse, they might keep running and go to ground in the forest. After today, there would be no more hunting for months. It was too close to the dragons' waking, and nothing was safe with them hunting the ice.

The cold burned as Toli allowed herself a long, slow breath. Her auburn braids dragged over the ice as she dug in her toes and pushed, using the tips of her fingers to pull herself forward across the surface. Luca had disappeared in the fog to her left. Pendar would be somewhere to her right. She caught sight of Spar's feet and, careful not to move too quickly, crept to her mentor's side.

The skin around Spar's dark eyes had gone tight—the telltale sign that her burns were bothering her again—as they often did out on the ice, but Toli didn't let on that she'd noticed. She'd made the mistake of asking about Spar's headaches only once, and had nearly lost her own head as a result.

Spar's eyes gleamed as she turned her face to Toli, her voice so quiet Toli could have convinced herself it was her imagination if the huntress hadn't been looking right at her, her lips moving.

"Prepare as I told you."

Toli froze. "Me?"

Spar's eyebrows moved toward her hairline.

Several moments passed as Toli tried to remember her training over the babble of her thoughts. *Come on, Toli. You've waited a year for this.* A crease had begun to form across Spar's forehead by the time she gave her teacher a stiff nod.

She slipped off her gloves, the freckles on her pale hands dark against the ice. *Which one?* Toli wondered, turning her gaze to the bison. The females and the young would be deep inside the herd. She didn't need to worry about hitting one of them. Few things were as important as feeding her family and her people, but that didn't mean she enjoyed this part. A baby step, Pendar had called it, for someone who dreamed of opposing dragons. She looked over the herd of bison for one that was big, but older, or injured—weaker.

A large bull, his horns gray with age and his back leg stiff from some old injury, stood scraping the ice just outside the fog line. Toli steeled herself.

He's had his time. If I don't take him, the dragons will—or the ice. She lifted a bone-tipped arrow from the quiver at her side, moving to place it in the bow on the ice in front of her.

Quick and quiet as a dragon's wings, she rose into a crouch and sent her arrow flying through the air. She aimed a little high, knowing that the twang of the arrow leaving her bow would reach the bull before the arrow itself. "Sorry," she mouthed with numb lips.

She couldn't see well in the dim, but she imagined the bison as he startled.

The soft thud of his body hitting the ice never came. Her stomach fell as his sharp alarm bellow echoed across the ice. After that, the only sound was the pounding of hooves thundering toward them.

CHAPTER TWO

Toli stared at the bison racing toward her. She had missed. *She had missed!* The thought was fleeting.

Spar cried, "DOWN!" Air whooshed from Toli's lungs as the hunt master threw herself on top of her, covering their heads with her scale-clad arms. Then the bison were everywhere as the herd's instincts drove them back toward the forest.

Toli trembled, cringing as the huge creatures filled her vision, their hooves pounding the ice around her. The ice next to her head shattered, its sharp splinters bouncing off her cheek. She squeezed her eyes shut.

Above her, Spar grunted as hooves brushed her back. If they were lucky, her mentor's dragon-scale armor would be strong enough to deflect the bison's hooves as they leaped past, but Toli knew the hunt master could still be injured, or even killed. She hoped the others were okay as the heat of the bison surrounded her, the acrid smell of fear a bitter taste in the back of her throat.

Breathing hard, Spar rose as the last of the bison ran past, their silhouettes fading as they beat their retreat. The hunt master raised her bow and took aim at the last bull's shifting shadow. The arrow hit its mark and the shadow stumbled, slowing. Spar ran toward it, firing another bolt, and then a third.

The bison fell.

Toli hung her head.

The other hunters emerged out of the fog. At least they hadn't been injured—or worse. Luca strode past, hurrying to Spar's side. Neither said anything to her. Pendar huffed up behind Toli, clapping one meaty hand on her shoulder and giving it a small squeeze. "Thank Nya's stars—you're safe. You'll do better next time, Princess," he said softly.

Spar would tell the queen about this for sure. A surge of panic washed over Toli as she imagined first her mother's face, and then her sister Petal's.

"If there is a next time," she mumbled. *There has to be.* Her heart stuttered. Spar had to keep teaching her in case the dragons attacked. Her father's death demanded it.

Pendar didn't answer, but moved to help the others.

It took all of them to get the bison back to the sled. They'd stopped almost a mile from the hunting grounds so there would be no scent of the foxes to alert the herd. Now as they approached, the huge sled foxes, in anticipation of their share, sent up happy yips into the icy sky, their long tails lashing the air.

At least they had brought Toli's sled. That would save some time. Spar lifted the carved bone horn from the front of the sled, blowing it hard to let the rest of Pendar's team know the hunt was over and they could return to the meeting spot. All that remained was to head back to the safety of the Southern Wall.

The sled had been a gift from Toli's mother just a week ago, for her twelfth birthday. It was special, salvaged from the deep ice fields by one of her great-grandmothers and handed down. Unlike the other handful of box-shaped leatherleaf sleds that had to be replaced yearly, hers was shaped like a long, shallow crescent and made of a dark material she'd never seen anywhere else.

Petal once told her that it was called a ship—that it was from the times before the ice. Toli didn't know if she believed all that, but there was no doubt it was different. The sled was larger and heavier than the leatherleaf sleds, but a team of the Queendom's waist-high snow foxes could still pull it without strain. The front arched gracefully up into the carved head of a dragon. Scales ran along the edges to the back and twisted up into a tail. Like the other sleds, it had two runners of stiff braided leatherleaf stems.

When Queen Una had presented it, just the thought of racing over the barrens in its dark belly made her breathless. It was the kind of sled that even the ice couldn't stop. It was the kind of sled that might outrun a dragon.

If only she could manage to feel like she deserved such a gift.

She hurried to make herself useful, working to load the bison. There would be fresh meat now for several days. She should feel elated, but her fingers were sore with the cold, and her heart ached. She didn't need Spar to tell her she'd endangered them all. *I'll do better next time*, she thought, but the stubborn lump wouldn't leave her throat.

Wix and the rest of the hunters melted out of the fog from the east, jogging to warm themselves. His shadow, lanky and leaning, jumped and shook along the surface of the ice, as if it was eager to go off and hunt on its own. His dark curls stuck out of his braids. She forced a small smile, despite her mood.

He hurried up to her, grinning, his rich brown cheeks flushed. Wix's wide smile offered the only warmth in the vast expanse of ice. "I couldn't see a hail-blasted thing with Justo and Mara blocking my view," he began. "Great work though! It's a big one. They wouldn't tell me what happened. Who took it?"

She fought to keep her smile. "Spar."

Wix came from a carving family, and although ice carving was highly honored in Gall, he longed, like Toli, to become a hunter. She'd known him since they were children. Wix understood her better than any other person could. His grin faltered as he met her green-eyed gaze. "What's the matter?"

"There was a stampede."

His hazel eyes turned dark with concern. "What happened?"

"I missed."

He went quiet, then gave her an awkward pat on the back. "Sorry."

"Yeah."

He tried again. "It's okay. It could have happened to anyone."

She arched a brow at him.

"Well, yeah, okay, not *anyone*. But me. It could have happened to me too."

Toli snorted, but her mouth twitched into the semblance of a true smile as they moved to help load the sled.

Pendar was talking about Rasca's cooking, as usual.

"I bet she roasts it," he said.

"Of course she roasts it," Luca laughed. "You don't expect the woman who cooks for the queen to boil it when it's fresh."

"She cooks for all of us," Pendar chuckled.

"No more ice root," one of the other hunters called from the back of the sled.

"No more ice root," Pendar sighed. "At least not for a few days . . . and maybe she'll make one of her sauces too," he said, and slurped at the thought.

"Pendar," Spar interrupted. "Stop worrying about the nightly gathering and go hitch up the foxes. Toli, Wix—you help him. Everyone else, load up."

"I don't s'pose you could have a word with Rasca, could you, Princess?" Pendar gave her a hopeful look. "The old bat seems to like you well enough."

Wix laughed, answering before Toli could. "Maybe that's because Toli doesn't call her 'the old bat.'"

Pendar shrugged. "I mean it in a nice way."

Toli rolled her eyes at him.

The way back to the Great Hall was quiet. Wix sat nearby, but knew enough to leave her alone. She closed her eyes, and for a moment, her thoughts were whipped away by the wind, unable to keep up. Her shoulders relaxed.

The return trip was slower with the extra weight in the sled's belly, and she was glad for the time. The foxes leaped forward, their narrow forms racing shadows across the dark gleam of the ice fields. Ahead, the dim smudge that was the Southern Wall rose against the horizon.

She could almost hear Wix grinning next to her, but the only real sound was the breath of the foxes, the shushing rush of the sled's runners, and the beating of her heart. Darkness closed in behind them. The stars, each one a dream cast down by Nya-Daughter Moon on her travels, shone in the bowl of the sky. When Father Moon came along, any time now, his green light would obscure many of the dimmer stars as if they were nothing more than Nya's toys and he was gathering them up.

At least the fresh meat would help get the people through the dragons' waking. Her gaze rose to Nya's wide, pale face. Did the Daughter Moon see them, racing for home across the ice? Not for the first time, Toli wondered if Nya had really sent the dragons to Ire herself to heat the planet from the inside. If she did, had she known what it would cost her people—in food and in fear—and in loss? Nya had wanted to keep her creations alive. Toli understood that need. Like Nya, she would do anything to keep the people she loved safe, but couldn't the

Daughter Moon have found some other way? Why did it have to be dragons?

A bitter taste rose in her throat, and Toli closed her eyes. As they skimmed along the surface, she tried to imagine what it would be like to spread out giant wings and ride the lights. Where did the dragons go when they vanished into the stars? Did the aurora actually carry them across the sky, as it seemed?

Her skin prickled as she reprimanded herself. What difference did it make where they went? She knew enough.

They had killed her father.

Every living thing knew their nature and ran. It made no difference that they could think and speak. They were predators, their every thought steeped in the instinct to kill or destroy from the moment they entered the world.

She tightened her grip on the side of the sled until her knuckles ached. One day when they attacked again, she'd show them they had crossed the wrong princess when they killed her father and his hunters. She would deny them everything.

She tried to listen to the rush of the wind, but all she could hear was the grating persistence of her thoughts.

Her father's face, carved among the dead's in the Hunters' Shrine, flashed before her eyes.

They moved north, watching the stonetree forest grow larger as they approached. The hundred-foot-tall trees swept down from the black stone bluff over the Queendom of Gall, spilling across the ice fields and into the east like a shadow. The wind picked up, pushing against the sled as though trying to turn them back. Toli could just make out the hollow, soothing song it sang as they passed by the tubular ice caves pressed between the edge of the forest and the Southern Wall. She shivered. Sometimes she imagined the wind was alive, sending up its angry howls to make the caves ring like bells.

Spar pulled the foxes to a stop just outside the Southern Gate. They stood panting, tongues lolling from their narrow muzzles. The massive blocks of ice gleamed. Huge frozen statues spread out across the top edge of the wall.

Carving families were granted additional food and other items; then each year when the dragons returned to molt, the carvers of Gall competed for the honor of having their statue rise to look out across the ice. Sometimes they were elaborate scenes or fallen hunters. Sometimes they were quiet tributes to the harsh beauty that surrounded them every day.

The one of her mother, the queen, was so detailed it had taken Belgar Walerian himself almost a year to ease it out of the ice, and he'd let no one see it until it was finished—not even Wix, his own son. Of all the statues, only the one of the queen had been allowed to grace the wall for a second year. She loomed above Toli, looking out across the empty landscape.

On the other side of the arched entryway a dragon statue took flight. More statues lined the wall, stretching out until, at the farthest edge, where the wall met the rise of the stone ridge breaking through the ground, there stood the last statue—a delicately carved stack of delicious but dangerous foot-long ice beetles. Toli's stomach was always impressed by the detail, even from a distance, and gave a hopeful growl.

She closed her eyes and allowed herself a small sigh, imagining what it would be like to put a lid on the afternoon, letting the quiet promise of the evening simmer, like one of Rasca's soups, into something better—something perfect.

The sound of Spar's voice snapped Toli back to the reality of her failure. The master hunter passed the reins to Wix. Spar's black dragon-scale armor held pinpricks of starlight. "You take the foxes back to the stable and get them settled for the night. The rest of you tend to the bison." She turned to Toli. "You stay a moment, Princess. I have something to discuss with you."

Her stomach fell. Spar was going to tell her she was done hunting—that she'd ruined her chances and would have to stay home from now on. She could feel it coming like a sickness.

Toli watched the hunters. They were amiable with the prospect of the meal to come as they towed the sled toward the outbuildings at the outskirts of the Queendom. Maybe if she didn't look at Spar, she wouldn't have to hear the disappointment in her mentor's voice.

Wix cast a sympathetic glance at her over his shoulder as he led the foxes under the Southern Gate and into the Queendom.

"Anatolia." Spar's voice was soft, but Toli knew her eyes would be hard.

She swallowed and turned toward the inevitable.

"Your shoulder was too tight. I've told you a thousand times—hold the bow as if it could turn and bite you! Also you shifted your foot after you rose from the ice. The pause cost you. You held your breath! What were you thinking?"

Toli's cheeks heated. Only children and stark beginners held their breath to shoot. "I—"

"The answer is, you weren't. You could have gotten them killed—then where would your Queendom be, with half as many grown hunters to bring in food. People would starve."

"I know, I—"

Spar took Toli's upper arms in a tight grip. "Worse, Anatolia, *you* could have been killed." Spar narrowed her amber eyes. "Why should I continue to teach you? My queen, your mother, would sigh with relief if I refused. Why should I continue to teach you when your stubborn desire to follow in your father's footsteps distresses her?"

Toli's throat was almost too tight to speak. "Because you have to."

Spar's face hardened.

"Because you want to, then. If you don't, I won't be good enough."

The skin of Spar's burns shone in the dim light. Her eyes flickered. "Why should I feed a child's foolish whim?"

"I'm not a child!" Tears filled Toli's eyes. She gritted her teeth. "And you know why," she said angrily. "Because they killed him in cold blood. Because they killed all our best hunters that day, like they were nothing." Her voice rose. "He brought them the tithe—a whole bison that could have fed our people well for days." She tried to blink away the tears, but a single fat drop escaped to roll down her cheek. "You killed one, but one escaped, and—"

Spar's grip relaxed as she met Toli's eyes. "Anatolia—"

"Why did they do it? The queen says they were hungry, that they were out of their minds—but we were hungry too. Why didn't they just take the bison and go, like always?"

Something flashed in Spar's eyes, but then it was gone again, so fast Toli couldn't tell if it was pain, or regret, or just her own imagination.

The hunt master dropped her hands. "We may never know what really drove them to do what they did," she whispered, looking away across the wasteland. "But we know what drove the bison today—don't we, Anatolia?"

The weight of Spar's words settled on Toli's shoulders like a layer of ice, cold and immovable.

On the day her father died, Spar had been the only survivor of the Tithing party. She'd suffered her devastating burns killing one of the dragons, and trying to save the queen's consort—Toli's father. The second dragon had escaped with nothing but a torn wing.

Everyone knew the huntress had never forgiven herself for failing Toli's father, but in all the Queendom, only Spar knew the truth—Toli was the one to blame. Spar knew Toli had been there that day, and she alone had lived through the distraction. The huntress had never said a word about it.

Not to Toli.

Not to anyone.

Toli met her mentor's amber eyes, her throat too tight to speak.

Spar's mouth hardened. "I'm afraid we still have some unpleasant business ahead of us."

Toli's stomach dropped. "Couldn't we . . . not . . . do that?" She hugged herself as she looked up into Spar's face with its ruby burns. She poured all the hope she could muster into her eyes.

The hunt master just arched a brow at her. "I'm sorry, Toli. Your mother has to hear about what happened. You could have been killed. It must be done."

Petal could talk Spar out of it, Toli thought bitterly. Her little sister could talk anyone out of anything.

In the dark times, when the world went cold,

Nya the kindhearted, bright and clever,

Sent creatures born of fire.

Raised a mountain from the frozen sea.

Showed them the task.

Heat in perpetuity. Heat for the living.

Heat for the young.

She placed hearts of fire in them,

And gave them breath of flame.

—Anonymous

CHAPTER THREE

Toli tramped through the Great Hall toward the empty throne. The rhythmic thudding of Spar's steps reminded her to slow down, steady her pace—be calm. Petal was in the far corner of the room by the hearth, surrounded by a gaggle of friends. Her sister's cascade of black hair hid her conversation, but her laugh rang through the rafters. Oil lamps hung along the walls, their light dancing across the floor like fox pups begging to play.

Her mother would make them wait. She made everyone wait. Spar moved to speak with a cluster of young boys playing off to the side of one of the long hearths—no doubt telling them they should still be busy getting peat in, manning the fishing holes, or off in the melt house getting water.

Toli turned back to the throne. Raised on a platform in front of the fire, it cast a long shadow across the floor, flickering in the glow. It was carved to look like the trunks and branches of the stonetree forest. Across the tops of the trees, the head of the Dragon-Mother peered out at them. When the queen sat down, it would lean over their mother's shoulder—a sign of their ancestral debt, and of their perpetual danger. As if they needed the reminder.

Toli fidgeted as Rasca shuffled in from the dimly lit root cellar. The cellar served as a larder for Gall's precious stores of honeywine—fermented from the excretions of stonetree ants and for all the Queendom's food. Rasca's closely watched supplies of dried meat, mushrooms, lichens, ice beetle eggs, ice root, and snowflower stocked the shelves. The efficient and exact records of the Queendom's food supplies were the old woman's pride and joy, and woe to any who entered the storage room without permission.

Years ago, before she'd been given control of the supplies and the cooking, Rasca had been their mother's nanny. The old woman was bent nearly double, and her skin was as pale and wrinkled as an ice root. But though she wore only simple clothes, she needed no other mark of respect than the single white feather in her hair.

Every year when the dragons returned, they would molt, shedding feathers and scales over the stonetrees. Petal often liked to gather them in the forest near the Queendom. Rasca's feather, however, had come from the Dragon-Mother herself and was a gift from Queen Una. Everyone with half a brain took it as a warning. Rasca was valued and for far more than her supremacy at the hearth.

The old woman said something to Petal, and though Toli couldn't make out the words, Petal spun around and hurried toward her. Petite and pale, Toli's younger sister wore silken dresses, all grace and air as they floated around her. Maybe that was how Petal always managed to make walking look like gliding.

She's so quick and light on her feet, Toli reflected. *She would have made a good hunter.* Her sister's spirit was too gentle for that work though, however necessary it was to their survival. A smile snuck across Toli's face as she watched her sister glide, like nightfall in her deep-blue dress, with her black hair flowing behind. She looked like a queen.

The thought made Toli drop her gaze to the scuffs across the tops of her boots.

"Are you okay?" Petal asked. "I heard what happened."

Toli grimaced. "How could you have heard what happened? I *just* got back."

Petal shrugged, her star-blue eyes wide. "Rasca always hears things first." She glanced toward where Spar was lecturing the boys. "Was she mad?"

"Not exactly. More . . . disappointed."

"Oh," Petal whispered, moving closer.

Toli sent a wistful look back at the wide double doors of the Great Hall. Their dark surface gleamed an invitation. It would be so easy to avoid the coming lecture—just push them open and be gone.

She dragged her eyes away. The Daughter Moon would set soon. Then it would be too cold to be out on the ice without shelter. The wind would rise, sharp and bitter, and sometimes strong enough to shred clothing and tear at flesh. Without protection, the nighttime frost could burn skin as surely as dragon fire.

Rasca shuffled to Toli's side, her eyes twinkling as she placed one soft hand on top of Toli's.

Toli let her hopes out in a whisper. "Maybe the queen will let me hunt again."

Rasca cocked her head. "Maybe she will, but your mother's no fool. She'll never let you fight a dragon."

"A dragon?" Petal frowned, and for an instant the rare expression made her a stranger.

Toli blanched. "Who said anything about fighting a dragon?"

Rasca just shook her head. "Defending the Queendom's not for you, girl. Anyway, dragons aren't for killing. They're for keeping our world alive. Use your brain, and turn your thoughts to something else." She let out a soft chortle as she walked away. "Your brain is that mushy thing between your ears . . . in case you forgot."

The old woman's laughter only grew louder as Toli sputtered at her, reaching up to twist the end of her braid. Rasca was almost out of the room when she paused to look back at them. "It's a pity they killed him. Your father was something special, Princess—you'll get no argument from me there, but no one fights a dragon and lives to tell of it."

Spar did, Toli wanted to say. *Spar lived.* She bit her tongue. *Yes*, argued a soft voice in her head, *but what kind of a life does Spar have, really?* The hunt master had never been the same. Her disfigurement was a constant source of pain. There were times, too, when her mood turned dark—slippery and black as the deepest ice. On those days, Spar was more likely to break a person in half than have a conversation.

A tingle of cold foreboding lifted the hair along the back of Toli's neck. It *was* her job to defend her sister and the rest of her people. She began to pace. She had no intention of starting a fight with dragons. She simply had to be able to finish one, if the chance came.

The fact was, if she had to choose between defying their heritage—the stories of the Queendom—and protecting her family and her people, she knew what she would choose. If the dragons attacked again—Spar would say *when* they attacked—she wouldn't hesitate. She had to be ready.

She spun to stomp past the throne in the other direction. Everyone knew Petal didn't have a fierce bone in her body, and thanks to Toli, they had both lost a parent. Protection was the least of what she owed her sister, and she owed her father justice.

Toli shook off her doubts and turned to pace the other way again. Her mother understood the danger. She might be worried for Toli's safety, but she couldn't keep her from doing her part to protect them all. She couldn't keep her from the chance to learn from Spar, at least.

Petal slipped her smaller hand into Toli's as she passed, forcing her to lurch to a stop. She'd been so lost in her own thoughts that she'd forgotten her little sister was there too, watching as she took her anxieties out on the floorboards of the Great Hall. Around them, people came and went, preparing for the evening by bringing water and baskets of ice root through to the larder, or stacking peat bricks along the sidewall.

Petal's fingers wrapped tight around Toli's. A year had passed since their father's death. Petal had been only eight at the time, and Toli, just eleven—too young to affect the outcome. Or so they'd been told, but Toli knew better. Her father would still be alive if it weren't for her.

Petal's face was pale as the ice, her eyes wide. "What did Rasca mean about you wanting to fight dragons?"

"She's just talking." Toli smiled.

Her sister narrowed her eyes, but let it go. "The dragons will be awake again soon."

Toli didn't answer. When the dragons woke, just as they did every year, the queen and a chosen few would take a portion of their food—what her people called the tithe—from Gall and give it to the dragons as a tribute. The dragons would gorge on whatever they could find on the open ice, and for months everyone in Gall would take cover and pray to the Daughter Moon to keep them safe.

Once the dragons flew south, everyone would breathe a little freer, at least for a few months, until they returned again to molt, preparing to hibernate all over again. What would it be like to travel as they did, skimming the world? Where did they go?

Toli twisted her hands and pulled her attention back to her sister.

"What if they do attack us again?" Petal's voice dropped as her eyes met Toli's.

Toli gripped the smooth curve of her bow, her knuckles whitening. "The dragons will be hungry when they wake up . . . and irritable, as always, but the herds have recovered. The hunting is better this year, Petal. The dragons won't be starving like last year. They'll take the tithe, hunt the deep ice, and fly south. They won't need to attack again. And if they do, I swear you'll always have me to protect you."

They were hungry every year though, and everyone knew it. Why had they attacked? The truth was simple: It didn't matter why. Maybe it was just because they could. Maybe it was because all that mattered to them was killing and eating. Spar told her that despite what the story of the Telling said, there was nothing in the dragons but predator.

Her sister gave her half a smile, but Toli thought she saw fear flicker in her eyes. It disappeared as quickly as it had come.

Petal grabbed her hand again, tugging her toward the kitchen. "You should eat something. Have you eaten? You have to take care of yourself, Toli."

Toli shook her off and frowned. "Never mind that. The queen should be here by now. Where is she?"

As if she had just been waiting for her to ask, their mother strode past them like a rush of wind, climbing the dais and lowering herself onto the throne. She wore bison hide and leatherleaf with dragon scale of gold and green. Her hair, long and dark like Petal's, was twisted into a tight knot at the nape of her neck. Toli's stomach dropped, and her gaze fell with it. She studied her feet, fighting the urge to launch into her defense.

Toli twisted the end of her braid. Her mother's face was like a storm, but one glance wasn't enough to know if the queen was pale with anger—or just disappointment. Toli didn't want to know. The first was bad. The second, worse. She swallowed and lifted her chin.

Her mother's eyes shone, but her emotions, unreadable as the ice, would only be revealed in a slow melt. Her words might quench deep thirst or frost bone, but there was no telling which until she spoke them.

Toli was grateful that only a few people came to and went from the Hall at that hour. Nonetheless, Spar had taken one look at the queen's face and ushered those few out—all but Rasca, who no one told what to do. At least they would have a few minutes of privacy.

Wix appeared out of the storage room behind Rasca and assessed the situation between one step and the next. He caught Toli's eye and ducked behind a stack of peat. Spar either didn't notice or decided to let it go. Given her mother's expression, it was probably the latter.

Spar's movements were fluid as she shifted around a pillar and marched toward the queen. "A word, my queen?"

The queen frowned. "What is it, Sigrid? You know I'm here to speak with my daughter."

Spar shifted her weight, her eyes on the floor. "The dragons—"

"What about them?"

"They're up to something."

Toli moved closer, away from Petal, unable to look away. Toli's attention sharpened as she realized what was wrong. Her mentor seemed nervous.

The queen let her breath out with a whoosh. "Not this again. What proof do you have?"

Spar lifted her face to the queen, and her expression was so raw Toli took a step back and bumped into her sister. Petal had moved forward with Toli as if they were tethered together by some invisible cord.

Spar stood taller. "I saw one flying this morning, from a distance."

"Is that all? An early riser?"

Spar paused before she gave a stiff nod. "They've already taken so much—the blood of our hunters, the blood of your companion." Spar held up her scorched palm, the skin tight and shining in the lamplight. "We cannot trust them, my queen. Not ever. This is the proof."

Toli couldn't tear her eyes away. Helplessness rooted her to the floor as she watched her mentor plead. Petal's expression was carefully blank.

She had to do something. Her throat tightened as she forced herself to approach the throne. "Spar's right," she said. "The dragons can't be trusted. We should prepare for them to attack again."

The skin around her mother's eyes pinched, and Toli fought a stab of guilt. Her mother looked tired. "Listen," the queen said. "Both of you. We've lived with the dragons for hundreds of years, perhaps even thousands. In all of that time—"

"They've taken people off the ice before," Spar growled.

The queen tapped a finger on the arm of her throne. "Our law tells us to stay under cover, under the bluff or in the trees when the dragons wake, and again when they return to molt. It's true that on occasion, some have died—if they were foolish enough to venture out in defiance of law and good sense. It's a terrible—"

"We cower here like prey. Is it any wonder they treat us that way?"

"In all those many years, hunt master, they've openly attacked the Queendom only once."

"That we know of," Spar ground out.

The queen's mouth hardened. "Very well. Once, that we know of. We know why they did it."

Petal nodded. "They were starving. The herds were sick, and—"

Toli's hands began to shake. "We were starving too! And we still gave them the tithe. They *killed* Father! And look what they did to Spar! How can you just accept—"

The queen's voice could have frozen burning coals. "Enough, Anatolia." She rose and moved to take Spar's hand, ignoring the huntress's wince as she examined her palm. "The burns still pain you." It wasn't a question.

"Always," Spar hissed, her voice dropping. "And I hear her— the Dragon-Mother. I hear her, whispering in my head."

"What does she mean?" Petal whispered in Toli's ear.

Toli shook her head, leaning into the press of Petal's shoulder against her own.

The queen studied the huntress for long moments before she let go of Spar's hand. "I'll speak to the healer. Perhaps Petal can help gather the herbs she'll need for a soothing balm."

Petal darted forward. "Yes! I can do that! I know exactly where—"

But Spar had already spun away, storming out through the small door at the back of the Hall without another word.

The queen pinned Toli with her bright-blue gaze and returned to sit on the throne. "Now. I have some things to say to you, Daughter."

Toli froze. Words flew through her head, but none of them connected to thought, and none were able to reach her mouth. She nodded.

"There's more to ruling a Queendom than hunting, Anatolia. It's time for you to learn that."

Words stuck in Toli's throat like snow flower burrs. Her father's warm smile flashed in her mind, and the way his eyes would sparkle as the early morning ice crunched under his feet.

She shifted her feet. "I'm not ready."

Her mother's lip curled. "Nonetheless, you must learn. Being the heir is a responsibility."

Toli's voice tightened. "Father told me I would make a great hunter one day." She crossed her arms. "He really did say that. That I would be a great hunter and protect the Queendom—like him."

The queen scowled. "I don't doubt he said it, Anatolia—he saw himself in you. Hunting is important, but there are many ways to protect Gall. As heir to this Queendom, you will learn to excel at all of these tasks. You must learn how supplies are stocked, tracked, and parceled out. You must learn about the tanners, and the carvers—about the weavers and the ice fishers."

Toli glared at her boots. How could she explain to her mother that wanting to walk her father's path wasn't just about glory and adventure on the ice? Didn't she understand that it was about preparing for the worst—about somehow *denying* the dragons something? Protecting what they had left was as close as she could get to revenge. Her father deserved that much justice, at least.

A lump rose in her throat. She would never see his kind brown eyes again. She tried to answer, her voice a whisper. "But Father said—"

The queen sighed, her face softening. "Whatever your father might have said, Anatolia, you're not a child anymore." She waved Toli up the dais's two shallow steps to stand close, her voice dropping as she reached out to grasp both her daughter's hands with her calloused fingers. "Your father was proud of you and he loved you. He wanted great things for you." She let go, tipping Toli's chin so their eyes met. "But he would not disagree with me on this. As my eldest daughter, you must learn what it is to be Gall's queen."

Toli's thoughts spun as she tried to find words to change her mother's mind. She knew there were none. She wanted to scream in her mother's face, but instead, her cold fingers wiped the tears from her eyes.

The queen peered into Toli's face like she was looking for

cracks. "You could come with me for the Tithing. You could do the Telling, even judge the carving when the dragons return to molt—there are many things you *could* do."

Toli hadn't known that despair was so much heavier than anger. It was as though her body weighed three times more than it had a moment before. She shook her head. Of all the things her mother could have asked of her, the Tithing was the one thing she couldn't do. She couldn't celebrate the dragons, couldn't offer them a portion of the Queendom's food. That had been her father's job that day, and they had killed him. She didn't care what the stories said. The dragons didn't deserve the tithe, and the Telling only glorified them.

There was, of course, no way to tell her mother that, no way to explain that even the *thought* of offering a gift to the dragons made her stomach sour—not when it was the sacred duty of their family.

Instead, she crossed her arms. "No. I wouldn't be any good at it."

Behind her, Petal's breath caught.

Her mother's gaze iced over. "Wouldn't be any good—*psh.* You're a Strongarm, and heir to the throne. You've heard the Telling since you were a babe in arms. You could tell the story in your sleep, and the Tithing—"

The blood drained from Toli's face. "I can't give the tithe."

The corners of the queen's mouth pinched into a frown. "This insistence you have—this determination to defy your path—it must stop, Anatolia. The ice cannot bend. It can only break."

"The ice never forgets! I can't give the dragons the tithe. I won't."

Her mother's face grew hard. "You *won't*. I see." Her gaze traveled the back wall of the Great Hall. "Pendar!"

Toli spun, falling back to step down from the dais. Her cheeks warmed. While they had been talking, the hunters had filed in, lining the wall at the back of the hall. Wix had come out from his hiding spot to join them. He gave her a nod, but his expression was grim.

Pendar moved to her side, one hand tugging at his beard. "Queen Una."

The queen lowered herself in her throne, signaling to a fire-keeper that it was time to build up the hearth fires. "Father Moon is rising. The lights will begin and the dragons will wake. We must be ready. Is the tithe prepared?"

"Yes, my queen."

"A whole bison?"

"Yes—a large bull. It has been placed in the butchering shed to thaw."

"Good. Since my daughter refuses to join us for the Tithing, you'll assist me. Choose three more from your team to help. The last hunt is complete. Tonight we'll complete the Telling, and when Father Moon crests the Mountain, perhaps the day after tomorrow we will take the tithe out on the ice. We will be more cautious this year. Once we reach the Tithing ground, I will blow the horn and return to the Queendom. You will remain there, at a safe distance, until they come to take it."

Pendar nodded. "Yes, Queen Una."

"And, Toli."

Toli lifted her eyes from the stonetree boards of the floor. "Yes, Mother," she whispered.

"Now that the last hunt is over, the time has come for you to rise and do your duty as my heir. You *will* recite the Telling this year! Do I make myself clear? Hunting may be part of what you do as heir to this Queendom, but it will not be the whole. The way you're acting, I'm beginning to think—"

Toli fought to keep her voice from breaking. She couldn't just let this happen. "Once the dragons go south, Spar will start her trainings in the pavilion. You can't keep me from that!"

She swallowed the words as her mother slowly rose to stand, gripping the throne's dragon-carved neck with one hand.

"I can do as I see fit, Daughter, and I advise you to *remember* it."

Toli's heart thunked low in her chest, sinking like a prisoner as she struggled to keep breathing.

Petal moved forward a step. "Why now?"

"You're interrupting, Petal," the queen snapped, but her face turned away from Toli.

Petal reached out to give Toli's arm a quick squeeze, then let go.

The queen paced. "It's time. That's all. There are ways to serve Gall other than hunting. I'm tired of repeating myself, Anatolia." Her face eased, and her voice fell. "You remind me of her. Have I told you that? You remind me of my sister, your aunt Rel."

Toli shifted her weight. Her mother rarely spoke of Aunt

Rel, but every now and again, she could glean something about her mother's younger sister besides the fact that she'd died before Toli was born.

"You would have liked her. She wanted to be a hunter too." Her mother's gaze frosted over as she turned back to Toli. "She went out one day to scout the herd and never came back."

"I know, but I'm not—"

"I wish I could give you what you want, but I wish a lot of things. I wish my sister had never left. I wish things were easier for all of us. I wish your father wasn't dead." She straightened. "But the past is like the ice. It will never bend."

"Father wouldn't have made me do this," Toli ground out. "He would have understood."

Pain flashed in her mother's eyes, and Toli cringed. Fear crept through her veins like an animal trying to hide in any dark corner it could find. If her mother knew what she'd done—how she'd cost her father his life—what would she say? She would stop pretending Toli was fit to be heir, but she'd also never forgive her. Their relationship would crack, and the fissure would never seal. Toli forced down her guilt. Her mother's love was too steep a price.

The queen trailed her hand along the back of the throne, her expression thoughtful, as if she could stroke the scales of the Dragon-Mother. Her face was cold again. "Tonight at the evening gathering, you will give the Telling. I'll complete the Tithing myself when the time comes. After that, you'll stay by my side and learn from me. We'll organize food collection in the forest. We'll delegate the ice, water, and peat crews within the wall. You'll help judge the carving and weigh in on any issues or claims of injustice among the people—"

"But that's—"

"Hush. You'll collect lizards and beetle eggs. You'll learn to drill the holes for fishing so that when the dragons hibernate again you can participate in that work."

Petal nodded. "And we can go out and dig ice root in the forest together—like we do every year, Toli."

"But—"

"You may have until I return from the Tithing to do as you choose. Then I will expect you to be as close to me as Nya's light is to the ice." She moved to leave.

Toli stepped closer as if she might block her path. "The dragons will awake anytime."

"Exactly. The time to hunt is over. Your time to hunt . . . is over."

"What about Petal?" Toli pleaded. "I need to be able to protect her."

Petal frowned. "I can take care of myself."

The queen gave Petal a gentle smile. "No one's asking you to do that, Anatolia. Your sister knows her duty, and she's stronger than she looks."

Toli stood a little taller, fear etching her words. "And if the dragons attack again?"

Their mother's small smile faded to nothing. "And if the dragons attack," she said without looking away, "what I've told you to do or not to do won't matter anymore, but I'll expect you to do your duty and provide for the Queendom to your last breath. Let the grown hunters do the fighting." She brushed her hands against the rows of black scale on her thighs, as if to say she was done with the discussion.

Toli looked up at the paintings across the beams of the ceiling, tears pricking at the backs of her eyes. She gritted her teeth, hating the quaver in her voice. "Fine."

Spar understood. Dragons were not to be trusted. It didn't matter what the Telling and the old tales said. They were vile and vicious. Why couldn't her mother, of all people, see that simple truth?

Disappointment crept like frost, numbing her from the inside out. How could she do the Telling? How could she tell the story of her people—a story full of gratitude to the creatures that killed her father? She couldn't. Nor could she give a tithe to them. And if she couldn't keep the Telling, and wouldn't do the Tithing, she couldn't be queen. Not now, and not ever.

CHAPTER FOUR

Wix knew her well. Toli hadn't seen him leave the Great Hall, but he was waiting for her in front of the Hunters' Shrine. He must have left well before her to beat her there. Maybe he even ran the whole way, despite the narrow, slippery pathways through the Queendom—all the way to the eastern edge of the ridge where it stretched up to cover the leatherleaf houses.

He had known that after that conversation with her mother, she would be missing her father.

Above the houses, stars winked and sparkled like dragon scales shed across black ice. The wind whistled its warnings over the ridge.

Toli slowed as she came toward the two round buildings made of alternating blocks of stonetree and ice. In one, the House of Remembrance, there were life-size statues carved in ice of the Queendom's citizens who had died in the past year. The statues would remain there for a full dragon cycle, then be towed far out onto the ice fields to stand in the Necropolis, taking their place on the Queendom's memorial ground. Toli's father's had already been moved there.

Toli had never been that far out on the deep ice—had never seen the great field of statues, the ancestors of her people, going back centuries. From what she had heard, all the statues stood together, facing Nya's rise, until the wind and frost wore them down, first defacing and then destroying them.

The second building at the eastern edge of the Queendom was the Hunters' Shrine. It held the statues of the hunters, five men and four women, who had fallen in the dragon attack. It stood as a permanent memorial, as a way for people to pay their respects. Wix's father, Belgar Walerian, had carved the second statue of Toli's father.

She lifted her hand as she walked toward Wix, the snow creaking under her feet.

Wix exhaled. "Figured you'd head here. You okay?"

Toli shrugged.

He hopped down from the top of the two steps in front of the shrine to land next to her, knocking her sideways. "You're fine. Don't be stupid."

She caught her balance but couldn't help laughing.

He grinned. "So, you'll do the Telling tonight?"

Her smile faded. "It looks that way."

"You're not worried about it, are you? You know that story better than you know the ice."

"It's not that." She lowered her voice. "I just don't want to celebrate them. The dragons aren't a gift. They're a curse."

Wix's brow furrowed as he studied her. He gave a small nod. "I have something to show you. It might even cheer you up." He pulled a small sack off his shoulder and dropped back down to sit on the step.

Toli moved to sit next to him. "What is it?"

"You're going to love this." From the bag he pulled a wide stonetree goblet. Across its face, a long-tailed fox chased a hare.

Toli's eyes widened. Wix was always trying to pull some kind of prank. "That's Pendar's cup. What are you up to?"

He pointed inside the cup, where Toli could just make out a small hole. Wix flipped it over. The hole opened into the stem of the goblet, which Wix had sealed at the bottom with an ice cork.

Toli pulled a face. "I don't get it."

Wix waggled his eyebrows. "When Pendar goes to fill it with honeywine, it will all drain into the stem. He'll think it's empty."

She nodded. "*Annnnd?* Won't he just fill it again?"

No one was around, but Wix leaned in to whisper anyway. "*Annnnd* that's the best part." He spun the cup and pointed to a second tiny hole. "See, the extra liquid will pressurize the wine in the stem. When I add the little ice tube I'm making on the other side . . . the wine will shoot right out of the cup at him!"

Toli stared at him. "How are you going to make an ice tube that small?"

He shrugged. "Hollow out an icicle."

"One of the tiny ones? How?"

"Easy. Drops of hot water . . . and patience."

A slow smile spread across Toli's face. "He'll see it."

"No he won't. He's going to be thinking about the honey-wine."

"Okay, well, he's going to be madder than when you rigged his feast chair."

Wix wheezed a laugh. "I almost forgot about that one."

Toli joined him. "Maybe his . . . face will . . . turn purple again," she said between laughs.

When she caught her breath, her throat burned from the cold night air. She was warmer now, as if some icy thing inside her chest had thawed and loosened. "Seriously though, Wix. He'll be expecting you to pull something. You always mess with him at the Telling feast."

Wix smiled. "Yeah, but this is the best yet. He won't be expecting *this*."

Toli turned the goblet in her hands, admiring his work. "He really won't. It's genius."

Wix's cheeks colored. He reached up and snapped an icicle from the roof line. A thin blade appeared in his other hand. "Everybody needs a hobby. Messing with Pendar is mine."

She snorted. Wix's cheeks reddened as Toli watched him shave and etch the icicle in his hand, then spin it around to work the other side. "Will the queen make you judge the carving this year too?"

"Maybe." Toli sighed. "Probably." Laughing with Wix had

helped a little, but the thought of the evening in front of her made Toli's heart sink.

He bumped her with his shoulder. "Well, do me a favor. If she does make you judge, don't pick my father's work. His ego is unbearable as it is. There are hardly any statues on the wall that aren't his." Wix dropped his voice to imitate the deep rumble of his father. *"Carver's wisdom, Wix. Carver's instinct. Our lore never lies."*

She laughed, but her heart wasn't in it.

They fell quiet. After a minute, Wix looked at her, his hazel eyes thoughtful. "Remember the first time we played together?"

Toli nodded. "If by *play* you mean when the pack of wild foxes attacked us while we were gathering lichens at the edge of the forest. Yeah, pretty sure I remember that."

One corner of his mouth twitched. "Yeah, well, we were collecting tree conks, but other than that, you've got it right. Anyway, we had each other's backs then, didn't we?"

"We were only seven, Wix."

He whittled away more ice at one end of the icicle, and for a moment they sat in silence; then he bumped her again with his shoulder. "Still. We had each other's backs."

She bumped him back. "Yeah. We did."

He etched a last sliver of ice from the back of a small carved fox. "Okay, then," he whispered. "Good talk." Wix held the fox up for both of them to admire, turning it in the starlight. Rising from the step, he settled the little creature neatly on the low edge of the shrine's roof where the icicle had once been. "Ready?"

Toli stood up with a frown and brushed the snowflakes from her pants. "As I'll ever be." She stretched her arms up and out as if she could invite all the stars of Ire to gather in her embrace. The rich scent of the bison being cooked over the fire wafted through the air like an invitation. Her body ached from sitting in the cold. She had steeped in her own worry for too long, and now her thoughts were near-frozen too.

Wix sniffed the air. "I smell Rasca's bitter lichen-and-deer-berry sauce."

When they reached the Great Hall, Wix hustled to replace Pendar's cup among the others on the hunters' shelf, and Toli took a seat at one of the long tables along the far end of the room. Bowls of hard-boiled beetle eggs had been set out, and she popped one of the thumb-length eggs into her mouth, rolling her eyes with a sigh at the sweet burst of flavor.

Some of the Queendom's musicians had come in and stood unbundling their instruments at the back of the hall. Mistra Fen emerged from the shadows in the corner of the room, her dark skin glowing. She'd already tied back her coiled black hair, and now she began tuning up her bone fiddle. Banta Ru, his dark eyes narrowed in concentration, rested the edge of his largest drum against the even larger curve of his belly and tapped a lively beat. He moved to stand next to Mistra, his round face so pale that he glowed like the Daughter Moon.

Toli searched the hall for her mother, wanting to gauge her mood. The queen was seated at the head of one of the long tables, with room on either side for Petal and Toli. She wore her red scale dress, as she always did for the Telling. There

were no signs to indicate her mother's thoughts or feelings—
and Toli knew better than to try to guess.

As people came in out of the night, cheerful voices called
across the huge rectangular hall, glad to get out of the cold.
A couple of people linked hands to stomp and swing to the
music. Most, like Toli, watched them with bemused expres-
sions. Wix danced past, lifting his knees laughably high. On his
second time around, he grinned at Toli. "Come on. It will make
you feel better."

Toli shook her head but couldn't help smiling as he
shrugged and grabbed hold of Petal as she passed, whirling her
toward her friend Willa.

She should be anxious and excited about her first Telling.
It was a way to show her people who she was and who she would
become. Instead, her whole body was heavy, as though it were
having its own quiet revolt. A year ago she would have jumped
at the chance to feel the warmth of her parents' pride. Now
there was just an overwhelming sense of uneasiness—and a
little nausea.

She knew every word of the story by heart. But to go before
them all and tell the story of their beginnings, and to praise the
coming of the dragons, seemed wrong when. Because of them,
her father wasn't there to hear the tale—when all that was left
of his laughter was an echo in her head.

Dancing next to Willa, Petal looked like a small piece of the
night sky, her long, dark hair swaying. The light from the oil
lamps sparked on the smattering of dragon scales in her dress.

Petal, laughing, caught hold of her friend, and the two of them stomped a merry counter-rhythm that encouraged a few others to join them. Toli dropped her eyes at the little pang in her chest. Maybe one day, she would laugh like that with her sister.

Dust sifted down from the rafters from the force of all the jumps, lifts, and hollers. Across the hall, Rasca's white hair glowed in the light from the hearth. The meat sizzled.

"Food's ready," the old woman hollered over her shoulder as if she were calling them all to war.

Toli sighed and moved to take her place next to the queen. She and her family had their own narrow table and bench nearest to the main hearth, where they could look out across the room. A young boy brought their plates.

Once the Strongarm royals had been served, everyone else could gather around the serving table to collect their portions and find a place at one of the long tables or, failing that, on the floor. Dinner was a cacophony of grunts and sighs punctuated by the rattle of knives on plates.

The silence between Toli and the queen thickened as the noise around them grew louder. As she ate, Toli listened to the hollow wails of the wind picking up outside. Around the huge gathering room, adults sat elbow to elbow. Children gathered on the floor around all three hearth fires that stretched down the middle of the room. Toli's gaze fell on Pendar, elbow-deep in his plate and surrounded by hunters.

Petal shifted in her seat, her star-blue eyes traveling from Toli to their mother and back again. The queen glanced at Toli and her eyes hardened. "The Telling is yours tonight, Anatolia." She rose to refill her plate. "No excuses."

Toli could feel Petal's eyes on her as the queen walked away. She avoided her sister's gaze, but couldn't avoid the extra portion of bison Petal took from her own plate and plunked down on Toli's.

"You should eat it, Petal. I don't need it."

"No. It's yours. You don't want your stomach to growl in the middle of the Telling." She watched until Toli gave up the fight and took a bite, then a brief smile brightened her face. There was a long pause as Petal thought through whatever it was that she wanted to say. Toli could almost feel the weight of her sister measuring her words.

Petal cleared her throat. "You could teach me to hunt in your place."

Toli stopped chewing and looked up. "You want to hunt?"

"Why not? You'd be free to help Mother. Let me help. I can do it." Petal folded her arms, spots of color darkening her cheeks. "You think I can't."

Toli picked up her cup and downed some water, trying to think of what to say. She met her sister's eyes. "It's my job, and anyway . . . it doesn't seem like your thing, Petal."

Her lips thinned. "My thing."

"Yeah, you know. It doesn't seem like something you'd enjoy . . . or . . . be good at . . ." Toli wanted to snatch the words back, but it was too late.

"Fine. Spar can teach me, then, if you won't. I bet I'll be a great hunter."

Toli stared at her. "Petal." She struggled to keep the agitation out of her voice. "You won't even step on spiders."

"We don't eat spiders, Toli," she growled.

Toli raised an eyebrow. "Right. That's why you don't like to step on them. Because we don't eat them."

"You're just mad because you know if I asked, she'd let me."

Toli's heart pinched. "Of course she would. You're the youngest. You can do whatever you want, whenever you want."

"Is that what you think?" Petal hissed.

The queen returned, setting her plate down with a crash. "What are you two bickering about now?"

"Toli says she doesn't think I'm capable of hunting."

"That's not what I said."

"It might as well have been."

The queen pinched the bridge of her nose. "Toli, your sister has never trained as a hunter."

"Exactly."

"And, Petal, since when have you wanted to learn to hunt?"

Petal bit her lip. "I don't know. Why does that matter?"

The queen put her hand on top of Petal's. "Since before or after I said Toli couldn't?"

Petal gritted her teeth, then exhaled. "I'm just trying to help! And I could if I wanted to."

Toli scoffed, "Look at your dress!"

"I wouldn't hunt in my dress, Toli. I'm not stupid."

A shout from across the room made everyone jump, and Toli spun to see Pendar, sputtering and dripping with honey-wine. It ran out of his hair and eyebrows and streamed from his beard. He was staring at his cup like it had a monster in it. Around him the hunters roared with delight. Wix rocked gleefully.

Pendar took one hand and drew it across his face, scattering drops of wine everywhere. Luca smacked him as the droplets rained down on her. He turned the cup over, poking at the plug of ice wedged into the stem. His eyes fell on Wix.

"Uh-oh," Petal whispered, reaching across the table to grab Toli's arm.

With a roar like one of Nya's bear-cats, Pendar charged. Wix stumbled backward off the bench and ran to the far side of the table. Pendar followed.

The queen sighed.

"I've got to distract him," Toli muttered.

"The Telling," her sister mouthed. "Do the Telling."

She would have to do it anyway, so it was as good a time as any. Before she could change her mind, Toli rose and smashed her cup down on the table. "Gather!" she cried. "Gather, and hear the Telling—the tale of our people—the tale of creation."

Pendar froze, then moved slowly toward his place at the table, but not before shooting Wix a "you'll pay for this later" look. Wix gave her a grateful nod as he returned to his seat.

As voices quieted and people began to turn toward her, Toli's mouth went dry. Her mother leaned back, her expression a strange combination of irritation and pride. Luca dragged Pendar down to his seat on the bench, and Rasca shuffled to throw more peat bricks on the fire.

As Toli walked toward the main hearth, she struggled to

focus over the loud rush of her pulse. The flames flickered, casting long shadows as she moved. She took a gulp of water when Rasca offered it and almost choked.

You know this story by heart, she told herself again. There was no reason to be nervous . . . if she stuck to what she'd memorized. The problem was she couldn't do that. Not now, after what the dragons had done. If it made her mother angry—so be it. She closed her eyes for a few seconds, willing her heartbeat to catch and slow. The children settled into their spots on the floor, pulling out hides and furs to wrap around themselves. Silence fell.

"In the time when Ire—when our world was much warmer— when more than half the planet was covered with that thick, dark water called the sea, Nya grew tired of her father's rules." Toli drew out the name of their beloved moon—*Neeeya*—lifting her hands as if the Daughter Moon's light poured down into her palms, warm and golden. "Nya grew tired of the cold universe, with its stars that sparkle but never answer." She glanced at her mother. "There was only the water below her, and the Daughter Moon wanted someone to talk to that wouldn't tell her what to do or how brightly to shine."

Toli struggled to imagine the might of the sea. She suddenly wanted her people to picture it with her. "Imagine the ice," she began, straying from the story she had been taught. "Imagine the deep ice. How slick it is, and black, like an endless night that even Nya's light cannot touch."

Some of the people smiled or nodded. She swallowed. "Well, imagine it could move beneath you like a living thing, all of it heaving upward. It could turn and swallow you whole in an instant. That was the sea—and it was all Nya had for company."

A boy at Toli's feet had gone pale, his eyes wide. His full attention gave her confidence. "Night after night," she went on, "Nya lost herself in dreams. She dreamed of *us* . . . of humans, and that she was one too, and she loved those dreams with all her heart. There, she imagined conversations, heard strangers' hopes and fears—their tales of bravery and kindness, shared with her across great distances, until they were no longer strangers at all, but family. Then she would wake to find herself alone again."

Toli watched as the flames licked at the peat bricks like small, famished creatures. Her people had been telling this tale, the story of their birth, at this time of the year for as long as anyone could remember. The weight of it settled on Toli's shoulders as the fire crackled and the wind howled outside the Hall.

From across the room, Petal gave her a nod of encouragement, and Toli had a sudden flash of memory, of hunkering down with her sister, watching with open awe as the queen rolled out the story of their Queendom like a gift.

She pitched her voice to echo in the rafters. "So in the season when Father Moon sleeps on the far side of Ire, Nya decided she would do something about her loneliness and make the creatures of her dreams.

"She stretched her light down and planted her dream in the heart of the sea. She shone on it through the dark waters, night and day, sending it her love, showing it the way to the surface, where it could become. And just as her father was beginning to rise, the surface of the water split wide, and black rock rose up, a wide ridge bursting up toward the sky."

"The rock ridge that shelters our Queendom," a little brown-skinned girl whispered, her voice tense, though even at her age, she'd heard the story many times before.

"The very same." Toli smiled at her. "And under that ridge rose a queen. The first queen of Gall. Her dark-blue eyes were the only reminder of that deep sea where she was born."

"The first Strongarm," a boy with pink wind-burned cheeks called out. The crowd chuckled.

"Yes. My ancestor. And after that, with each passing cycle of Father Moon, Nya made new souls to join the people, hiding them all from her father on an island of sand and stone under the black rock ledge."

Toli's breath caught as her mind went blank between one heartbeat and the next. Her pulse began to race. She tried to look calm, racking her brain to remember what came next. To buy time, she shot a meaningful look around the fire.

Wix's father, Belgar Walerian rose. Perhaps he sensed that she'd lost the thread, or perhaps he just wanted peoples' eyes on him. His umber skin blended seamlessly into his shadowed beard and the embossed leatherleaf of his artist's apron. The master carver called, "Our Nya was an artist like me!" He smiled and sat back down as several other carvers reached to pat his back.

Thank goodness for his pride, Toli thought as the next part of the story rushed back. "A great artist," she agreed. "She wanted no two of her people to look the same. She made some of us tall and thin as moonbeams, and some of us lumpy as tree conks. She made women and men. She used basalt, and sand, and shell. She chose shapes, and colors, and talents to suit each new soul."

"She gave you freckles," Wix shouted to laughter.

"And she forgot to give you sense," Toli shot back, beginning to enjoy herself. Wix grinned.

"Then she made the forest," someone called.

"Yes . . . yes, don't rush me." More laughter.

"Then she made the forest, and filled it with creatures. Wide and green the trees were, they say, and tall enough to reach up to her in the night, as if she could take them into her arms. Nya was no longer lonely."

"Until Father Moon saw the people out hunting one day," Wix called again from the back.

"Humph," Toli grunted, accepting a cup of water from Rasca. The old woman's wrinkled face wore a wide smile.

Toli looked around. "I think you've heard this story before," she teased.

Chuckles echoed from around the room as the children protested for her to continue.

"Father Moon was very angry. He was so angry that he kicked Ire over—kicked over the world, and knocked it far out of its path, away from the sun and stars that were its family."

The room grew quiet with the weight of listening.

"Denied the warmth of the sun, the wide seas of Ire froze, and the world Nya had made began to die. The trees didn't want to un-become, and Nya showed them how to turn to stone—how to be cold on the outside, and hard, but full of life deep under the bark. The stonetrees were born. And she guided the people, showing them how to hide from the wind, where to dig the peat for their fires, and she sent them the giant leatherleaves from the stonetrees for our homes. But the planet still lay dying. It was too cold. There could be no life without heat."

Toli paused again, dragging out the dramatic finale to the tale. Her mouth twitched as the little girl reached out to grasp her ankle as she passed. "Then what?"

Toli took a deep breath. Sweat beaded at her temples.

As a child, she had believed every word, understood the Tithing as an answer to the Telling, and as a tradition that expressed the peoples' gratitude to the dragons, and to Nya for providing them. But now—now she wasn't sure she believed it, and worse, she wasn't sure she could encourage others to believe it either. Nya wouldn't have created something that could so carelessly destroy her own creations.

"Go on," the girl breathed.

Toli swallowed and continued. "So Nya lifted the floor of the sea once more. She built the mountains—Dragon Mountain— and the force of her breath made it hollow. It became a path to the core of the world."

"And then she made the dragons," a pale boy curled against one of the hearths whispered reverently. His mother, seated behind him, gave him a tolerant pat.

Toli exhaled. She was supposed to agree—was supposed to talk about their beauty and fierceness, and say, "Yes, and then she made the dragons," but she couldn't quite bring herself to do it. She kept her eyes turned away from her mother, and said, "Made them. Brought them. Called them. Maybe the dragons know for sure. I don't."

There were some whispers as her changes registered with her listeners. Some nodded. Others frowned. She heard one woman tell her husband not to worry—that it was the princess's first time giving the Telling, and she'd get it right next time.

Toli cleared her throat. Time to finish the Telling for another year. "From that day forward, Father Moon had a second name—the Dragon Moon. For when he rises, they wake, and the people must hide away under the ledge of stone. And when the dragons return from their travels and settle themselves in the heart of the Mountain, only then will the Dragon Moon leave his daughter and her people alone. Only then will it be safe once again to hunt the ice."

As the people rose and began to filter out of the Hall, a hand fell on Toli's shoulder. She spun around.

The Queen of Ire stared into her daughter's eyes. "I'm not sure I *liked* what you did with the end, Anatolia, but the people seemed to like the way you included them."

"Are you . . . disappointed?"

Her mother's brow furrowed as she exhaled. "Every teller has their own way. In any case, you'd do a fine job leading the Tithing, I'm sure. We could ride together out to the Tithing ground. Once the ceremony is over, we could return to the Queendom together. Pendar would stay to see it received. Are you sure you won't even try?"

Toli's heart thunked at the flash of sadness in her mother's face as she shook her head.

"Very well, then." The queen moved past her toward the door.

"Mother, wait. I just—"

The Queen's profile was stern, cold even, as she paused in the shadow of the half-open door. "I have duties to attend to, Anatolia. One day you'll come to understand what that means."

Then she walked away, and though their Queendom was small, Toli couldn't help wondering if her mother was out of reach for good.

Our people cannot exist without the dragons. Neither can we know them. They are like the ice in that way. Vast. Unyielding. Dreadful.

Yet over time, we may learn.

Of the dragons' many ways, we know they value strength and loyalty over all else. To show uncertainty, or fallibility, is to deserve nothing, and less than nothing. It invites dishonor, and even death.

The idea is flawed, but perhaps it is this unbending belief— this inner strength—that makes their scales so beautiful, and strong.

—From the journals of Queen Larat (great-great-grandmother to Queen Una)

CHAPTER FIVE

The nighttime chores were winding down when Toli noticed Spar had returned. She paced awkwardly just inside the doors of the Hall, her hands tucked behind her back. Her mentor caught sight of her and came to a halt with a grimace that was almost like a smile.

A stab of alarm cut through Toli's exhaustion. Spar never smiled. Perhaps her mentor's disagreement with the queen earlier that evening had finally broken her.

Toli hurried over. "What's wrong?" She couldn't be certain, but it might have been the first time she'd ever seen her mentor's teeth. The sight made her jaw ache. "Spar? What's going on?"

Her mentor held something out to her. "It's your birthday gift. I know it's late, but I was saving it for after your first hunt—"

Toli didn't take the gift. Her chest tightened. "No."

Spar shifted, her shoulders tensing. "No?"

"I don't deserve it! I caused a stampede! I failed."

Spar exhaled. "We all fail, Anatolia."

"And that day, with Father—" she whispered.

Something unreadable passed in Spar's eyes. She shook her head. "Even terrible mistakes have roots and reasons. Making them doesn't mean we get to give up." Spar took Toli's chin in her calloused fingers, lifting her face so she had to meet Spar's sharp amber gaze. "*You* don't give up."

Toli's eyes burned with unshed tears. She gave her mentor a stiff nod.

Spar released her chin. "Take it from me," she said, holding up her burned hand. "Your life can change faster than the weather, Anatolia." She held out her gift again. "You should look like the queen you will one day become."

Toli gave a weak smile. "What is it?"

"It's camouflage," Spar explained, shaking out a white cape. Toli stared as the soft white folds shifted and fell. "Happy belated twelfth birthday, Anatolia."

People came and went, preparing to close up the Hall for the night. Every one of them cast soft, knowing looks as they passed. It seemed Spar's gift had been a well-kept secret.

Toli reached out to take the cloak from Spar's burn-scarred hand. It was white rabbit fur, soft and warm on the inside, the outside covered in white dragon scales, rare as ice melt and gleaming in rainbows. There was only one white dragon she'd ever heard of—the Dragon-Mother.

"Where did you get these?" Toli breathed, lifting the

feather-light cloak. The scales were warm and smooth under her fingers.

"I collected them—from the forest and the ice." Spar paused. "It took a few years. The Dragon-Mother doesn't leave the Mountain often." She gave a soft chuckle at Toli's expression. "Don't look so shocked. Even the Mother molts, just like the others. So you like it, then?"

Toli nodded, whirling the cloak so it settled onto her shoulders. She pulled the hood over her head. The weight of the scales kept it up. "It's perfect," she breathed. "I'll never be seen in this. If the queen lets me hunt again, I'll be able to sneak up on anything."

Spar's eyes narrowed. "That's the idea—*eventually*. Until then, it will help protect you—keep you hidden."

Toli studied Spar's face. "You mean if the dragons attack again." An image of her father turning toward her with wide eyes flashed in her mind, and Toli paused. Spar had never said a word to her about it, and now here she was, giving her the most beautiful gift she'd ever received. She struggled to get enough air to speak. "After everything that's happened, I thought you might have given up on me."

Spar's focus sharpened. "No. I haven't. And from now on, whether you're hunting or not, I expect you to wear it."

"I will! I love it. Thank you." Without thinking, Toli did something she had never done before. She threw her arms around Spar's neck and hugged her tightly. The hunt master gave a woof of surprise. The black scales of Spar's armor were cool against Toli's skin, and for an uncertain moment, she thought she might have made yet another grave mistake.

Several uncomfortable seconds later, Spar gave Toli's back an awkward pat. Toli let go, her cheeks burning.

Spar cleared her throat. "Go on. The queen is staring, and your sister looks like she's about to burst."

Toli looked around the Hall, only spotting her mother after Spar pointed her out. She stood in the shadows at the back of the Hall, in conversation with Rasca.

Spar moved away to talk with the last of the hunters where they stood at the doors of the Hall. Petal rushed up to Toli's side. She brushed her palm down the soft fur side of the new cloak. "Toli, you look beautiful!"

Toli grinned.

Petal's fingers were so pale they almost matched the smooth white dragon scales along the edge of the cloak. "It's even more beautiful than I thought it would be."

Toli looked up. "You knew about *this* too?"

Petal giggled, her delicate blue gown rippling in the light. "Sorry."

Toli looked over at her mother. When she looked back again, Petal was watching her. "Come on," her sister said, moving toward the back of the Hall.

Rasca watched them come, and when the queen turned and saw them, her mother reached out to touch one of Toli's long braids. Her eyes were sad. "I miss your father too, Anatolia. Like Ire misses the sun—but missing him changes nothing."

There was a sharp pain, like something in her snapped

clean through, but before Toli could think of anything to say, she felt the queen's attention shift, and looked up to see her staring after Spar as the doors closed behind the hunt master. "I know you're angry with me, Anatolia. And I don't expect you to come to me, not for help or—for anything really—at least not for a while." She scoured Toli's face. "But I want you to steer clear of Spar for a while. Give the hunt master some space. If you need advice, about anything—I want you to listen to Pendar. Let Spar be." She pushed Toli back a step, gripping her shoulders and pinning her with her fierce star-blue gaze. "Swear it."

Toli squirmed but gave a stiff nod.

"Say it."

She glanced at her sister's somber expression, then back to her mother. It took a moment for the words to creep across her teeth into the room. "I'll listen . . . to Pendar. I promise."

"Good."

Then their mother swept from the room, leaving Toli holding Petal's hand in the middle of the empty Great Hall.

Toli hung her head as the doors swung shut behind the queen. The gift from Spar had been a brief gleam of hope, but her mother would never let her hunt again, which meant she would never learn how to defend her Queendom the way Spar had that day when she killed the dragon. A bitter gust of wind ripped through the open door into the room, stealing the breath from Toli's lips.

Petal put one hand on her arm. "Spar will be okay, Toli. I promise. I'll help get the herbs for the balm she needs and . . ."

It wasn't just Spar. It was everything. Toli didn't trust herself to answer. She tried to be calm and confident for her sister's sake, but her face felt tight. "I think I just need some fresh air," she said, cutting off Petal's assurances.

"I'll come with you."

"No! I just . . . I need a few minutes alone."

"Okay," Petal whispered, taking a step back.

I'm always disappointing someone, Toli thought with a pang of regret as she left the Hall. *If Petal is smart, she'll just keep her distance.*

The air outside was thin and bright with the smell of snow coming, but she knew the cold would be worse beyond the wall. Toli shot a grateful look up at the thick black ridge of rock that jutted out over the Hall and the scattered homes. It protected the whole Queendom from the worst of the wind.

The Daughter Moon had sunk down beyond the horizon for the night. Only the thinnest sliver of her light remained, pale and wide, giving everything a cold, starlit glow. The leatherleaf walls and roofs of the little circular huts, in hues of gold, red, and brown, were laced with frost and lit by the gleam of a few hanging lanterns. Almost everyone was tucked away in their own small homes, warm as could be expected, for the long cold night.

The only sound was the lonely song the wind sang through the bones and bells that hung at people's doors.

Toli closed her eyes and took a deep breath, opening them again to watch the massive white cloud of her breath float away in a gust of wind. She was about to try for an even bigger one when Rasca's scream from the far side of the Great Hall froze her blood.

Toli ran, scrambling down the narrow path toward the sound of wailing. Doors opened around her, alarmed faces gazing, first out, and then up toward the empty sky. Her feet brushed the ice, shallow as starlight, as she ran. She turned the corner, her feet skidding. Pendar appeared like a bison stampeding from around the opposite corner. Toli toppled toward him, almost colliding. Luca, right on his heels, reached out and yanked her upright. Toli caught sight of Rasca.

She stood sobbing, pointing at the dark sky, where streaks of colored aurora light had begun to shine. More people poked their heads out the doors of their little round houses or stepped into the narrow roads from the workshops and outbuildings to see what was going on.

Toli squinted, peering in the direction Rasca pointed. In the distance, growing smaller, she saw the glint of blue scales, and something else—something hanging from the dragon's talons. Her stomach flipped. Not something. Someone.

CHAPTER SIX

"It came over the ridge," Rasca panted, tears running down the creases of her face. "I saw the whole thing. Queen Una was up on the wall over there, looking out like she does. There was no warning—just a rush of air. It picked her right up. She didn't even have time to yell for help. I just stood here," the old woman wailed. "I just stood here."

Toli's heart stopped.

Behind her, Petal gasped and burst into tears.

A middle-aged woman standing nearby turned ashen, her fingers gripping her young son's shoulders like talons.

Pendar's eyes widened. "A dragon took the queen?"

As if from far away, Toli could hear him telling people to get to the Hall. "Get everyone inside!"

Petal grabbed her hand, but Toli shook it off, Pendar's voice echoing in her head. People jostled past, crying, calling for their children—looking at the sky.

Toli's thoughts fell away as a curtain of red dropped in front of her eyes. Before Pendar's words had stopped ringing in her ears, her legs were churning, carrying her forward. She heard Petal cry out, but it would have been easier to stop her heart than to stop her feet. Racing for the Southern Gate, her blood rushed in her ears like the beating of wings as she prayed for Nya to show her where the dragon had taken her mother.

She registered the beating of footsteps behind her only a moment before Pendar wrapped his thick arms around her and slid forward, lifting her up off the ice.

"Stop it. Stop it now, Princess. Getting yourself killed isn't the answer."

Toli struggled, striking backward with her heel. She had the satisfaction of hearing his curse of pain, but he didn't set her free.

"Let go! Pendar, let go! I won't let them take her! I won't—"

"She's gone already, child. You can't help her."

Toli let loose a roar as tears streamed down her cheeks. Still, Pendar held on. At last she stopped struggling. Her body went slack.

Toli wept. "They take everything."

Pendar spun her around and crushed her in a hug. "I know. I know it, Princess, but listen now. They didn't kill her. She's not dead. They took her, alive. I don't know what this is, but they took her alive."

"Why? Why would they do that?"

"I don't know, but Nya willing, we'll figure it out." He held her away from him. "Now come on. We need to get to the Hall."

Despair and rage competed to take hold of Toli's thoughts as she and Pendar walked back. The hunters, well armed, had taken up positions around the outside of the long building. Toli stared at Luca as she passed, and the huntress met her eyes with a tight nod and cold fury. "I won't let them through, Princess. If that dragon comes back, I'll deal with it myself."

Toli shuddered.

Petal stood by the doors, shivering. Wix had joined her, his normally cheerful face solemn. Toli tore off her cloak and wrapped it around her sister's shoulders. "Go inside, Petal," she whispered. "You'll freeze."

Petal shook her head. "You need it, Toli. You'll get cold." She tried to hand back the cloak, but Toli crossed her arms.

"I won't, I'm too angry. Besides, you're shaking so hard your teeth are going to fall out."

Her sister nodded, her eyes moving to stare at the place in the sky where their mother had disappeared. She pulled the cloak closed, but didn't move to leave.

Wix shifted his weight. "What . . . what can I do?"

Toli met his expression of helplessness with one of her own. They all had the same question, but no answers.

Petal grabbed Wix's arm, her voice matter-of-fact. "I know. Broth."

"What?"

"Broth. It's strengthening and warm."

Toli blinked.

"Don't look at me like that." Petal crossed her arms. "It's what everyone needs, and it will give Rasca something to do." Petal gave a determined nod. "You'll see." Her eyes sparked as she spun and walked through the doors of the Great Hall with determined steps.

People streamed into the Hall. Toli caught a glimpse of Rasca through the open door, still weeping, as Petal took her by the arm and pulled her toward the fire.

Spar appeared out of the fog and growled, "Is it true?"

Toli couldn't bear to look at her—she hadn't been prepared. She had failed her father, and now she'd failed her mother too.

Wix put out a hand as if to shield her, but Toli stepped around him.

Pendar answered. "It's true. A dragon took the queen."

Spar's eyes flashed. "Ready our hunters to go after her."

Pendar's mouth fell open. "Certainly not."

Confusion flew across Spar's face, anger rising in the hunt master's eyes. She stepped closer. "What do you mean, 'certainly not'? Surely you aren't suggesting—"

Pendar stared down the hunt master, his face grim. "What I'm suggesting is that going after her now is stupid."

Spar sneered. "And you propose what? We let the dragons have her?"

Pendar snorted. "Of course not. No."

As they fought, Toli noticed Petal handing out cups of steaming liquid to anyone still standing outside. Her body grew heavier. She wanted to close her eyes and make all of this go away.

The sudden weight of Pendar's hand on her back drew Toli's attention back to their argument. "No. Listen. If they were after a quick meal or wanted her dead, they would have killed her. They could have done that, but they didn't. I'm telling you, I don't understand it, but they took her for a reason."

Spar's jaw tightened. "You propose we bow to their will. You propose we lose what's most precious to us." Her amber eyes sparked like embers. "We need to strike now. Kill the Mother and get Queen Una back."

Toli moved closer to Spar, glaring at Pendar.

Petal arrived with a trayful of steaming cups, her face falling as she took in the scene.

Pendar gripped Spar's arm, lowering his voice to a growl. "Don't be a fool. If you want to get killed, do it by yourself."

Petal bit her lip, and Toli quickly reached for a cup, startling as Spar barked her name. Hot broth spilled on the ice at their feet.

"Listen to me, Princess," the hunt master hissed. "Your mother has been taken. That makes you the acting queen. What do *you* say?" Spar's eyes narrowed. "Do you want your mother back . . . or not?"

Toli's mouth went dry. "Of course I do," she whispered.

A smug smile grew on Spar's face. "Then choose."

"Anatolia." Pendar's face fell. "Don't do it. Listen! We'll talk to them. We'll get to the bottom of it—when we take them the tithe. We'll reason with them."

The tithe. Toli squeezed her hands into fists at her side. She opened her mouth to tell Spar to get the sleds ready, but Petal spoke before she could, her voice soft as new snow. "You promised."

"What are you talking about?"

"You know what. Your promise—to Mother."

Toli's shoulders slumped as she remembered the last words she'd spoken to her mother. She had promised, not just her mother, but her *queen*, that she would listen . . . to Pendar. To *Pendar!*

Toli narrowed her eyes at Petal. "I thought you went inside."

The tray of cups began to shake in her sister's hands. "Don't change the subject. I heard you promise our mother. About listening—"

Toli sent Spar an apologetic look as her heart sunk lower. Her mentor would hate her for this. Her voice was thick as she held back her tears. "Fine," she mumbled. "Pendar, we'll do it your way."

Spar's face turned deep red, and Pendar looked flabbergasted.

Toli went numb. Her thoughts spun out like thread unraveling, slipping away into nothing. She could hear her breath, but not her heart. It was as though it had forgotten how to beat.

She seemed to float away from them, drifting through the doors of the Great Hall without any conscious choice.

Crowds had gathered in small clusters. Some people wept.

Some worried at one another with hushed whispers. The air in the room felt heavy, like a blanket of thick snow had been laid over the entire Hall. Toli, unable to stop shivering, hurried to the back of the Hall, and the long ladder that would take her up to her bedroom in the high reaches under the roof. All she wanted was to be alone.

Wix caught up, jogging backward. "You okay?" He shook his head as she pressed her lips together. "'Course not. 'Course you're not okay. Stupid question. The look on Spar's face when you took Pendar's side. Hailfire! Did you see—"

A sob burst from Toli's lips.

"No! I didn't mean that. Don't listen to me. She looked great. That's just her face. I—I'm sure she's fine." He banged into someone, then tripped over his own foot. Toli kept going.

He caught up again, limping now.

"Go. Away. Wix."

She strode past the hearths, past her mother's throne where it sat in shadow.

Wix cleared his throat. "Listen. Toli. About your mother—"

"I don't want to talk about it."

They reached the bottom of the ladder.

"No. I can see that." He rubbed the back of his neck. "Is there anything you need though? Water? Weapons, maybe?"

Toli leaned in and his eyes widened. "I'm getting her back," she said, willing him to believe her. "I don't know how yet, but I'm getting her back."

There was a pause; then he cleared his throat. "Not tonight though. You hear the wind, right?"

"I hear it," she said through gritted teeth as she began climbing.

She reached the platform outside the bedroom she shared with her sister.

"You know you can count on me to help," Wix called up.

Toli paused, and then closed the door behind her.

Her head ached. She should be down in the Hall, talking to people—reassuring them, but she didn't have it in her. She couldn't even reassure herself. The dragon must have taken her mother to the Mountain. Was she there now?

The oblivion of sleep would be sweet, just to fall into darkness and pretend none of this had happened, but the still, quiet bedroom was too full with thoughts of her mother. She moved to look out the single tiny window. Its pane of thick ice, the size of her palm, gave her a view all the way over the deep ice wastes. What did the dragons want with the Strongarm queen? Pendar was right. They could have just killed her. Why hadn't they? What did it mean?

Below her, the shining roof of the Great Hall, tiled with dark dragon scales, glittered where its roof beams curved upward toward the sky. Farther out was the Southern Wall, and beyond that, the miles upon miles of empty ice that led to the mountains. On the horizon, the black silhouette of Dragon Mountain loomed. The Dragon-Mother was there, and whatever was going on, she was sure to be at the heart of it.

She touched a warm finger to the pane of ice, watching as a single drip of meltwater formed and ran down the window. Toli was in charge now. Her mother was counting on her. She squeezed her hands into fists at her sides. "Get the peat bricks in," she said under her breath. "Check the stores with Rasca." What else would her mother want her to do?

Toli wasn't sure. She should have paid better attention. Her pulse throbbed behind her eyes, as if she'd been staring far out across the ice for too long. Maybe she had been.

If she had just followed Spar's lead, they might be on their way to get the queen right now. In her head, she had already packed the sled. She had fed and harnessed the foxes. She had stowed water and food and weapons.

She pressed her lips together. Of course, that was the one thing her mother had told her—the thing Petal wouldn't let her forget. She'd said to listen to Pendar. And Toli had agreed.

Her mother's voice rang in her head. *Steer clear of Spar for a while.*

So she would listen to Pendar. For now.

A draft seeped up from the Great Hall through the cracks in the floorboards. She pulled a fur wrap from her bed and threw it around her shoulders, shifting the few steps back to their small stone hearth. They were lucky to have it. True rock was precious—rare, and difficult to dig from the frozen ground. The extra warmth it lent their small room was a welcome thing.

Toli chewed at her lip and picked up a black peat brick to place on the fire. Was her mother cold? Toli pushed away the sick feeling that rose with the thought. "She's alive," she whispered aloud, willing herself to believe it. Pendar had said so. She had to be.

Toli watched a streak of red light dance across the sky

through the tiny window. She'd need to check the peat stock and make sure there were enough ice blocks cut to melt into water. They'd need extra of both to get through the coming weeks after the Tithing.

The Tithing.

She would play no part in honoring the dragons—this, at least, was her choice. Pendar could do as he pleased. Toli threw herself down on her bed, watching the fire glow. Their beds— hers and Petal's—took up the far wall of the room. Built head-to-head, and made of stonetree that was cold to the touch and dense as rock. Each bed was enclosed to shield the girls from drafts. Only the side facing the fire was open to the room.

As the fire crackled, the urge to take action boiled at the back of Toli's mind, scorching her thoughts until they were dry, ungrateful things.

She had spent many quiet nighttime hours lulling herself to sleep, staring at the drawings that Petal had made to cover the inside ceiling of her bed—a herd of white bison out on the ice fields, a dragon in the distance, a sky filled with stars. Worry rattled through her like wind through bare branches.

She heard a gentle knock on the door before it opened and Petal slipped in. Petal leaned against the closed door, staring at Toli.

Petal's voice was tight. "Toli, what are we going to do?"

"*We're* not going to do anything. *I'm* going to figure out a way to get our mother back."

Petal slumped to the edge of Toli's bed. "Can I stay with you?"

Toli held out her arm, and her sister climbed up next to her, curling her knees to her chest. Petal's dark hair spread like shadows between them.

Toli's voice softened. "We'll get her back. I'll do whatever it takes."

"I want to help."

Toli didn't answer. There was nothing Petal could do.

Her little sister turned to face her, reaching out a hand to pick at Toli's soft lined tunic. "Why didn't they kill her?"

Toli closed her eyes. "I don't know."

Petal didn't say anything, but Toli heard the sharp sniff that meant her sister was about to cry. Words spun through her head, but none of them seemed right. She pulled her sister close and held her, trying to offer her one thing that was certain and safe. After a while Petal quieted, draping one slender arm around Toli's waist. Toli's thoughts slowed, and she let herself fall into the silence of sleep.

It was the wind that woke her, no longer raging, but sending up howls like a forlorn child.

She lay there, eyes wide, remembering what had happened and itching to do something—anything. At last, she slipped out from under her sister's arm. Petal looked so peaceful, and Toli felt a pang of regret that she couldn't make it last.

Outside, Nya-Daughter Moon was still below the horizon, and only a thin green glow—the promise of Father Moon's arrival—edged the black shadows of Dragon Mountain.

She'd take her sled out on the ice—not too far, just to clear her head. As long as she was back before Nya's first light, no one would miss her, and if she was lucky, maybe the wind would bring her a plan.

The lined tunic and leggings embraced Toli's body as she swept her white cloak off the bed where Petal had draped it. She snapped her bow off the wall. Out on the ice, the aurora lights would be wrapping the world in the season's first dance.

Toli slid down the ladder to the Hall floor, walking quickly through the carved doors into the frost-stung air. Everything sparkled—the sky with stars, the ground and houses with thick webs of frost. Soon the lights would spread, and the sky would be on fire with dancing colors, their reflection mirrored on the ice fields below.

She hurried toward the edge of the Queendom, along the walkway between the last of the houses. The stable where the sled foxes were housed was a large rectangular building that leaned against the towering ice blocks of the Southern Wall and its arching gate. Through the gate beyond were miles of wind, ice, and snow. She looked up at the statue of the queen, and her heart skipped a beat.

She heaved open the stable door and managed a smile despite herself as the large white foxes spun and jumped up to lick her face, banging into one another in their hurry to get to the harnesses. Raised among people since birth, they were smart, affectionate creatures. Their long tails whipped at the backs of her legs as Toli pulled the gear from the wall. Once she had the foxes lined up, they tugged to get going, huffing steamy clouds that hung in the air like little wishes. They were eager to be gone, and that was a feeling she understood.

She pulled up her hood. The dragon scales at the hood's edges were warm and smooth against her skin. Once through the gate, Toli climbed onto the sled's front bench. A moment more to yank a blanket of fur up over her legs and they were away.

"Hup!"

Beyond the arch of ice that served as the Southern Gateway, the starlight reflected off the ice in sharp blue pinpricks of light. They sparked and gleamed like eyes as Toli raced across the surface. She shivered. Out here the world felt bigger and stranger. Out here she could hear her thoughts as they gathered to whisper together under the clear, starry sky.

When the aurora danced, the dragons would wake, and when they did, they would expect their tithe from the Queendom of Gall. This year, the dragons could starve for all Toli cared.

Toli went as far and as fast as she dared, listening closely as the cold wind bit at her cheeks and frosted her eyelashes, but she still didn't know how she was going to rescue her mother. Pendar wanted to wait—for what? She *had* promised to listen to him, but for how long?

She could prepare supplies for the long journey and go herself. If she went alone, maybe she could sneak into the Mountain and find the queen. But then what?

Toli looked out across the ice as the fog rose around her like steam. Yeah, no problem. Just trek across the ice, stumble her way into the Mountain, get past a bunch of dragons, find her mother, and get them both home again. That's all. Her shoulders slumped. Oh, and don't get burned alive or eaten.

Toli snapped the reins and the foxes turned back toward the Queendom. This was stupid. The wind wasn't going to bring her a plan. It wasn't going to help her at all. She needed to return home, talk to Pendar, and decide what to do.

As they turned back, Toli glanced up at the sky. Dark clouds rolled in from the east. It would be better not to be caught outside if it began to hail. She could press on, but she had run the foxes hard, and a brief rest, just to let the squall pass, would give her a little more time, and space, to think.

Her route back to the Queendom took them past the ice caves. It had been a long time since she'd been inside, but it was out of the wind, and would give the foxes a chance to catch their breath. Hopefully the storm would change direction or move past quickly.

The caves lay a half mile from the Southern Gate, just out of view of the Queendom, where the silhouettes of the stoneforest trees loomed over them like curious giants. The long tubes of ice swept down under the line of the forest. There were several caves, most no more than a hundred feet long. A few opened into the forest on the other side. A few tunneled through the ice and opened into caverns. As the wind blew over the entrances, they played their hollow song, inviting her closer. In true storms, the wind grew so strong that the ice at the mouths of the caves sometimes shivered and hummed as if their stormsong could sing away the danger.

Toli slowed as they passed, tugging at the reins until the sled came to a stop a hundred yards from a cave that curled down into the ice under the edge of the forest. The entrance gaped open, its mouth lined with icicle teeth. Toli stared into the dark, then reached down to grab a torch out of the sled, lighting it from the small clay bowl of coals that was always kept alive in the belly of any sled that braved the ice.

She led the foxes inside, just out of the wind. The walls and rounded ceiling of the cave gleamed, smooth and bright in the flickering light. They beckoned her to look farther inside, and she picked her way forward, watching for anything that might be hiding in the shadows.

As she walked, her reflection walked next to her, appearing a step ahead on both sides. The hair along the back of her neck rose as she moved to where the tunnel opened onto a small empty cavern.

She turned to go back to the foxes. A few steps from the entrance, a spark of red in the snow caught her eye. Soon, when the aurora arrived, red would be common enough in the sky, but red on the ground meant blood, and blood on the ice almost always meant something had died.

She crept closer, her steps cautious.

There.

A gleam, just above the piles of snow that had blown inside, catching against the walls. Heart pounding, Toli reached out one hand to brush away the drifts. It was a long, oval-shaped stone, sparkling like a jewel. She'd never seen anything like it. Toli dug into the snow around it to get a better look.

When all the snow was brushed away, she could see the whole thing. It was about the size of her forearm, and it took both her hands to lift it up. She held it high and it caught the light, sparkling and shining.

She'd heard of people finding jewels sometimes, though those were deep in the forest and in the ground, not in the snow. Sometimes the stoneforest trees crystallized, she remembered, but those jewels were black. She peered closer. The warm cloud of her breath fogged its surface. She gripped it tighter before wiping away the moisture with her glove.

Her breath caught as its weight somehow shifted, threatening to topple the stone from her hands. Her grip tightened instinctively as the light on its surface changed. Toli frowned at it. How could a stone change its weight in your hands? She leaned closer.

Under the surface of the stone, something moved.

When, at last, a seethe is born,

Some have feather, some have horn.

Of royals there are only three.

One fights to lead, the others free.

In every seethe, they must obey.

To sleep, to hunt, to toil, or play.

The firstborn girl is named for Frost.

The second named for Stone.

The third to hatch makes due with Sky.

The rest take their names alone.

—Dragon Ranking Creed

CHAPTER SEVEN

The weight within the stone shifted again, but Toli held on. She peered into the bejeweled depths, leaning closer. A sweep of scales brushed past before a bright golden eye blinked up at her. Its vertical pupil narrowed. Toli yelped and tossed the stone back into the pile of snow at the cave's edge. It vanished with a poof as a burst of snow flew into the air.

Choking, Toli stared at the place where the thing had disappeared. A single word ran through her mind like a storm. *Dragon. Dragon. Dragon. Dragon. Dragon.*

She shivered. The wind rang through the caves as she reached out and pulled the dragon chrysalis from the snow. Its weight shifted. One golden eye narrowed at her accusingly.

Her thoughts jumbled, and Toli swallowed hard as her hands slipped over the smooth crystalline surface. She stared.

She couldn't help it. If she looked close, she could make out red scales glinting inside, the outline of a leg, a talon—a long muzzled face.

Her heart hardened. She should leave it. Let it stay here in the cold. Anyway, what would she do with it? The dragons would want it back—wouldn't they?

Toli paused, chewing her lip. *The dragons would want it back.* Could keeping the chrysalis help get her mother back? She bent down and grabbed a woven sack partly frozen to the bottom of the sled. A small hole tore in the bag as she pulled it free of the icy surface. The inside was covered in bits of fish and frozen scales, but it would have to do. Her hands shook as she shoved the chrysalis inside, along with some rags and fur. She'd take it to Spar. She had promised to listen to Pendar, but if he didn't know about the chrysalis, he'd have nothing to say about it. Spar would know what to do.

Toli leaned one hand against the outer lip of the cave. She peered out at the snow, and then up at the sky for any clue as to where the baby dragon had come from. Her hushed voice seemed loud in the smothering fog. "Why aren't they looking for you?"

Hearing the words sent a jolt through her. Maybe they *were* looking. *Of course they were!*

She couldn't wait on the weather. She had to leave. Now.

Toli tugged her white cloak tight around her shoulders, pulled the hood up to cover her hair, and then rolled her eyes at herself. *She* might be harder to see, but the sled wasn't.

She stashed the sack under the seat, out of sight, and where she wouldn't have to look at it. She'd show it to Spar. They could figure out what to do with it together. Her heart pounded as she jumped into the sled and slapped the reins, racing for the safety of the Queendom as fast as the foxes could carry her.

As she left the caves behind, Toli tried to calm her thoughts, but they whirled like snow in the wind. A baby dragon. She'd found a baby dragon, not even hatched. She'd never seen a dragon chrysalis before. What was it doing out here all by itself, and how had it gotten there? She had no idea how unhatched baby dragons were supposed to be cared for, but she was pretty sure that lying buried in the snow at the mouth of an ice cave— alone—wasn't it.

The foxes slowed, whining.

"Hup! Hup!" Toli cried, rising to her feet. She had hardly left the cave. They were still thirty minutes from the Southern Gate, and she was eager to find Spar. She frowned as the foxes dragged to a stop, whimpering and cringing. Something was making them nervous.

Goose bumps broke out across Toli's skin. There was nothing—just fog and the first pale hints of morning moonlight on the ice. She got out of the sled, moving slowly, her eyes flicking from the fog to the foxes, but she couldn't find any reason for them to be alarmed.

She crouched down next to the lead fox. "What is it, girl?" She sank her hands into the fox's fur to comfort her. "Listen," she let her voice drop to a whisper. "I'm nervous too, but we have to hurry. We need to get home now, okay? Please?"

The fox crouched down on her haunches with a low snarl,

and as she did, Toli caught a scent on the air. It was a sharp electric smell. The last time she had smelled it, her father had died.

A whoosh of wings, and Toli slowly lifted her eyes to the sky.

Two dragons, one huge and black, the other smaller and green, hovered high above her, looking down. Instinct took over. Toli threw her arms over her head.

The black dragon hissed—a female, then.

The green one snickered, touching down to the left of the sled, blocking any escape toward the forest. "It sees us, Sister. Should we fear for our lives?"

The foxes cowered as the black dragon dropped down to land, so close it shook the ice under the sled. The scales along the front edges of her wings glittered in the starlight. Slit pupils dilated in large sapphire eyes as she peered at Toli. "I am Krala Frost, firstborn female of my seethe. This is Dral—my twin. Name yourself."

Words stuck in Toli's throat for several long seconds. It was the green's cough of laughter that shook them loose. "T . . . Toli. I'm Anatolia Strongarm, uh, firstborn female of the Queendom of Gall."

The black dragon—Krala—seemed to smile, her mouth so full of piercing teeth that Toli almost missed what she said. "You were right, brother mine," she hissed. "It is one of them. And the firstborn. The thing they call a *princess*."

"What do you want?" Toli croaked.

The brother dragon, Dral, cocked his head at the foxes, his crescent pupils widening. Toli had the fleeting thought that he wanted to eat them, but it was drowned out by the rushing sound of her own blood. She fought to stay still, as some still-observant part of her brain noticed Dral's feathers. He had more than his sister—a wide collar at his neck, and long, green and copper pin feathers along his spine that rose and fell when he breathed.

Krala dipped her shoulder, knocking him aside. "We're here for something else, Brother. These little bags of bone will only stick in your teeth. They never satisfy."

Dral narrowed his slit eyes at her, but fell back a few steps.

"What do we want?" Krala's chuckle sent a tide of shivers down Toli's spine. The dragon gazed back at her brother. "The better question is, What don't we want?" She chuckled again, leaning forward to peer at Toli. "In fact, we are . . . looking for something."

There was only one thing Toli knew of that they might be trying to find, and no matter how she might feel about the chrysalis itself, she would be charred to ash and bone twice over before she would give these dragons anything they wanted. Her heart lurched, remembering the sight of her mother being carried out of sight, hanging from a dragon's talons, and the pain of her father's shout as he ran across the impossible distance of ice between them. If there was something she had that they wanted—good. She would deny them at every turn. She'd have nothing to do with helping dragons.

Even as rebellion flickered in her head, her body recognized the danger. Every muscle tensed, and her breath turned shallow as she struggled not to make any sudden moves, and not to check under the bench where the dragon chrysalis was hidden. She kept her face blank, but her skin broke out in a cold sheen of sweat. "What are you looking for?"

"Just a small thing," Dral simpered. "A small red stone. It belongs to the Mother, and—"

Krala hissed at him, edging him back. "It is of no value," she said, her head whipping back toward Toli. "It's only . . . sentimental. Tell us. Have you seen it?" She leaned closer. "You must have passed by the caves quite recently. I am certain it was there. Do you have it? I smell something . . . familiar."

Toli couldn't keep her gaze from shifting to the belly of the sled where her bow lay waiting, the chrysalis a handsbreadth away from it. Her fingers twitched. *Breathe, Toli,* she told herself as she moved to stand in her sled, closer to her weapon, and to the chrysalis.

Toli forced her hands to relax, clasping them to her sides, so the dragon wouldn't see them shaking. She'd never get to her bow in time. And she was outnumbered. She'd be dead in a heartbeat, and then what would her mother do—and what about Petal?

Her thoughts whirled. She wasn't about to give them the chrysalis. However it got there to begin with—and whatever they wanted with it—helping them wouldn't do the Queendom any good—or get her mother back. If they already knew she'd found it, they wouldn't be *asking* her. They'd just take it.

"I don't have your stupid stone," she snarled. "All you smell is my cloak." She held up the edge of it. "Scales! See?"

Krala huffed, and Toli gritted her teeth. *How dare they take everything and then ask for more?* "Why should I help you? Where's *my* mother? Is she alive? Bring her back!"

The dragon lifted a claw and gave an idle flick toward one of the foxes. "Unimportant."

Rage lanced through her. "Not to me! Did you do something to her? Where is she?" Her mother was in danger. Was she dead already? Had they killed her?

Toli's skin crawled as Krala craned forward, her rank breath steaming against Toli's face. "So distrustful. Be careful, Anatolia Firstborn. You may offend me." She leaned forward another inch. A drop of saliva fell, steaming, to the ice next to Toli's foot. "I think you do not want to offend me." The dragon pulled back. "Your mother is alive enough, most likely. Ata collected her. My Queen had some foolish notion that she might be *useful*." Krala's mouth widened, her teeth glistening. "It is weak of her. She might as well bare her throat."

Her mother was *alive*. A rush of dizziness threatened as relief coursed through her. She could almost hear the seconds pass as her thoughts churned. It wasn't too late. Her mother was alive. *It isn't too late.* She had to keep them talking, had to somehow make them reveal something—what the Dragon-Mother wanted, why they'd taken the queen—anything that might help Toli save her. "What do you mean, my mother might be useful?"

Krala blew fire at the sky. "I agree. It is absurd. Our Dragon-Mother makes a fatal error." She craned forward, her lip curling back in a sneer. "Imagine thinking such puny, stupid bone bags could be useful to us." Krala's neck arched toward the sky like a serpent as she let out a roar. "She is fire-addled if she thinks we—*we*—could need anything from such puny bites."

Toli cringed as the other dragon—the brother, Dral—let out a matching roar that shook the ice. She forced herself to stand her ground.

"If the Dragon-Mother thinks we're useful . . ." Toli didn't realize she'd spoken until the words tickled across her lips. She tilted her head as the rest of the question escaped. "If she wants our help with something, why didn't she just ask us?"

Krala launched forward like a shooting star. Toli stumbled, falling to her back on the bottom of the sled. Krala leaned down to stare Toli in the eyes.

She froze in the dragon's glare, her body going cold.

"We are dragons," Krala began in a low whisper. "We do not *ask* for anything. We take what we want, and what we want is ours. In this, our Dragon-Mother is correct." Krala stepped back, allowing Toli to get up.

"Your queen is the mightiest of your people." Krala continued. "Take her, and we take her power. Take her, and the rest are ours—loyal."

"What power? What does the Dragon-Mother want with our loyalty?" Toli cried out as Krala snapped her jaws inches from Toli's face.

"I don't like your tone." Krala let out a low hum that was

almost a purr. "But your questions show a sliver of wisdom, puny one. She should not show you such regard. *Bone bags* have no use at all."

Dral snorted a puff of smoke. "It is good that we did what we did, Sister."

Toli's thoughts caught on his words. *What we did.* What had Krala and Dral done?

They obviously didn't think much of people—or of her. Maybe she could use that, if she was careful. They didn't see her as a threat. To them she was just a bag of bones, dumb as stone. She took shallow breaths. If she stayed quiet, maybe they'd forget she was even there. Maybe they'd talk too freely and tell her something she could use to help her mother.

Krala chucked. "I am always right. The bone bags should fear us and stay below our notice, where they belong. This notion that their queen could help us is offensive! Absurd!"

Toli began to shiver as Dral leaned his face close, studying her. "I do not understand why our Dragon-Mother wishes a partnership with these creatures. Can you see it, Sister?"

"See it?" she hissed. "I can almost smell it—like rot. Puny bites ruling the land. Puny bites telling us what we can eat, and what we can't." Krala moved closer to Dral, her disgust rolling across the ice like wind, carrying the scent of smoke and death. "Listen to me, Brother. This error in judgment will open this Dragon-Mother's veins in the end—the solution is simple. I will destroy her so I may my rightful place."

Toli's breath hitched. *Krala wants to rule the dragons.* At the same moment she saw Dral's eyes widen, and for just an instant, a flash of fear. She wondered what he was afraid of, but cast the question away. The important part was that Krala wanted their Dragon-Mother dead—or gone.

Toli chewed her lip. She hoped Krala was telling the truth about her mother being alive. Dragons didn't ask for help, Krala had said. But apparently their Queen, the Dragon-Mother, might. But help—with what?

She looked up and startled. The dragons had stopped talking. Krala looked at Dral expectantly, but Dral was watching Toli with narrowed eyes. She froze as he inched closer.

"Answer me," Krala rattled. "Am I not a Frost? So what would you have me do, Brother?"

Dral's lips peeled back, revealing two neat rows of jagged teeth. "We could just finish all the bites in their tiny Queendom, starting with this one."

Toli's blood turned cold as Krala tipped her head back and laughed, her throat rippling. "Such hardship! All those bones in our teeth, and our seethe would hunger still, my brother. Though it would almost be worth it to see the looks on their faces. No, I think it must wait. I do not wish to call attention to us at this time."

Toli didn't trust any dragon, and she never would, but these two seemed even less trustworthy than most. They had just threatened to turn her Queendom into a snack. It was long past time to escape—to return home and plan her mother's rescue, but if she made Krala angry now, the dragons' only quarrel would be over her bones.

"Are . . . all the dragons awake? I'm sure with everyone looking for the stone—"

Dral huffed steam. "We rose early. But soon the rest will rise."

Toli wondered if there were other dragons that agreed with Krala and thought the Dragon-Mother was weak and, how had she put it . . . fire-addled?

"Hush, Brother," Krala hissed. "It is past. I am done with searching. I suppose you may eat this bone bag now if you wish, and the little four-footed bone bags."

A gust of hot, putrid air brought her eyes up. Dral had moved closer, his inhale dragging at Toli's clothes. "Are you certain, Anatolia Firstborn? Are you certain you have not seen what we're looking for?" he asked.

Krala whipped around, crashing into him with her head and blowing a long blast of fire past his shoulder. "Dral! It is time to let the stone go. Its fate is sealed by now. It will be broken and d-dust. We can't return it! Not now. Not ever!"

If it was so important, why wouldn't Krala want to keep looking? Why wouldn't she want the others looking when they rose? Krala had said she was a Frost. There was something familiar about that. The thought danced at the back of Toli's thoughts, but she couldn't quite catch it out of the past.

She saw alarm flash over the green dragon's face and watched as Dral drew back, his pupils narrowed. "Sister," he rumbled, "you said we would return it—that once the Mother suspected Bola and the others of conspiring to take it, we—"

"No! We cannot return it! Nor do I wish to. She needs no more brethren! She needs no more first—"

"But, Sister—"

"No. It will be as I say. The Dragon-Mother will believe what we tell her, and so will the others. The stone no longer matters."

Toli let out her breath. *They* had stolen the chrysalis! They put it there and for some reason wanted the Dragon-Mother to suspect other dragons.

Whatever the Dragon-Mother had planned for Toli's mother, it had upset Krala enough to do something about it.

Toli's eyes slid to the foxes where they huddled in a shivering pile, as far from the dragons as they could get. Her heart had given up being in shock, but it still threw itself painfully against her ribs, again and again. She pressed one hand to her chest, certain it must be bruising.

It's just like I felt on the hunt, she thought. *Just like when I missed.* She closed her eyes, shutting out the dragons, forcing her pulse to steady.

"Look at it, Sister. What is it doing?"

"The firstborn calms itself," Krala hissed, and Toli thought she imagined a hint of respect.

Past time to get out of here, Toli, she thought, and opened her eyes. "So, the Mother sent you to look for this red stone thing?"

Krala dipped her head. "Of course," she hissed. "It is as you say."

"And she sent you because you're—"

"Her sister," Krala hissed.

"Her servant," Dral said.

Krala spun, snapping, and this time she drew blood. A thin

line blossomed across Dral's shoulder. "It is both, of course," she explained, turning back to Toli. "We all serve the Mother. We are all . . . loyal."

Toli's brows knit. *Loyal* wasn't a word she would use to describe either of the dragons.

Krala had settled into what Petal would have called "a sulk."

Toli's voice was carefully soft—humble. "The Dragon-Mother isn't your . . . mother?"

Dral's eyes didn't leave Krala, but he steamed his breath and answered. "It is a . . . title, like queen or empress. She is mother to some."

"But not to you and Krala."

"The Mother was thirdborn of our seethe," Dral snarled, the green of his scales sparking light off the white of his teeth. His gaze shifted to Toli. "We will trade for it, Firstborn. If the stone is found, we will trade you for it. A fair trade." He glanced at Krala. "We want it back."

"You waste your time, Brother. It will never be found."

Dral cringed, his head sinking toward the ice. "It pains me, Sister, to disagree with you. I will try to find the stone—to return it to its place of belonging." He turned, lurching toward Toli. "We will bring you food," he said, "in exchange for the stone. If you or your bone-bag brethren find it."

Toli shook her head. "I don't under—"

Krala gave a sigh that ended with a cough of flame. "If you must, but you must speak more slowly, Brother. It does not understand you."

"We. Will. Bring. Food."

"What food?"

"It does not matter what it is," Krala hissed. "What matters, little bite, is that my brother says he will bring some. But I will give none of my own food."

Toli wasn't certain, but she thought she heard Dral snarl.

"I will give you enough to help your people not go hungry in the hiding season. It is a sacrifice I make . . . willingly."

Toli narrowed her eyes. "If you have stored food to spare when you're done hibernating, why don't you eat it?"

"I will bring it. I did not say I had it now," Dral muttered.

Krala chuckled and craned her scaled neck forward, her blue eyes narrowing. "It thinks it's clever, Brother. A clever bite." She turned away. "Come. Forget the stone."

Dral ignored Krala's words and lumbered forward until he stood right next to her. Shoulder to shoulder, they crowded out the sky. "If you find it," Dral added, his eyes pinned to Toli, "you must keep it warm."

Krala snarled at him, beating her wings. Dral's taloned forelegs gouged the ice as he worked to stand his ground. The gust of wind carried the scent of dragon over Toli.

"And my mother?" Toli asked, lifting her chin as her heart fluttered in its cage. She held her breath. "What about *our* queen?"

Krala drew back. "Wise girl. Clever bone bag. Time will tell, but we will not." She turned to make an awkward, skipping run across the ice, her heavy body lifting into the sky.

"How do you know I'll help you find it?" Toli called to Dral.

He grinned as he too turned away. "We know because we are wise and clever also." His green and copper feathers brushed the ice with something like affection as he left the ground. Toli could hear him chuckling as they melted back into the morning fog.

CHAPTER EIGHT

Keeping a baby dragon warm was the last thing Toli had expected to be doing. The two dragons hadn't thought much of her intelligence, but she'd never been so happy to be underestimated. Thanks to Spar, she'd been taught long ago how to pay sharp attention, even through a cloud of fear. Thanks to her mentor, she had learned a lot from the dragons. More, she thought, than they had learned from her.

Toli gritted her teeth. While she'd been debating the dragons, the wind had risen, bringing in the squall she had noticed out on the ice. Their enormous winged bodies had provided a strange kind of shelter. Now that they were gone, cold raged against the sled, pushing the foxes back and tearing at her clothes. A thick layer of cloud made her wonder if Nya had yet risen. Surely the Daughter Moon had crested the horizon by now, but with the wind against them, she wasn't sure they could make it back to the Queendom.

She could turn the sled over, drag the foxes inside, and shelter there until the fog cleared and the storm passed, or she could turn her back to the wind and make their way the short distance back to the cave.

She turned toward the caves.

Something Dral had said caught at her thoughts. They had taken the chrysalis because they were angry at the Mother, but there was more to it than that. Toli was sure of it. Dral seemed to think the Dragon-Mother would want it back, but why take it if they were just going to return it? Krala seemed just as determined to leave it in the snow as her brother was to return it. Yes, Toli thought, the chrysalis had value. It meant *something* to all of them, which meant she had leverage.

What if she took it back herself? What would the dragons give, Toli wondered, to have the chrysalis back again? Would the Dragon Queen return her mother if she explained how she had found it—that Krala and Dral had taken it—if she delivered it back safely?

The chrysalis might at least get her into the Mountain, and buy her time to find where they were keeping her mother.

Toli lifted her chin and glared at Dragon Mountain. It might not be a plan, exactly, but it was better than no idea at all. It was better than waiting. She would get her mother back—if it was the last thing she ever did.

It's not about helping the Dragon-Mother, she told herself as she pulled to a stop outside the cave and gathered the bowl of coals and the small store of peat bricks out of the sled. *It's about getting our queen back.*

Inside, she built a fire and placed the sack nearby. The flames were enough to warm the cave a few degrees and make the walls glisten. Torn between looking at the dragon again and ignoring it, Toli watched the bag.

She leaned down with a scowl and peeled back the furs from around the chrysalis. A flash of red scales. Toli pressed her lips together. Could it hear her? She glimpsed the gold shine of the dragon's eyes following her movements. It could definitely see her.

What was it thinking in there? she wondered. It was probably as suspicious of her as she was of it.

She stared a moment longer, then flicked the furs back over the chrysalis and sank down on a blanket next to the fire.

There was no telling how long it would take for her to get all the way to Dragon Mountain. She had never even been as far as the deep ice fields, never seen the Necropolis, where the statues of the long-dead greeted Nya each morning—never spent a night on the ice. Still, she would return to the Queendom and prepare the sled as best she could.

If she told Pendar about what she'd found, would he change his mind and let them go get the queen? If she told Spar, would she bring Toli with her to the Mountain?

She couldn't risk it, couldn't risk either of them saying no.

Better to keep the chrysalis a secret, for now at least, until it was too late for them to stop her. The dragons had gotten the better of her for the second time. But this time, they hadn't left her unconscious in the snow.

Storm light shown outside the cave. The light from Toli's peat fire flickered against the slick walls. She eyed the sack that held the chrysalis as if it was plotting something.

"Dragons killed my father," she told it, glaring. "Dragons took my mother." She poked at the black brick on the fire with the tip of an arrow as she edged closer. "So don't think for a second that I'm doing this to help you." She flicked back the edge of the bag. A gasp stuck in her throat.

Thin cracks lanced across the red crystal. They spread as she watched, lacing the chrysalis like frost. Toli scuttled back with a cry, pressing her back to the cold sheen of the cave wall. The chrysalis shattered like splintering ice, and a slender, sparkling dragon the length of her arm slipped out. Its scales shone red as the aurora that streaked the winter sky. It shifted to its feet fast, shaking itself, ruffling the damp red and gold feathers at its neck.

It hissed at her.

Toli shook her head so hard, her vision blurred. This couldn't be happening.

The dragon zipped closer, pausing to stretch her wings open and then close them.

"Stay away," Toli hissed back, pressing herself against the ice.

The dragon paused, cocking her head as if she were listening to something far away. Her talons clicked against the ice as she hustled up the wall next to Toli, clinging to the ice above her, peering, upside down, into her face. An electric whiff of dragon washed over her.

Toli shot to her feet, hitting her head on the ceiling of the cave. Her breath came in short bursts. She stumbled away, but the dragon followed, faster than wind, across the cave floor. She scampered up Toli's leg, her talons pressing hard but not quite piercing.

Toli yelped a curse, dancing and waving to break free. "Get off me!"

The dragon raced down again, cringing toward the fire, her golden eyes wide.

"Don't come near me!"

The dragon shivered, fluttering her wings. They looked at each other, another shudder moving over the dragon's body, bouncing light off her red scales. She blinked up at Toli.

Toli frowned. If the dragon died, she'd never get her mother back. She waved her hand at the baby. "You're freezing. Get back in the furs. Go on."

The dragon slunk around and nudged the now-gray husks of chrysalis out of the way. She whipped inside the sack, burrowing in among the furs until only her head poked out. Her eyes stared accusingly at Toli.

Toli fought the urge to stick her tongue out at it. "I suppose you're hungry too," she muttered, brushing her hands against her legs. "Never heard of a dragon that wasn't." She walked backward as she moved toward the front of the cave. "Well, I don't have much. I wasn't expecting to have to feed you. Just . . . just stay there."

She gritted her teeth, walking faster. She'd left the sled just inside, where the foxes could be out of the wind. It was a good thing no one went out on the ice without emergency supplies—just some dried meat and a few mushrooms, but it would have to do.

As Toli leaned over the sled, a quiet voice at the back of her head whispered, *What if it attacks you?* She paused. Her hand shook as she hesitated over the handle of her long knife where it lay quiet in the belly of the sled. After a moment, she shrugged and picked it up, slipping it into the outer wrap of her boot. A child of the ice is prepared for anything.

The dragon was asleep, or pretending to be. Toli watched it for a while, then dumped the food on top of it and closed the sack. The dragon hissed in what Toli imagined was a questioning way.

"I can't very well leave you here and pick you up on my way back," she ground out. "Someone else could find you, and then what?" She picked up the sack, pinching the bridge of her nose with her other hand. Keeping an actual dragon a secret was going to be a lot harder than hiding a red stone, no matter how pretty it had been.

I don't think I can do this, she thought, dropping her forehead into her hand and cradling it there. There was a strange kind of comfort in the gesture, like there was someone who would catch her when she fell, even if it was just herself, and only for a moment.

She glanced outside. The clouds had passed, and Nya was up. Time to go.

Toli lifted the sack over her shoulder, dragon and all, and dropped it into the deep pocket of her hood with a sigh. The dragon shifted, curling inside with a contented rattle. Toli climbed back in the sled and headed toward the walls of the Queendom, but she couldn't help feeling as though, somehow, she had lost an argument she hadn't even known she'd been having.

She traveled fast, stabled the foxes, and left the sled just outside the wall, hurrying toward the Great Hall. She needed to collect her belongings for the trek across the deep ice. Maybe in the privacy of her room she could at least hide the dragon under her bed for a time, or—

Toli stopped walking, tipping her head back to stare at the color-streaked sky. The problem was the same. The dragon could creep off and attack someone. Worse, someone might accidentally creep up on it, and then what? What if Petal found it? No. The dragon had to stay with her, where she could keep an eye on it.

"Where have you been?" a harsh voice spun her around.

"Spar—"

"Up and gone—where?" Spar rasped.

"Nowhere! I just . . . I was checking the caves for . . . for—"

Spar's eyes narrowed as she pointed up at the morning sky. "Do you see what time it is?"

Toli lifted her face. Above them, blue and red streaks of

light raced one another, weaving across the sky. Over the dark silhouette of Dragon Mountain in the distance, the green light of Father Moon's rise cast a sickening pall over the ice.

"Dragon time," Toli whispered. *All* the dragons would be awake now. She shivered. Somewhere out there, her mother was fighting to stay alive. The lights gleamed back at her, streaking the sky.

"Come with me." Spar scowled. "We need to talk."

Toli didn't move. She didn't have time for this. She had to pack the sled and go—had to get across the ice before any more dragons went searching. Still, she thought, Spar knew the ice better than anyone. If she told the hunt master about what she'd found, maybe Spar would help her, maybe—

"Still dreaming?" Spar spat. "Still thinking the dragons are just going to pop your mother back here like she'd been invited for tea?"

"No! Spar, listen—"

Spar leaned into Toli's face. "If she's alive, the queen is in the Mountain, with *her*."

"You mean the Dragon-Mother."

"Yes. And taking our queen—that's a declaration of war."

Spar's footsteps crunched on the packed snow as she strode away, expecting Toli to follow.

"I—I can't come with you right now."

"Why not?"

"Toli!" Pendar's voice cut through the frosty air. "Nya's blessing, child, I've been looking for you everywhere."

Spar's jaw tightened, her eyes flashing.

Toli backed away from both of them, her heart racing. *Please, Nya, let the dragon stay asleep.*

"What do you want, Pendar?" Spar asked through gritted teeth.

"I have a plan."

"*You* have a plan."

I have one too, Toli thought. *And it starts with getting this dragon out of the Queendom.* Still, Toli paused despite herself. If Pendar had a real plan, maybe she wouldn't have to go. Maybe everything would be okay. "What is it?"

Spar sneered. "Trust me, Princess, whatever it is isn't worth your time. There is only one answer."

Pendar ignored her. "The Tithing is tomorrow at moonset. If the queen hasn't been returned to us, Spar and I, and a few of the other hunters, will go to meet them. We'll give them the tithe, as usual—to show our respect. Then we'll demand answers."

Spar began to laugh, a high tight sound that put Toli on edge. She shook her head at Pendar, and began to edge away from them again. "Your *plan* is to . . . wait and *ask them nicely?*"

Toli didn't have time to wait two days. She didn't have one day. Her mother needed help *now*.

Pendar reached toward her. "Listen. We have no real information. We can't make a decision until we do. Not with the Queendom at stake."

Toli had stopped listening. It would likely take at least two days to reach the Mountain. Pendar could have his *chat*. She'd be long gone.

Spar's black mood smoldered, dark as smoke and almost visible around her. Her burns seemed to glow in the cold, and her hair hung dark and lank across her shoulders. "Your plan is absurd," she ground out. "I told you. There's only one answer: We muster our best hunters. We go to the Mountain, and we kill the Dragon-Mother. We kill her, once and for all." Spar's words lurched Toli to a stop. She couldn't be suggesting they go to war with the dragons.

Pendar's brown skin darkened with rage. "You're insane," he growled.

Spar's words had lurched Toli to a stop. She couldn't be suggesting they go to war with the dragons. "We wouldn't survive," Toli whispered, her voice steadying. "It isn't just her. There are hundreds of them, Spar! Maybe thousands!"

Spar's eyes flashed. "Then we die, Anatolia," she hissed. "But we take that vile worm with us."

Toli's mouth fell open. She met Pendar's equally shocked gaze.

He turned his back on Spar. "Toli, I'm so sorry, the truth is, Toli . . . anyone—*anyone* goes to the Mountain, the chances are they won't come back alive. Listen to me. You and I will take the Tithing—"

"No!" Toli and Spar said in unison.

"We must think our actions through. We must learn more," Pendar pleaded.

Spar fisted her hands. "No tithe this year." The hunt master moved past Pendar, reaching out as if to take Toli's arm.

Toli drew away as the weight in her hood shifted. Her pulse

fluttered in her neck and she bit down on the urge to cover it with her hand. She had to get out of there.

"Listen to me," Spar said, moving with her as she backed up. "The moment they took Queen Una, our decision was made for us." Spar held out her hands to her, imploring. "*You* are the acting queen now, Anatolia. I don't care what promises you made to your mother. Some promises are made to be broken."

"No," Pendar said, his voice soft as new snow.

Toli moved toward the Hall, turned half toward Spar and Pendar as they followed behind.

"You can't allow it, Anatolia," Pendar continued. "It will be your death. The death of us all. You promised your mother you would listen to me." He turned to Spar. "Hunt master—please. You're . . . something's wrong with you. You're ill. You're not making sense."

"I have to go," Toli whispered as the snow creaked under her feet. The dragon shifted again, sending a bolt of adrenaline through her. She had to get out of there before they saw the baby.

"Fools!" Spar ground out. "There are no more promises!" She pointed a calloused finger at Toli, and the embers of her amber gaze pinned Toli to the spot. "I'll do what I can to keep you safe," she snarled. "But wear your cloak—at all times. Don't take it off. The scales will protect you from their fire. Did you know that?"

"I—"

"They will. Though Nya knows I hope you never need it." She sucked in a sharp breath, lifting one hand to her forehead.

Toli noticed the hunt master's hands were shaking.

She knew she couldn't help her mentor. She needed to go. The dragon could wake at any moment. But worry for Spar crowded out her thoughts. "Is it . . . is it your burns?" she stammered.

Pendar's face darkened. "Are you in pain, hunt master?"

Toli stepped closer, placing a hand on Spar's arm. It was like stone. A heartbeat passed before Spar shook her off. "When does the ice forgive?"

"The ice never forgives," Toli whispered, wishing she knew how to make things better.

"When does the ice forget?"

"The ice never forgets." She intoned the words the hunt master had taught her, but her thoughts spun away. If she didn't leave soon, she'd be stuck on the ice through the night. And if the dragon woke now—

"Will you bend the ice's will?"

"It cannot bend. You will break trying."

Spar's hand reached up to touch the scars on her face. "Good. Then you'll understand."

Pendar huffed. "Understand what?"

Spar didn't answer. The huntress stared into the distance, toward the sharp silhouette of Dragon Mountain. Her eyes glittered like ice in her scorched skin as she turned her head to study Toli. "If you won't kill that creature, it will have to be me." Spar paused. "It *should* be me."

Toli's voice stuck in her throat. "Wh-who? The dragon that took Mother?" She'd never seen Spar like this. Pendar was right.

Something was wrong with her. The pain of her burns, and of all that had happened, had affected her mind. "We . . . we can't just kill her. How will you even know which one it is?"

Spar grinned, her eyes fever-bright. "Perhaps we'll end them all."

Toli shook her head numbly. Hating the dragons was one thing. Protecting her people from them—saving her mother—all those she could defend, and would, and in doing so, find some measure of justice for her father.

But attacking a mountain full of dragons, young and old, and trying to what? Wipe them from the face of Ire? It wasn't just murder. It was a death wish for every man, woman, and child in Gall.

Her knuckles tightened on her bow. She had to get away from here. The weight of the dragon pulled at her. Given the chance, Spar would kill her, and Toli would lose whatever small power having it gave her. She looked at the two of them, and the truth hit her like the snap of a cord breaking. She might never see them again.

She took in Spar—with her shoulders thrown back, confident—and Pendar's gentle eyes. She spun without a word, unable to look at either of them any longer. Her feet pounded the ice like drums as she ran for the Great Hall. They both meant well, but she was done lying to herself—done listening to ridiculous threats and unacceptable promises. Saving her mother was up to her. She was on her own.

CHAPTER NINE

Toli hurried toward the Great Hall. She would slip up to her bedroom and get what she needed for the journey across the ice while the dragon was still asleep. In her head, Toli made a list of everything she would need as she ran. Extra clothes, food and water, of course, and some of the leatherleaf bags hunters took out on the deep ice. Waxed over with animal fat, they would protect what they held against dampness and frost. Peat bricks. What else? Weapons. The sleds were all stocked with beaters and spears, but she'd bring her bow too, and a good knife. She'd need strong embers.

She threw open the doors to the Hall, surprised at how quiet and peaceful it was inside. The fires crackled, merry and unaware. Everyone was out fulfilling the tasks of the morning.

Rasca had begun setting out bowls of beetle eggs on the

long tables so people could have food in their stomachs during the day. With only a few hours of moderate moonlight each day, there was no time to be wasted.

Toli wondered how long dragons slept as she hurried toward the ladder to her room, pausing only to pop a beetle egg into her mouth with a sigh. The dragon rattled deep inside her hood. She froze. *Go back to sleep*, she thought. *Go back to sleep*.

The dragon shifted. Of course. Now it was awake and probably hungry. Toli feared she was never going to get out of here! She looked around. Did dragons eat eggs? She had no idea.

Rasca shuffled by with another bowlful of hard-boiled beetle eggs. When the woman's back was turned, Toli picked up a handful of the pearly beetle eggs and dropped them into her hood. She hoped it was enough to keep the dragon distracted.

Toli hurried toward the back of the hall, but the dragon shifted again with a hiss, pulling Toli two steps sideways as she gobbled the eggs.

Wix came through a side door ahead of her, blocking her path with the barrow load of peat bricks he'd brought in to fill the fuel boxes at the back of the Hall. Toli let out a groan and stepped into the shadow of a pillar.

Petal followed behind him, wearing one of her favorite dresses, soft leather embellished with bright dragon feathers and scales she'd collected herself from the ice after the dragons returned to molt last year.

As they came closer, Toli tucked herself tightly against the pillar. Once they had passed, she'd make a dash past them and climb the ladder to her bedroom.

The dragon turned a circle in Toli's hood, shifting her weight again, forcing Toli back a step. Toli twisted around and caught a glimpse of red scales as the dragon climbed up the tall post into the rafters.

Her heart pulsed. *No, no, no, no, no. Where is she going?* "Get back here," she hissed upward, glancing over at her sister and Wix, who stood by the fire. "We have to go!"

They hadn't noticed her yet, but any second now they would. Toli held her breath, peering upward, and found the dragon's golden eyes peering back at her. "Come back," she mouthed, pointing toward the ground.

With a flick of her tail, the little red dragon slipped across the rafters like a breeze, zipping down a pole halfway across the room, on the far side of Petal and Wix. Her taloned toes reached out, grasping eggs out of one of the bowls. She shoved them into her mouth. Bits of egg flew everywhere. Rasca was going to have a fit when she saw the floor.

Toli gritted her teeth, and tried to catch the dragon's eye again.

"Toli!" Wix shouted, catching sight of her. "What are you doing here? I figured you'd be out training with Spar while you still can."

"Spar's not . . . feeling like herself." From the corner of her eye, she saw the dragon wrap herself up another post, this time coming down directly behind Wix. She shot Toli a wide-eyed blink and emptied another bowl of eggs into her scaled cheeks.

Next to Wix, Petal frowned. "I'd say Spar is more herself every day."

"No. I mean, she's *off* somehow."

"Yes." Petal nodded. "That's what I mean too. She's off."

Toli spotted a flash of red scales right behind Petal. She reached out, then startled, dropping her arm quickly as Wix narrowed his eyes at her. The dragon was gone again.

Hailfire! She tried to strike a casual pose.

"Anyway, I'm glad you're here," Petal said. "Did you hear? Pendar's going to talk to them—to the dragons—at the Tithing. He's going to ask about Mother. And I think you can help settle our argument." She glanced at Wix meaningfully.

Toli grunted. She wanted to tell them about her plan, but she couldn't. For one thing, they'd only try to stop her, and for another, finding the blasted dragon in the rafters was taking every ounce of her attention. So she said nothing.

It didn't matter anyway. Whatever Pendar intended, she was going to the Mountain. There would be no more waiting. She tried to smile at Wix but caught sight of the dragon, so it came out more like a grimace. When Toli looked behind him again, she was gone.

Where had that blasted creature gone?

Petal was looking at her earnestly. "We want Wix to go to the Tithing too, so you have to tell him I'm right. He would look older if we changed his outfit. At least mended all the tears in his tunic."

Wix lifted his chin and patted his curls and braids. "Forget it. I don't care how bossy you get. You're not touching my fashion."

Toli barked a laugh, despite herself.

Petal scowled. "Fashion isn't funny. Anyway, you have to be there so you can come back and tell me what happens." She cast Toli an apologetic look. "Toli won't go, and sending you is the only way we can be sure we're getting the whole story. If you want the hunters to take you seriously when you ask to go, we should make you look older. I have a bowl of black scale. With one of Father's old tunics, I could—"

"I don't need to look older. I just need to look tough. All the scuffs and tears on my clothes are from training and hunting and—"

"Yeah," Petal said. "I know you've got *a look*, Wix, but—"

A hiss from the rafters spun Toli around. A flash of scale. *There*—behind the throne. The dragon scrambled across the floor. Toli moved to intercept it. Trying to look casual, she threw a peat brick on the fire as she passed. Just as she was almost close enough to reach out and grab her, the dragon caught sight of another bowl of eggs—the last one—and veered away. She had the sense to look ashamed as she poured them into her gullet, then shimmied up another pillar.

Toli glared as the dragon came down behind Petal, pausing to let out a belch that shot flame across the edge of Petal's dress. The dragon slipped under the nearest bench as Petal spun around, screaming, "My dress!"

Wix gaped as Toli raced to the water barrel. Sparks shot up

the spines of the long feathers, filling the air with putrid smoke. Toli filled the scoop, running to toss all of the water at her sister.

Petal stood, dripping cold water and glaring at Toli.

"You were on fire," Toli explained, though she couldn't see why Petal would need this explanation.

Wix scratched his head and frowned, rattling a poker around in the peat embers. "It must have been a spark." He paused. "But it's such a small fire. And did either of you hear that noise?"

Toli shook her head.

Petal just sighed as she looked down at her scorched dress, the feathers singed black and crumbling. Dark circles stained the skin under Petal's eyes. "Guess I'll change," she grumped. "You," she added, pointing at Wix. "Wait here. I'm not done with you."

Wix gave her a solemn nod, apparently resigned to Petal's efforts.

Toli wanted to say something, but instead, she bit down a yelp as the dragon zipped up her leg and under her cloak, slipping back into the hood. The weight pulled her off-balance, and she threw out one arm, catching hold of Wix to steady herself.

His hazel eyes widened. "Toli, what's going on? Are you okay?"

Toli nodded, blowing out a deep breath. "I'm fine," she said, forcing a smile. "I've got a . . . a lot on my shoulders, that's all. I—I just—I have to go." Wix watched with a hurt expression as she backed slowly out of the room, turning away just in time to catch a glimpse of Rasca's perplexed stare as she shuffled in and saw egg on the floor, and all the empty bowls.

Toli waited for her sister to finish changing and leave to find Wix before returning to their bedroom. Sated, the dragon slept again, still and warm, curled behind the crook of Toli's neck. Toli packed as fast as she could, moving quickly to run supplies out to the sled without being seen.

It took her most of the remaining hours of Nya's light to finish. At last, she stocked the bowl of coals from the little hearth in her room. In normal circumstances, she wouldn't dream of leaving in a sled so close to nightfall, but these weren't normal circumstances.

Toli paused to take a look around before she shut the door behind her for the last time. This was it. She was going to try to accomplish the impossible—cross the ice and make a bargain with the Dragon-Mother.

She might die. The ice might kill her, and if it didn't, the dragons probably would. She bit her lip. She didn't want to leave Petal, or Wix, and she certainly wasn't interested in dying. *Maybe you should wait*, a voice at the back of her head tried to persuade her. *What if Pendar really can find out something important at the Tithing? What if they just give her back?*

Toli thought of Krala's sneer and knew she and Dral

wouldn't be waiting. She set her shoulders. No. There was no time for games, and no room for lies, even comforting ones. She would save them all—or die trying.

Her mother should be here, sitting on the throne where she belonged. Toli's throat tightened as she closed the door behind her with a firm thud.

She couldn't say goodbye to Petal and Wix, not with the dragon in tow. The ache in her chest grew. They would be mad, and hurt, but there was no other choice. She'd just have to explain it later, when she got back.

If I get back, she thought.

But there was only one person she needed to say goodbye to—one last thing to do.

Toli blew through the front doors of the Hall, hurrying back along the narrow paths, weaving around the small houses and outbuildings toward the far eastern edge of the Queendom. The lights danced over the ice, calling her to hurry.

The nine statues stood in a half circle along the back wall of the small building, four to either side of her father. Not for the first time, she wished the ice could have captured him better. His eyes had been green, like hers, and full of laughter. She remembered that, though the statue couldn't show it. She remembered his shaggy red hair and his rough beard.

She remembered his voice as he would lean over her bed to put her to sleep. It had been his job ever since she had left her mother's arms, and he continued to do so long after she was too old to need it. He tucked Petal in for the night, then made time for Toli, wrapping the blanket edges in tight around her. They talked about their day or their thoughts—asking questions, or posing them to each other, sometimes until long after bedtime.

"How far does the ice go, Father?" she had asked once, sinking her fingers into his crinkly beard. He pulled the furs close around her.

"The ice goes on for days . . . for forever, perhaps. It goes all the way to Dragon Mountain, and farther still."

She stared up at the painted ceiling of her bed, frowning. "All that . . . nothing."

His expression had turned serious. "You're wrong. The ice is not nothing, Daughter," he said, giving her cheek a stroke with the back of his hand. "You must respect it, as you respect all dangerous creatures. It is unpredictable—cruel as any dragon, fickle as any storm. It just holds its secrets even tighter than the dragons do."

She shook herself, releasing the memory, and put one hand on the statue's icy foot. It burned her skin, but she left it there anyway. "I should have listened to you," she whispered.

She closed her eyes.

Her parents' room had been warm that morning—their small fire singing with a merry crackle. He'd stared down into her face, her hands on his shoulders.

"What if something goes wrong?" she'd asked. "Why do you always have to be the one to give the tithe?"

His eyes had sparkled as he pushed her gently away. "Nothing will go wrong. The dragons have never hurt us before, Toli love, and they're coming, one way or another. My hunters need me to lead them. Your mother needs me to do my part." The black scales of his armor had caught the light, turning them deep blue.

"I can come too."

"You will stay here," he'd said, and she knew there would be no changing his mind.

Toli couldn't explain the weight of her foreboding, but it tugged at her like deep water, heavy and unrelenting.

She'd moved to block the door. "I won't let you go."

"Anatolia, please—"

"You can't."

"Toli, I'm the queen's companion. It's my task to do. The herds are so sparse this year—we have a tithe, but nothing left for our people. Your mother's doing her part. I must do mine."

Anatolia had willed her feet to root to the floor as he lifted her up. She tried to make herself stiff and heavy as a stonetree as he gently moved her away from the door. Tears had filled her eyes, her heart a dull throbbing ache as he engulfed her in his arms. She'd caught the sharp, icy scent of hail. Then he put her down, and it was gone.

She should have stayed there—like he'd told her to. If she had, perhaps he'd still be alive. Instead, she ignored his instructions. She followed him, and he saw her, and the distraction got him killed.

They'd offered the tithe even though the herds were scarce. *Why* had the dragons attacked? The dragon's hunger had always been the explanation for the attack, but something just didn't add up.

Toli blinked away tears, getting colder with every passing moment. "I'm sorry, Father."

She pulled her hand away from the statue and turned to go.

The wind outside whipped her braids behind her. She could hear the caves singing, half a mile outside the Queendom. Their mournful storm song rose and fell like the keening wails of a family when a loved one has died. Toli shivered.

White fog hovered just over the Queendom, getting lower, sifting over the edge of the black stone bluff to fall like water. Snow twisted down and around her. If she hadn't known her way through the Queendom by heart, she could easily have lost her bearings. She growled at the wind. *Another hail-blasted storm!*

Her skin itched to leave, and every moment she stayed was another moment her mother was fighting for her life—another moment she wasn't back on the throne, where she belonged.

She was prepared to brave the cold and the open ice wastes without Nya's light, but halfway to the Southern Gate, she knew she couldn't leave the Queendom. The air was thick with snow. It whipped around her head and eyes, blinding her. If she left now, she'd never make it to the deep ice, never mind all the way to Dragon Mountain. She had to be smart and consider each action carefully, as Spar had taught her. Leaving in this storm would be death. *Another blasted delay.*

Toli stomped toward the stables, leaning into the wind. The dragon shifted and rumbled. Perhaps it smelled the foxes, though they didn't seem bothered by her. Toli grabbed a leatherleaf tarp from a high shelf in the stable and hurried back through the Southern Gate to throw it over the sled waiting just outside the wall. It was loaded with supplies now—ready to drive out onto the ice wastes. The cloth would cover it, and once the storm moved in, there would be a thick layer of snow and ice. The sled would look like just another drift in the storm.

Toli turned on her heel and, just through the Gate, spotted Spar pacing toward her—coming to check on the foxes, no doubt. She could barely see her mentor through the barrage of wind and snow, but Toli tucked herself behind the edge of the stable, unable to look away. Spar's eyes were cast down, her forehead gripped in one hand as she passed, and Toli could see her lips moving as if she were talking to someone.

When the stable door had shut behind the hunt master, Toli slipped out from behind the building. She peered through the Gate into the storm until her eyes stung and her head began to throb.

"If you cause any trouble," she hissed at the dragon, "I'll have Rasca turn you into soup."

The dragon's only response was a low rumble as she shifted in the deep well of Toli's hood. She couldn't turn her into soup, of course—not if she wanted her mother back—but what the dragon didn't know wouldn't hurt her.

Toli knew if she left now, she wouldn't get far. The wind would tear her to shreds, and the foxes along with her, if the cold didn't kill them first. A bitter taste filled her mouth as she turned away from the ice and trudged back toward the Hall.

The ice would not bend. She would break trying. She had to wait out the storm, but even the ringing of the ice caves faded away against the turmoil in her mind screaming for her to go—and go now—while there was still time.

CHAPTER TEN

With the storm raging, the quiet of evening settled in fast. Toli gave the fire in her bedroom a vicious poke. She had no choice. She could leave and spend the night huddled with a dragon and seven foxes under her sled, hoping for the best. Or she could spend it in her bed. Her heart gave a sharp pang. Where was her mother spending this cold night? Was she scared? Did she think they'd all forgotten her there?

Toli threw a brick on the fire. Wherever she was, one thing was certain: The queen of Gall wouldn't give up.

Toli glared at the dragon curled on her pillow. She could see how someone like Petal might think there was something cute about her, with her wing tucked over her face like that, but Toli knew better. She was just another dragon—dangerous.

She stabbed the black peat with the poker until it broke apart, bursting into an angry glow.

With a dragon hidden in their bedroom, there was no way Toli could allow her sister to sleep in their room that night. She'd told Petal she needed time alone to think. Her sister, pale and weary, had accepted without question. It would be good, Petal had agreed, for her to sleep in their mother's bed. "Maybe I'll dream of her," Petal added with hope in her voice. And maybe she would. Maybe her sister would wake from her dreams somehow knowing their mother was alive and well.

Toli's heart had ached, powerless to help, as she watched Petal glide across the narrow ledge to the other side of the Hall, where the queen's room looked out over the ice.

Alone in the bedroom she and Petal shared, Toli managed to hide the sleeping dragon between a wall of blankets and the shadows at the back of her enclosed bed, just in case. She supposed she should be grateful that between hatching and all the mischief in the Hall, the creature seemed to have worn itself out.

Toli moved to sit on the edge of her bed and scowled at the dragon. "I'm not lying down next to a dragon," she muttered, gritting her teeth. She reached out and picked it up. Its scales were smooth and warm against her skin as she moved it to the floor under her bed.

The dragon squawked a protest as Toli dumped it on the ground and flopped into her bed with a sigh. *Maybe I should just put it back in the sack.*

Toli's eyes flew open at the sound of claws scrabbling against the stonetree boards.

Fast as wind, the dragon zipped herself back up onto the bed, curling up on Toli's pillow.

"Get. Off," Toli growled, shoving it off the pillow and flopping over on her side.

The creature gave a hiss. "Friend," she insisted.

Toli froze. Great, it was talking now. "I'm not your friend," Toli ground out. "I'm not your anything."

A few minutes passed before the soft pressure of talons told her the dragon was back on her pillow. Toli shoved it off.

The dragon waited, then climbed back on, curling in a tight ball next to Toli's head. She stretched one wing, her feathers reaching down to tickle Toli's nose.

Toli growled and shoved her off again, yanking the pillow to her side. The dragon curled up a little farther away, her eyes hooded, waiting.

Toli's eyes grew heavy.

She woke to a faceful of feathers and the dragon's long neck stretched out across her chest. Its heavy head was tucked up under Toli's chin, the sharp, electric scent shifting with her breath.

Toli could feel the dragon's heartbeat pressed against her own. Her hands itched to push the dragon off, but for a moment she paused. It wasn't hurting anything. Not really.

Thin green moonlight spilled into the room. Morning—or close enough and the wind had died. She shifted the dragon off her with gentle hands. All she had left to do was throw on her cloak and she'd be racing across the ice toward her mother with a dragon to trade.

Time to go. At last.

No sooner had Toli thought it than Wix threw open the bedroom door with a laugh. "Wake up, sleepyheads. Let's go collect some—"

He froze.

Toli shot up, shifting to block his line of sight. "Wix! It's not what you think."

Wix looked like someone had struck him with a rock. His eyes shifted from her to the baby dragon and back again. He lifted one hand to point at Toli's bed. "It's *not* a dragon?"

"A what?!" Petal appeared behind him. She stumbled into the room, one hand raised to point at the dragon. "Toli?"

"Okay," Toli raised her palms. "Okay, it is what you think . . . a little bit, but you don't understand."

The dragon scrambled up onto Toli's shoulder, despite efforts to discourage her, and gave her a wide-eyed look as if to say, "Yes, how *did* we come to this?" The narrow end of the dragon's tail wrapped around the front of Toli's neck like a necklace. Smooth scales warmed against her body. The creature sighed.

Petal shuffled forward. "Toli," she whispered. "There's a dragon on you." She stopped. "*Why* is there a dragon on you?" She mirrored Wix's crossed arms.

"Look. Both of you. I was on the ice early yesterday morning before Nya rose, and I found a chrysalis, okay? It hatched unexpectedly, and now it's a dragon. Easy. Done."

Petal blinked.

Wix rolled his eyes. "Uh-huh."

"Don't worry. I'm getting rid of it."

Petal came closer, her fingers reaching out to touch the dragon's tail. A small smile played across her face as she looked at Toli. "It's soft," she said. "And warm."

The dragon lifted her head, her golden eyes heavy.

"Petal," Toli warned.

"Right." Wix spun around. "I'll go get Pendar. He'll sort this out."

"No," Toli shouted. The dragon rose to crouch on her shoulder, arching her neck at Wix to cough a short burst of flame.

"Stop that," Toli snapped at the creature as Wix stumbled back. The dragon snorted and curled up again, shooting her a glare.

Petal stared. "Toli, what is going on?"

"Close the door," Toli instructed Wix.

Wix did as she asked. "Okay, the door's closed. Talk, he demanded."

Petal had moved closer and dropped her face down to meet the dragon. "She's beautiful . . . aren't you?" she purred, stroking the dragon's tail. "Aren't you just the prettiest thing."

Toli's jaw fell open. "Are you . . . baby talking to the dragon?"

"She's just the sweetest." The dragon gave a contented hum that vibrated her throat like a purr. Petal laughed. "Yes you are. Look at your pretty golden eyes. Yes, Petal thinks you're beautiful. Yes I do. What are you going to call her?"

Wix's eyebrows had disappeared into his hairline. He looked

at Toli, the question "Aren't you going to do something about this?" written all over his face.

"Petal, I'm not going to call her anything! It's not a fox pup. It's not some kind of pet. It's a dragon! It . . . it's dangerous."

"*She* doesn't look dangerous to me. She slept on your head all night, didn't she? And your hair doesn't even look worse than usual. I think she deserves a name."

Toli threw up her hands. "Fine. Name her. Just don't get attached. I'm giving her back—I'm trading her—for our mother. You remember her, right?" A stab of regret lanced through Toli at Petal's stricken expression. "They're not our friends, Petal. They can never be our friends."

"Friends," the dragon whispered, dropping her chin into Petal's palm.

Toli froze. Great. Now it was talking to *them* too.

"She's just a baby," Petal said. "She didn't kill Father. And she didn't . . . She didn't take Mother."

"Well," Wix said, joining them and watching Petal closely for any sign of impending implosion. "I guess that's true . . ."

Petal wore a smug expression. "Two against one. So. Her name's Ruby."

Toli tugged at her braids to keep from taking hold of Petal and shaking her sister's head loose from her shoulders. "*Ruby* didn't do those things, but her . . . her people did. I'm using her to get Mother back, Petal. The end. Now stop patting her—both of you. I'm supposed to protect the Queendom. And as your sister, I'm doubly responsible for you, Petal."

Petal frowned. "You can't protect me, Toli. Not always.

And besides," she added, cocking her head, "you're worth protecting too, you know." She rested her hand on the dragon's muzzle. Ruby rattled in her sleep. "Wix and Ruby and I think so, anyway."

Toli sputtered but couldn't think of a response.

"So," Wix began. "You're going to Dragon Mountain to get your mother back?"

"Yes. I told you. No matter what it takes."

The corners of his mouth drew down, threatening to fall right off his face. He stepped closer and reached into his pocket to pull out an ice beetle egg. Holding it up, Wix waved it slowly through the air until Ruby's nostrils flared and her eyes shot open. Her crescent pupils dilated when she saw what he held. Wix watched as her head wove back and forth, her gaze locked on the food.

He tossed it into the air. Ruby shot forward, snatching it before it could land. Wix stumbled back. "Whoa."

"Fast, right?" Toli smiled with unaccountable pride. The dragon's speed, after all, had nothing to do with her.

"Yup. She's fast, all right." He met her eyes, frown intact. "Now, what else aren't you telling us?"

Toli worried at her hair, considering.

Petal watched, her face guarded.

Wix huffed his breath. "All of it."

With a sigh, Toli told them about the twin dragons, Krala and Dral and how they were looking for Ruby, and about their offer. When she was done, the room fell silent.

"So," Wix began, eyeing Ruby, "why aren't they all out looking for Ruby?"

"Maybe they are," Petal whispered.

"I don't think so," Toli scowled. "I think those two took her."

Petal shook her head. "What did you say she called herself—the female?"

"Krala. Krala Frost."

Petal's eyes widened. "Like the poem Mother made us memorize? Remember, Toli?"

"What poem?"

Petal folded her hands in front of her. "'When at last a seethe is born, some have feather, some have horn. Of royals there are only three. One fights to lead, the others free.'"

Wix grinned. "Oh, I remember that one. Something about the rest of them all having to be loyal . . . then something else . . . something, something. What is a seethe, again?"

Toli pulled a face. "It's all the dragons born in a year."

Petal sighed. "Right, but they don't have a seethe every year. Only every . . . I don't know, every fifty years—maybe every hundred years. I don't know. Dragons live a long time."

"So a seethe is all brothers and sisters the same age?" Wix asked.

Petal nodded. "But only the first three female dragons hatched in a seethe have any power. They are the leaders of the seethe—kind of like the royalty. Only their strongest can grow up to challenge the Dragon-Mother. I mean, they don't *have* to challenge her. Mother told me this Dragon-Mother has been around for generations, since way before even our grandmother was born."

Toli unbraided and rebraided her hair, pulling out the knots from where the dragon had slept. "That makes sense. Dral said Dragon-Mother was a title. They use it the same way we use *Queen*."

Petal nodded. "Then some of the dragons were born to a different Dragon-Mother."

"How do you remember all that stuff?" Wix grumbled. "I bet you remember the rest of the poem too."

Petal rolled her eyes. "'In every seethe, they must obey. To sleep, to hunt, to toil, or play. The firstborn girl is named for Frost. The second named for Stone. The third to hatch makes do with Sky. The rest take their names alone.'" She put one hand on her hip. "Seriously, Toli? It's not like we know that much about them to begin with. None of this is ringing a bell?"

"Maybe," Toli muttered. "A small bell. In the distance."

Wix grinned. "So Krala is a firstborn. So when they hatched, if one of her seethe was going to challenge the old Dragon-Mother, it would have been Krala, right? Shouldn't that make her the Dragon-Mother?"

Petal shook her head. "Well, they seem to put a lot of importance on being firstborn, but you said this Dragon-Mother is Krala's sister. That means it wasn't Krala who challenged the old Dragon-Mother and won. Mother told me that this Dragon-Mother is a Sky. Thirdborn. I think any of the first three females born in a seethe *can* become the Dragon-Mother. One of them just . . . just has to take the old one's place."

Wix nodded. "Right. They fight for it."

Toli scowled. "So they fight their own mother for the throne."

Petal gave a somber nod. "Except for some, the Dragon-Mother might be an aunt or a niece . . . or—or a sister."

"Ugh." Wix gave a dramatic shiver. "That's horrible."

Toli gave her sister a tight smile. "Still think *Ruby* is just a sweet little bowl of bison butter?"

Petal sighed. "The point is, if those two dragons you met took Ruby, maybe it was because Ruby is a Frost too. If I was a dragon and I was planning on challenging the Dragon-Mother, and thought I could win, *and* I knew there wouldn't be another seethe born for fifty or a hundred years . . ."

Toli was nodding. "Then taking the firstborn would be a pretty good way for Krala to secure her position and seize power."

Petal scowled. "So if Krala believes she's supposed to be the queen . . . is she planning on killing the Dragon-Mother?"

Toli winced as the little dragon's talons dug into her shoulder. Ruby's expression was fierce. Toli's pulse skipped as she lifted Ruby's talons and peeled the creature off, moving her to the bed. "I think so, or at least getting rid of her somehow. She said that the Dragon-Mother taking our queen was a sign of weakness, and . . . rot. Oh! And she said something to Dral about wanting other dragons to get the blame for taking the chrysalis too."

"I can see why you didn't give her the chrysalis," Wix added. "I still can't imagine how you faced one of them, never mind two!"

"It's not as though I had a choice." Toli smiled.

Petal nodded. "Toli was right not to trust them. Besides"—she turned to Toli—"your plan is a good one. Having Ruby might help us get Mother back."

Wix stepped toward her. "So do you think the Dragon-Mother will talk to you?"

"It's my best chance," Toli said.

"Well, it's better than Pendar's plan, any day. I just hope it doesn't get us killed."

"*Me*," Toli cut in. "You hope it doesn't get *me* killed. You two are staying here."

"No," Wix and Petal said in unison as Petal lifted her hands to her hips.

Wix snorted. "No way, Toli. We all go together."

Toli's breath caught as Ruby scrambled up her leg, curling around the back of her neck. "Ow! Hailfire," Toli muttered.

Petal came over and tried to remove Ruby from Toli's shoulders, but the dragon clung on. Petal sighed, giving up. "We're going with you."

"Um. No."

Wix frowned. "Why not? She's right. You need us."

"I'm doing just fine. I don't want the two of you involved. You might get hurt."

Petal's lip quivered. "She's my mother too. And I can help. I know I can."

"No, Petal. I can't take care of everyone! Gall needs her queen and I'm going to get her. By myself. And if everything goes well, I'll bring her home, and then everything can go back to normal. I'll have proven to mother that I should be a hunter, so Wix and I can go back to training and you can do . . . whatever you usually do." Toli shifted her weight. She realized with sudden discomfort that she'd never asked Petal about her hopes and dreams. Maybe Petal didn't want things to go back to normal. Her sister always seemed so calm and . . . satisfied, just doing the things she did from one day to the next. Toli had always assumed that that meant she was happy . . . but maybe her sister wanted more. She shook the thought loose. Whatever the truth might be, Petal couldn't have this. It wasn't safe. Wix's huff of breath brought her attention back to the argument.

"Sure," Wix scoffed. "I mean, you taking a baby dragon to Dragon Mountain by yourself to bargain for your mother? That sounds like a brilliant plan, oh great queen. What could possibly go wrong?"

"Shut up."

"No." Wix squared his shoulders.

Petal was rubbing her fingers as if she were trying to clean the bones underneath. "Listen, I could do the cooking. I . . . I'll bring my herbs in case one of us, or the foxes, gets hurt. I can look after Ruby. Please! I can be useful."

"Yeah, don't be stupid, Tol. Let us help."

Toli crossed her arms. "Listen, both of you. I have the baby dragon. If Krala comes back—or worse, sends all the dragons, at least they'll only come after me. I can lead them away from the Queendom. Besides," Toli continued, "I'm not waiting. I'm going today—right now. The sled's all packed."

Wix began to pace, Ruby's golden eyes following him. "I'll go with you. Petal can stay—she'll be able to deal with Pendar and Spar."

"You're not leaving me behind!" Petal yelled. "And why didn't you just tell Pendar about Ruby, anyway?" she questioned.

Toli shook her head. "I thought about that, but he's committed to waiting—to trying to reason with the dragons at the Tithing. He'll just turn her over and hope for the best."

"It's not enough. I don't know exactly what Krala and her brother are planning, but I don't want to throw away our one chance to get Mother back. We have to take the dragon back *now*, and we have to give her to the Dragon-Mother—no one else. We don't know how many other dragons feel the same way as Krala and Dral.

"And before you ask, I can't tell Spar either. Believe me, I thought about it, but whatever is going on with her, one thing is certain: She'll kill *Ruby* the moment she sets eyes on her. Besides, I'm the acting queen. This is my responsibility. If anyone's going to get themselves brutally murdered, it's going to be me."

Wix blinked. "Your logic seems flawed."

Petal turned to grasp Toli's hands with cold fingers, her eyes pleading, but Toli pulled away. "Only I can be held responsible if something goes wrong. No one else."

Her sister's face went blank, as though she'd drawn a curtain across it. Her black hair swayed as she moved past Toli to the door. "You know, we might not be just a *risk*, Toli," Petal said, her voice strangely calm. "Wix is good at things . . . and I am too. It's not for you to decide."

Toli stared. "I didn't say—"

Petal held up her hand. "Remember when you wanted to learn to hunt? Mother let you, right? She even got the hunt master herself to teach you. And when she told you it was time to start your training to follow in her footsteps as queen, she didn't ask if you were strong enough, did she? No! She didn't ask if you were smart enough . . . or good enough. Did she?"

"Petal—"

"*Did* she? Because she trusts you! And you can't even trust your own sister and your best friend to have your back. Not even just for company. So fine. I give up. You want to do it alone? Do it alone." She spun on her heel and disappeared down the ladder to the Hall without looking back.

Wix glanced at Toli but wouldn't meet her eyes.

Her cheeks heated. *I can't lose anyone else.*

Wix turned to follow Petal, but before he slid down the ladder, he let out a long breath. "Be careful out there, Toli."

Then they were both gone.

Cold spread under her ribs, aching as she struggled not to call after them. She stood looking at the door with tears in her eyes. At last she swallowed against the lump in her throat and turned to fill her bowl with embers.

"Bye," she whispered back.

We are all fools. It cannot be helped.

—Ice carver Belgar Walerian

CHAPTER ELEVEN

People were usually busy about their tasks even this early in the morning, but Father Moon was up, and today they gathered outside to look at the streaks of red, green, gold, and blue as they wove across the sky and through the dim stars. The lights raced into the distance like dreams.

Toli, lost in thought, watched her feet as she walked along the packed snow of the path toward the Southern Gate.

As she passed the far side of the Hall, Rasca moved out of the shadows, startling her. She grabbed Toli's arm in a grip that would have left bruises if she hadn't been wearing dragon scale. "Look," the old woman gasped.

Toli followed the line of Rasca's gnarled finger just in time to see shining black feathers as they skimmed the ridge, low over the Queendom. Toli ran forward a few steps trying to see if it was Krala, but the dragon was gone.

"Must be hunting," Rasca said, appearing at her elbow.

Goose bumps rose on Toli's arms. Dragons didn't hunt over the ledge. That dragon had been looking for something—or maybe *someone*. Toli shuddered.

Rasca's watery blue eyes were wide. "Feathers like a whisper," she said quietly, staring up at the sky with fear in her voice. Her wrinkled hands trembled on Toli's arm. "Guess they're all up now," she sighed, then caught sight of Toli's clothes with a frown. "You're not going out there? Not today."

"Just . . . just collecting."

"Didn't you see what just flew past, girl?" Rasca lifted her weathered brown hands to her hips. "And you're not dressed for the forest. You're dressed for deep ice."

"No. Just collecting in the forest."

Rasca snorted, her wisps of white hair practically standing up with the force of her indignation. "Humph. Well, maybe that's where the hunt master was headed too—in her best armor. To the stonetrees . . . to collect conks."

"What do you mean? Why would Spar go out on the ice?"

"Your guess is as good as mine. But her sled is missing—according to Pendar—and the hunt master with it."

Toli's pulse fluttered. There was no good reason Spar would be out on the ice. She swallowed.

Rasca watched Toli's face carefully, her watery eyes narrowed to thin slits. Toli squirmed, and Rasca's scowl grew deeper, the lines in her face like cracks in the ice. "Humph." Her eyebrows scrunched together over her nose like a patch of moss on a tree. "I see. Well then, I'll make up a marinade—

sweet flower tea and a bitter lichen compote. It will be a proper feast."

It was Toli's turn to scowl. "Why?"

Rasca lifted herself up until her back was almost straight. She looked Toli right in the face without blinking. "I'd bet my last tooth you're headed to the ice. You ask me, it will be a Strongarm funeral." She turned to go back in the Hall, but paused, calling over her shoulder, "The least I can do is make your favorite sauce . . . in your honor."

"Make lots!" Toli called in her direction. "I'll be back!"

If Rasca heard her, she gave no sign.

The door to the Hall shut behind her.

Toli made her way to the Southern Gate. Had it really been Krala skimming the ridge? If so, why? Had Dral convinced her to continue looking for the chrysalis? Maybe Rasca was right and the dragon was just out hunting. Or *maybe* she was looking for Toli.

Regardless, the sooner Toli took Ruby out of the Queendom, the faster she could reach the Mountain—and her mother. She quickened her pace. Rasca would almost certainly be telling Pendar her suspicions. If she didn't go now, he might try to stop her.

She uncovered the sled and hitched up the foxes just as the green light of Father Moon reached over the edge of the Mountain to stain the ice fields like a sickness. The green moon would stay risen now until the dragons went south, battling with the clean light of the Daughter Moon's daily rise—the dragon time.

The conversation with Wix and Petal spun in Toli's head. She missed them both already, and Petal might never forgive her—Wix too. But she felt she'd done the right thing, and that was the end of it. She shook off her doubts like bits of frost that had overstayed their welcome. The supplies she'd loaded onto the sled didn't seem like much, all tucked away under a leather-leaf tarp, but it would have to be enough.

Ruby slipped out of her hood and dropped down to stand in the belly of the sled next to her. She placed one taloned fore-leg on Toli's foot. "Friend," she hissed, blinking her golden eyes. Toli forced away the tiny burst of warmth that bloomed in her chest.

Ruby cocked her head. "Food."

Toli frowned and pulled a bit of dried bison from her pocket. It wouldn't be long before the dragon used the words *friend* and *food* interchangeably, she thought.

She sighed. "Well, come on, then."

The little dragon climbed back up her leg, took the bison, and moved to a lookout position on her shoulder as Toli drove the foxes out onto the ice. The extra supplies she had packed for the deep ice weighed them down, the foxes working hard to get up to speed.

As hours passed, Toli lost sight of the Queendom, then of the stone ridge. By Nya's moonset, even the two-hundred-foot-tall stonetree forest would begin to look like nothing but a thin dark smudge across the landscape.

Low, heavy clouds moved in, covering the sky. Flickers of

aurora light shone through them, like storms in the distance. Bad weather was coming.

A muffled voice from under the blankets called out, "Could we stop and have something to eat?"

Toli yelped, nearly toppling out the sled as she yanked it to a stop and spun around, her knife clutched in her hand. There was a shifting sound at the very back as Petal clambered out from beneath the back bench. Ruby hustled over to scuttle up her arm, looking pleased.

Toli's mouth opened, then shut again.

"I could stand to eat too."

Wix climbed out from the other side of the tarp cloth, his face the picture of innocence.

"What are you doing here?!"

Petal stroked Ruby's head. "We told you. We're coming with you. We're not letting you do this without us."

Toli grasped her braids and tried not to shriek. "I told you not to come!"

"And we didn't listen!" Petal snapped back.

Wix shrugged. "Yeah, we thought we'd come anyway. Our lives. Our choice."

Hailfire. There was a selfish part of Toli that was relieved to see them, but she knew too well what selfishness led to. Her father had paid that price. She tried to think of a way to make them go home.

She looked at her sister. "I don't want you here!"

Hurt flashed across Petal's face, and Toli wished she could

take it back. She could see from the way her sister folded her arms that it hadn't done any good anyway.

"Tough." Petal scowled. "I know your cooking. You'll poison yourself, and Ruby too, if someone's not here to help."

"Look at it this way," Wix added, clapping her on the back. "Now, if the Dragon-Mother decides to eat us, we'll make a decent meal."

Petal dropped her head into her hands as Toli turned to stare at him. "That's supposed to make me feel better?"

He shrugged. "I think you're pretty much stuck with us."

Toli stared at each of them in turn, her thoughts churning. She was almost a full day's ride from the Queendom. Nya would be setting soon. People would have noticed they were missing by now. Pendar, Luca, Rasca—all of them would be worried—and angry. If she went back, it would be over. They'd lock her in a room before they'd let her out of their sight again. *And Ruby . . .*

After a moment Toli threw up her hands. "Fine. But when we get there, we stick together, and I do the talking. Agreed?"

Neither answered. The Mountain was dark against the horizon, larger and nearer than it had been when she'd left that morning—but the wastes still stretched into the distance ahead of them. Toli couldn't see where the ice stopped and the Mountain began. Father Moon's green light swept over the summit like a sickness.

"So," Petal asked, looking up at Father Moon. "How far do we still have to go?"

Toli frowned but followed her gaze. "Hard to say. I . . . I'm not sure anyone knows, except maybe Spar. She went at least as far as the pass. Anyway, I'm guessing it's farther than it looks."

"Did we pass the Necropolis? I tried to peek out of the blankets, but—"

Toli shook her head. "Can't be much farther now though." The thought made her shiver. A vast field of the dead carved in ice was hard to fathom. She didn't want to stop at all, but she especially didn't want to stop there. Her heart might not survive seeing her father's relic.

Wix tilted his head back, watching the lights dance over the bowl of the sky. He pointed to where four stars brightened, just to the west of where Nya sank below the horizon. "Nya's bear-cat." He turned and pointed in the other direction. "And I can just make out the Harvester. The Necropolis is just east of the Harvester, and as long as we don't get any closer to the bear-cat, we should be making straight for the Necropolis."

Petal shot an astonished look at Toli.

She shrugged. "Carver's wisdom," she explained.

Wix smirked. "What can I say? I'm good to have around." Then, as if he could hear what Toli had been worrying about, he asked, "Nya will be down soon. Should we stop for the night?"

She shook her head, motioning for them to sit down. "The wind's calm." She tossed the bag of dried meat and mushrooms back to her sister and slapped the reins. "Not yet. We're not stopping until we have to."

Father Moon hung just under the cloud layer, watching over the Mountain and the ice. The foxes raced forward, their breath coming in clouds as they pulled the sled across the barrens. They were farther now than any of them had ever been before.

Toli tried to remember everything she'd been told about traveling on the ice. Listen closely so it can tell you where danger lies. If you can't see, wait out the storm under a sled—or risk finding yourself miles away from where you want to be. Keep moving. Stopping for too long is death.

It was meager advice, and she raked her thoughts for more as the cold burned her cheeks.

When does the ice forgive?

The ice never forgives.

She tightened the hood of her white cloak around her shoulders, making sure it covered Ruby too. Had it really been only two days since Spar had given it to her? It felt like a lifetime had passed. Despite Toli's fears about where her mentor might have gone, and what she might be doing, the weight of the soft cloak around her shoulders gave her comfort.

Wix scooted up to sit beside her at the front, leaving Petal curled under furs at the back of the sled. He nudged her with his elbow. "You know," he said in a voice pitched just over a whisper. "You could give your sister a compliment now and then."

"What do you mean?"

"Well, it's just—you say some kind of mean stuff."

Toli stared at him. "I do not!"

Wix arched an eyebrow at her.

Petal's hurt expression flashed in Toli's mind and her shoulders slumped. "I'm not trying to be mean. I'm just trying to keep her safe. You know that!"

He bumped her gently. "Okay, but whatever your reasons are, it doesn't change how it feels, you know?"

"But if I say nice stuff, it will just encourage her!"

Wix looked at her, waiting for what she had said to sink in.

"Oh," Toli said.

Something sharp hit her cheek.

In the back, Petal yelped as something struck her hand. She glanced up. "Hail." Her eyes widened. "Should we stop?"

Toli shook her head. "No." She looked at the sky. "If we keep going, maybe we can stay ahead of the weather, at least as far as the Necropolis. If we can make it there, we should be a little more protected. We'll shelter there."

They were way out past the farthest hunting grounds. Spar had been out here, she knew, but Toli had never been this far. Other than the hunt master, only those the queen charged with placing the statues of that year's dead at the Necropolis had been out this far. It was their final resting place, a tribute to their ancestors. The statues were brought to the ice to bring Nya joy, and placing them there was an honor, as well as a burden.

It couldn't be too much farther.

The sled began to bump underneath them, tiny ridges and lumps pocking the icy landscape. An uneasy feeling crawled over her skin. Ruby crept out of Toli's hood, her body tense, as though she sensed it too. Above them, behind the clouds, streaks of color meandered, denying any urgency.

It started as a kind of rattling buzz. Toli turned and her eyes met Wix's. His brows knit together as he gave her a solemn nod. They both knew the sound of ice beetles under the surface, not from experience, but by reputation. It was one of the few things Spar had lots to say about.

Toli knew adult ice beetles were big, some as long as her forearm, and the edges of their iridescent wings could cut flesh to the bone. Their fist-sized heads hid in the shadow of enormous pincers. Bright reflective paddles flashed from the center of each leg. Beautiful to look at, and in a few months' time, harmless—once their pincers dropped and they affixed themselves to the bark of the stonetrees using their double rows of serrated teeth. Once a year, the stonetree forest sparkled with them.

Out here on the ice it was a different story. The giant insects were territorial and aggressive. There were stories of them forming swarms in the hundreds—or even thousands.

Spar had told her about sheltering under her sled once while on a hunt. The hunt master had watched as a bison bull wandered into the ice beetles' breeding ground, injured and bleeding from a fight. The way Spar told it, once the beetles had surrounded the doomed animal, it took twelve seconds before there was nothing left but bones.

The buzzing under the ice grew louder. A snarl stirred in the depths of Ruby's throat, low and questioning. The foxes whined.

Wix gave Toli a stiff nod, his eyebrows furrowing as he reached down to grab a beater. The beetles couldn't be shot with arrows. The weapons rarely killed them, and according to Spar, the beetles' carapaces just shattered in explosions of sharp shell pieces that rained down on the unfortunate shooter. Instead, sleds were equipped with long paddlelike clubs.

Wix handed Toli the other beater. She stretched to grasp the long pole of etched bone, slowing the sled to a stop.

Petal looked from one to the other. "What's happening?"

"Petal, I need you to do exactly as I say." Toli saw a flash of fear in her sister's eyes.

"Um. Okay."

The rasping buzz under the ice was a rare enough sound, heard only on the long hunts, but Toli and Wix both knew from the stories that once you heard it, it was too late to run. If there weren't too many ice beetles, they could fight their way through. Otherwise, they'd have to hide and wait out the beetles. That could take hours, or, if Nya's will was against them, the beetles might swarm for more than a day.

Her mother needed her *now*.

Toli reached under the bench seat at the front of the sled where she and Wix sat and handed him her spare dragon-scale hood and arm shields. He strapped them on without comment. Together, they unhitched the foxes and moved to unload the sled and tip it over. Working fast, Toli slid underneath and jammed layers of fur and leatherleaf in the gaps where the crescent shape rested higher. Then she crawled out and, just before setting the lip of the sled down, Toli turned to her sister. "Get in," she said.

Petal looked perplexed. "Under the sled? But—"

Toli began to push her toward the gap under the sled. "Just do it, Petal. I don't have time to explain."

"Okay! Don't push. Nya's promise, Toli, I'm going!"

Toli called the foxes in underneath with Petal, where they would be safe—as long as either she or Wix were alive to bring them all out again.

"If anything happens to Wix and me, hitch up the foxes and go back to the Queendom as fast as you can," Toli called into the darkness under the sled.

"But—"

She lowered the edge of the sled to the ice and turned to frown at Wix. "No. Tighten up your hood, and make sure the flaps cover your whole neck. And keep your elbows low to protect your middle." She watched as he made the adjustments, then gave him a stiff nod. "Now you're ready."

Toli looked around. There were bumps in the ice as far as she could see. There was no telling how large this swarm was—or how active. Pale, translucent wings sparkled under the surface of the ice.

Ruby gave another warning rattle and crouched low, her pupils narrowing as she watched the ice. Toli gave the dragon a grim look and widened her stance, stepping a few feet forward, away from Wix, so she could swing the beater wide. He followed her lead.

The first beetle flew out of the ice. Then another joined it, and another.

Ruby let out a long, low hiss as Wix squirmed.

"Now?"

Toli shook her head. "Wait."

A sharp clacking sound filled the air—the stuttering beat

of pincers as the air vibrated with swarms of wings. Beetles streamed from the tunnels.

Ruby let out a shriek and rose into the air, her wings beating furiously.

"Now!" Toli cried, swinging her beater to knock a beetle out of the air. She swung again. Her arm gave a painful throb as the beater connected with another giant insect. Two down.

Above her, Ruby let loose a swath of flame. Black beetles fell to the ice.

Still, more swarmed out behind the sled—all around them.

Petal cried out from under the sled. Toli heard growls, and then a clunking sound.

"Petal?" she called.

"I'm okay," Petal called back, her voice quavering. A beetle must have emerged underneath the sled, but it sounded like the foxes were dealing with it. Toli swung her beater, just missing a huge one.

Another burst of flame and falling beetles. From the corner of her eye, through the flickering pulse of wings, she could see Wix swinging his beater, knocking one after another to the ice. Moments later, he grunted, as pincers nicked his side. A small patch of darkness spread on his tunic.

Hailfire. They would smell Wix's blood.

The swarm thickened around him.

Ruby dived toward him, flame bursting from her mouth. The beetles fell, and as the dragon got close, she snapped her jaws, grabbing one out of the air and swallowing it in two bites.

But there were too many.

Toli ran to the sled and lifted one edge. "Wix! Here!"

He turned, grunting as a second beetle caught his upper arm and sliced. He didn't wait to be told what to do. Two long leaps and he slid across the ice and under the sled.

"Ruby!" Toli shouted, following behind. She held the edge of the sled up as Ruby zipped in, then dropped it behind them.

"What happened?" Petal whispered from the darkness.

Toli felt for Wix's arm. "Are you okay?" she asked into the shadows as Ruby slipped back into her hood.

"I . . . I think so."

"Twice, they got you. I saw it happen. I . . . I'm so sorry, Wix. I couldn't get to you."

Wix scoffed. "Of course you couldn't. You were crawling with them."

"But you're hurt. We should have just hidden. We shouldn't have tried to fight."

Toli could sense Petal's hand feeling for hers. "You didn't know what would happen, Toli. You were just doing what would get us to the Mountain the fastest."

Toli put her head down on her knees, her breath hot against her face. *I made the wrong call. If Wix was killed, it would have been my fault.*

Wix spoke suddenly, almost reverent. "I admit—I didn't expect your dragon to save me."

"I guess she did." Toli answered, her voice soft. The thought grew, taking up space between them.

They all sat together in the long, low space under the sled, listening to the panting of the foxes and the rasping of beetle wings until they were stiff with cold.

Toli must have dozed off, because she caught the image of her father turned, eyes wide, yelling for her to get back. It was this season, a year ago, when she and Petal had lost him forever. Toli pushed everything out of her head and focused on keeping her breath steady.

At last it grew cold enough that the beetles began to return to their tunnels. The thunking of their bodies against the bottom of the sled slowed, and then stopped. Toli wasn't sure how much time had passed, but when they crept out, it was into the stillness of night. Ruby slept across the back of Toli's neck, her tail wrapped so that it rested against Toli's pulse, as if for reassurance. Nya had set. The star-filled sky was streaked with colored light, Father Moon's green stain the only constant.

As they turned the sled upright to load everything back in, Toli glimpsed a patch of wetness along Wix's side and rushed to press her fingers to his tunic.

He cringed.

"You're still bleeding!"

"I—no, I'm fine."

"You're *not* fine! You're bleeding. Give me your arm. Is the other slice still bleeding? I thought it had stopped. Why didn't you tell me?"

"Toli—"

"How long has it been? How long were we under the sled?" She started to shake as she wrapped an arm around Wix, pressing one hand to his side. She led him to the edge of the sled and forced him to take a seat.

"Toli," Petal said, reaching out to take her arm.

Toli shook her off. "Think. Think about it. Nya's set now, but she was still visible when we first heard the beetles." She spun to face them, a wail building inside her chest. "Hours!"

Wix's mouth fell open. "Toli, I—I'm fine."

Petal appeared at Toli's side, blinking in the gloom. "He'll be okay," she said, her voice like snowfall. "I can sew it."

"What?" Wix stood up, backing up. "No you can't." He took another step.

"You! Stay put!" Toli pinned him with a look so wild, he froze instantly. Only Wix's eyes shifted, sending a desperate, silent plea to Petal.

Toli sucked in a deep breath of cold air. It settled in her chest, familiar—comforting as a lullaby. She considered her sister. "You can really do that? You can sew up the wounds?"

Petal nodded. "I've done it before. Rasca showed me how."

Wix scowled. "Rasca's a cook. What'd you do, sew up a roast?"

Petal pressed her lips together, her cheeks flushing.

Toli barked a laugh, then felt her eyes widen as Petal pulled something from her pocket that turned out to be a long bone needle wrapped in hide. She met Petal's unflinching gaze. "Be careful with that! The last thing we need is you stabbing someone with that thing."

"That's the idea," Petal muttered. She held the needle up to the starlight, threading it with a strand of sinew.

Toli's heart tripped at the sight of the wet black stain across Wix's side. Her dragon had saved him. Her *dragon*! Her best friend had gotten hurt—could have been killed—doing what she asked, and a *dragon* had rescued him. She reached up to touch

Ruby's soft scales. "Maybe you're not like other dragons," she whispered, but the dragon slept on, and her words fell like stones into the dark.

Wix studied her face, trying to get ahead of her thoughts. His eyes slid to where Ruby's head rested against her shoulder, and he shot Toli a wide smile. "She saved me from the beetles, so now it's your turn to save me from your sister."

Petal moved closer, waiting for Toli's instructions.

Be nicer to Petal. That's what he had told her, Toli remembered as she cocked her head at him. Her smile grew as his expression fell. "You should sew it right away, Petal. It's a good idea."

"Oh no," Wix took a step backward.

"Petal—I *encourage* you."

He sighed.

"We wanted to come." Petal shrugged. "And we can't have you bleeding everywhere, you know. Besides, if we don't take care of it, it could get infected." Toli lifted an eyebrow as Petal took Wix's arm and led him back to the sled, perching him on the edge.

"Come on," Petal said. "I promise I'll be gentle—and you're supposed to be a tough hunter, remember?"

Wix grimaced at her as she made the first stitch.

By the second stitch, Toli was standing behind them, watching. "Careful." She gritted her teeth, leaning over Wix's shoulder to see better.

Petal sighed and drew the third stitch tight.

Toli pointed. "Look. You don't have to do those small stiches. You can do big ones, just—"

"I've got this, Toli."

"Yeah, fine, but I'm just saying."

Wix grimaced as Petal's deft fingers worked along the wound.

"Petal"—Toli grumped—"you don't have to go so fast. You can slow—"

Her sister bent to peer at her work, answering through clenched teeth. "Speaking from your vast experience with sewing?"

"There's no need for sarcasm. I'm just telling you—"

"Done," Petal said, bending lower to bite through the sinew thread.

"Oh."

Wix let out his breath, and as Petal drew back, Toli found herself a little shocked at the sight of the neat stitching. She offered her sister a small smile as Petal cleaned her needle. The wind was rising.

The beetles and Wix's wound had cost them precious time. They no longer had a choice. They would have to stop to pass the coldest part of the night under the sled.

Wix must have been thinking the same thing. He was counting the peat bricks near the back of the sled.

Toli cradled her forehead in her hand and closed her eyes. "We'll build a fire and eat. Rest for a few hours. If we're lucky, the wind will stay calm."

"Thank Nya. I'm exhausted," Petal sighed, looking out toward the horizon. "Let's rest there," she said, and pointed. "The statues will help break the wind—a little."

Toli peered toward where she was pointing.

Wix's face fell. "It's the Necropolis."

Toli knew what he was thinking, and struggled not to step closer to him, not to even look at him, giving him as much privacy as they could afford. He felt the same way about the Necropolis as she did. He and his father had worked for weeks on the statue of Wix's mother. She would be out there now, among the other tributes to the dead, facing Nya's rise, and the endless winds. Toli and Petal's father was there too.

"Let's go," Petal said, breaking the silence.

Toli turned the sled with an ache in her chest. They would pass the rest of the night with their loved ones. The city of the dead waited.

Stay away from the pass.

—Spar

CHAPTER TWELVE

The statues of the dead grew against the horizon until it seemed as if the sled approached a crowd of people, backs turned, staring toward some shared dream.

Toli pulled to a stop at the outer edge of the Necropolis. The nearest statues were of those who had died most recently. They got older the farther out they stretched, those in each row becoming more worn and less recognizable. In the distance, the ancestors were rubbed to lumps, crumbling, their wind-scoured edges suggesting form and nothing more.

Ruby hissed.

Wix hadn't said a word. His face was still, but thoughts flickered behind his hazel eyes like a storm. He got out of the sled and busied himself setting up the raised stonetree base and platform where they would build their small cooking fire.

As Petal made soup, Toli walked among the statues. Ruby

had gone back to sleep across her shoulders, her stomach gurgling against Toli's neck.

The statues, raised on blocks of ice, looked down on her as she passed. Many she recognized. There was Roxanne the hunter. She had fallen while running after a bison and hit her head on the ice. Lazar stood next to her—an old carver who had died in his bed several winters ago.

Halfway along the next row she paused, goose bumps rising over her arms. Mykala. The little girl was only six when she died of a cough that had wrapped her up and sealed her in.

Somewhere nearby, there would be a statue of the queen's consort. Toli swallowed and moved away. She spoke to the permanent statue of her father in the Hunters' Shrine in Gall all the time, but that was different. The Necropolis was made just for Nya, and each statue would wear and fade. Just the thought of him standing out here, among all the rest, made his life seem smaller somehow. Her throat tightened.

She would leave this remembrance of him to the Daughter Moon. She didn't want to see it. Her heart couldn't take any more loss.

Toli moved out several rows. Five years back now.

She hadn't realized she was looking for Wix's mother until she came to Roma's statue. Roma had only been a little bit taller than Toli was now, but Toli remembered her as being taller. She wore her hair loose like Petal did, with every strand etched in loving memory. She held a bundle in her arms. A baby girl. They'd left the world that way—together.

It was, in every way, a masterpiece, as if Belgar Walerian, Wix's father, had poured all of his life force into it. And he had.

She'd seen it.

Roma's wide, kind face was so much like her, Toli instantly recalled the warmth of her laughter as she gave out handfuls of ice-worm fritters to the children—and the way her hands were always warm, no matter how cold the wind.

Toli startled as Wix appeared at her side.

He brushed away the snow that had gathered, sticking to his mother's hair and the shadows of her face. "She was the best mother I could ever have asked for."

Toli stilled, unsure of how to respond. Her hood grew lighter as Ruby slipped out. She let the dragon go. Toli glanced at Wix. His face was stormy. *Say something, Toli,* she thought, scrambling for words that would make him feel better. "Your mom made really good fritters," she whispered at last, edging closer to him.

Wix's mouth twitched. "Yeah. She did."

The aurora streaked the sky as they stood, side by side, in the gleam of starlight. Ruby scampered up one statue after another, peering into each face, sniffing at them and fluffing out her ruff of feathers. She was like a streak of fire—a streak of life in the field of gray and silver memories.

When the cold bit too deep, they returned to the fire and ate Petal's soup, which was much tastier than it had any right to be. Ruby wouldn't eat any, though her stomach growled louder than it had before they stopped. She slipped back into Toli's hood, curling up there with a low rattle. They huddled over the last bit of their fire.

Petal frowned. "I remember when I first heard about the sea. I was helping Rasca slice mushrooms for drying, and she told me that in the old tales—the really old ones—there were stories about the water that covered the world." She huffed her breath. "I never really believed there could be such a thing, you know? Even though it's spoken of in the Telling. Rasca said that in the old tales, the sea stretched beyond the mountains of Ire. She said it never lay flat and steady like the ice. She said it rolled."

Wix laughed. "What do you mean, it rolled?"

"I mean, the whole thing—all that water, filled with salt and dark as the sky. It was never still." She paused, staring past Toli. "It was like you said in the Telling. The whole thing could heave up and swallow you. I've tried to imagine it, but I can't see it."

Wix pulled a face.

"Rasca told me that the surface would rise up, again and again, into these long, racing swells. They'd travel across the surface toward the land like an army."

Toli shivered.

"She said the old stories talked about gigantic creatures deep under the water where the slosh and foam wouldn't find them." Petal looked up, her eyes wide. "Toli, what if that ocean is still there—still here—under the ice, waiting and watching?"

"It isn't." Toli shook her head. "It can't be."

"There's water in the fishing holes."

"That's different."

"Is it? I don't know. And what do you think happened to the people who first told those stories of the sea—the descendants of those early Tellers? Some of them must have lived in Gall, but what about the rest? Did they die? What did they do when the ice came?"

"Hailfire," Wix breathed. "When you think, you don't mess around."

Petal pulled something out of her pocket and held it out to Toli. "Look at this."

"What is it?" Toli reached out her hand.

"Rasca gave it to me for my birthday last year. She told me it's called Memory of the Sea."

Toli's breath caught as she took the shining object in her palm. It was a curling tube that wrapped around itself. Shaped almost like the moon, it glowed like the white scale of the Dragon-Mother but was made of something different altogether. It had a hollow entrance at the wide end, like the opening of an ice cave.

"I've never seen anything like it."

Wix held out his hand. Petal dropped it into his palm. "Nice work," he said, holding it close to his face. "Better than my dad's, even."

Toli shot Petal a look as she took Memory of the Sea from Wix's hand. "Do you just carry it with you everywhere?"

"I like it." Petal blushed. "I feel like it brings me luck. According to some of the oldest stories, there were creatures in the sea, before the ice came, that lived in homes something like this. I think it's called a shell." Petal's smile widened. "Put it to your ear."

Toli gave her a puzzled look but lifted the open end to her ear. Her mouth fell open. "The wind song! I hear the wind."

"It's not the wind. At least that's what Rasca told me when I first lifted it to my ear. That is the sound of water—the rushing of the sea."

Toli handed the shell to Wix as she turned to her sister. "How do you know so much?"

Petal shrugged, her star-blue eyes glued to Toli. "I pay attention, I guess." She slipped the cunning carving back into whatever hidden pocket she had taken it from.

Dragon Mountain was a sharp, black shadow, closer now than Toli had ever seen it before. It began to take up the horizon in front of them.

Toli itched to leave the dead behind. A dark thought crawled through her mind, threatening to leave her helpless in its wake. If she didn't reach the Mountain in time, her mother might soon have a statue here—watching Nya rise, but never seeing her light.

She looked out across the bitter ice. The howl of the night wind would only freeze their eyes and split the pads of the foxes' paws. She had to be smarter than her heart wanted her to be.

They would wait. Strengthen themselves while they could. Toli lifted her chin. She remembered Spar's lessons. She wouldn't let her fears rush her into failure.

Together, they spread out the furs and leatherleaf tarp under

the sled, lying down to get a few hours' sleep huddled together—
the kids and the foxes, and Ruby.

Toli awoke just as Nya's first light began to gleam against the
faces of the dead. Petal was already up and out. Ruby pulled
herself out from under the furs to climb up to Toli's shoulder,
her golden eyes blinking awake.

Wix lay curled in the pile of fur and foxes, his face younger,
somehow, in sleep. Instead of waking him, she grabbed a
handful of jerky and dried tree conks and went to find her
sister. It was time to go.

Toli called Petal's name, searching for her as she moved
through the glistening rows of statues. She stroked Ruby's tail
as she walked. The dragon gave a low rattle of satisfaction, and
Toli couldn't help wondering if she missed her Dragon-Mother
the way Toli missed hers. Did it matter that they had never
met? Would Ruby know her when they met?

She stopped, surrounded by the dead. How many rows were
there, she wondered. Had anyone counted? She was ten years
back now, where most of the statues had lost the sharpness of
their features. Their faces were worn. Some had piles of ice at
their feet where a piece had crumbled away. She called her sister
again. Where was she?

And then, in an instant, she knew where to find Petal. Her
stomach sank as she turned, walking back toward the newest
row of statues.

The sound of Petal crying caught on the wind, and Toli hurried toward the noise, past the statue of a woman hunter who she did not recognize, then around the bulky form of Pushku Damsin, who had been a good friend of Rasca's and had helped her in the kitchen for a time. She spotted her sister and stiffened, her heart lurching into her throat.

Petal stood, high on their father's frozen feet, sobbing against his icy shoulder. A painful ache filled Toli's chest as she stood watching her stroke his cheek, her black hair draped across his arm.

The sudden heaviness in her chest made it hard to breathe.

Their father's gentle face, unmoved and unmoving, stared into the distance at Nya's growing light.

A ping of hail hit the ice. "Petal?" Toli reached out.

Petal turned, tears streaking her cheeks. She dropped to the ground. More hail fell to the ice as Toli tried to think of something to say.

Ruby's hiss was their only warning. "Sissssster," the little dragon snarled as a heavy whoosh of wind drove them sideways, washing them in the sharp smell of electricity.

Toli recognized the sound of wings and was moving before she could think. She grabbed Petal's shoulders. "Hide!"

Petal ducked behind the statue, her eyes wide, as Toli raced toward the open ice where Wix slept beneath the sled.

My bow, she thought as a burst of flame blasted above her. It melted the hailstones into puffs of steam that hung in the air and clung to her clothes. Under the sled, the foxes gave terrified yips.

As Krala touched down, Ruby burst upward with a cry.

Wix appeared at Toli's side, two bows in his hands. He handed her one.

Deep, breathy laughter echoed through the air. The huge black dragon shimmered in the morning glow of the aurora lights. Above them, Ruby hovered, baring her teeth.

Toli's hair stood on end as she turned to face the enormous dragon. Wix, his face pale, stepped closer to her.

Krala's talons gripped the ice as she shook her wings in a sleek disturbance of blue-black feathers. Unlike her brother, and Ruby, she had no ruff. As Krala lifted her neck into a graceful arch, Toli noticed for the first time the two narrow black horns that crested her head.

"So you do have her," Krala hissed, her slit pupils narrowing. "You lied to me, Firstborn."

The dragon moved toward them, her talons clicking on the ice. Hail bounced off her iridescent scales with tiny pings. Ruby blew a scorch of fire, moving to block Krala's path.

Toli lifted her chin. Bright static crackled in the air as Krala's long snout split in a toothy grin. She opened her jaws with a roar, snapping at the young dragon.

"Ruby!" Toli cried, reaching out.

Ruby beat her wings, skating backward in the air, just out of reach of Krala's jaws.

Krala snarled, then inhaled deeply, eyeing Ruby. "What a delightful scent. It reminds me of my seethe." She paused, leaning slowly closer, her nostrils flaring. "And somewhat of dinner."

"Out running errands for your Dragon-Mother?" Toli shouted up at her. They hadn't had time to turn the sled over again, and hail pounded the underside like an army of drums. "What do you want?" she called, standing tall and refusing to flinch under the sharp onslaught of the falling ice.

Krala chuckled. "Bold words for a bone bag. The Mother still seeks her special little *stone*. I am not alone in the search."

Toli spoke through clenched teeth. "And you don't really want to find her—do you?"

Krala ignored her, her gaze falling on Ruby. "But of all the brethren, I alone found you. I alone know where the Mother's frostborn child is now."

"You can't have her," Petal cried, stepping out from behind a statue. A chunk of ice flew over Toli's head, pelting Krala in the chest. The dragon startled, coughing a burst of steam.

"You were never looking for a stone! Get out of here, liar!" Petal shouted, throwing another fist-sized block. "Go away!"

Toli gasped. "Petal, stop! Go back!"

Krala burst into a delighted snarl of laughter and blew a blast of flame over their heads toward Petal.

"Petal!" Toli screamed.

"I'm okay," her sister called from behind a dripping mass of ice that had been a person's likeness moments before.

"Stay where you are, Petal," Wix called.

"Your insult means nothing, puny bite," Krala said, rattling as she turned to Toli. "It is *you* who are the *liar*, Princess. And I see you've been . . . busy," she added, flicking her eyes toward Wix. The dragon's pupils dilated as she spotted the dried blood on his shirt. A thin strand of drool dripped from the corner of her mouth. "I see you met with beetles. They do love their snacks, don't they?"

Toli's throat went dry.

"What can we do for you?" Wix called up. He couldn't hide the shake in his voice.

"So polite! Very nice. Very nice manners . . . and in such bad weather." Krala huffed. "I did not think any of your people would be foolish enough to be out here . . . in the open . . . where anyone could spot you easily. I see I gave you too much credit. I confess, I thought the youngling lost, nor did I expect to find you here, Firstborn.

"But now I see you *do* have her, as my brother suspected, and so I wonder . . . I *wonder. What is it that you think you're doing, Princess?*" The dragon was perhaps two hundred yards away, but now she edged closer, her voice dropping to a hiss. "Tell me. Why are you *out on the ice*, when your people are at home by the fire?"

From the corner of her eye, Toli saw a muscle in Wix's jaw tighten, his knuckles taut where he gripped his bow. Toli's heart raced as Krala's face split in a wide grin, blowing another burst of flame over their heads. The dragon chuckled as the hail turned to steam, drifting down to soak their clothes.

The dragon lowered her gaze to meet Toli's. "Return her to me. I will give you food."

Toli glanced up to where Ruby hovered. "We don't want your food."

Krala's eyes widened. "Yes, of course you want food, stupid creature." She shot forward, cutting the distance between them in half. "It doesn't do to be rude to one's betters, you know." Krala paused. "Or so I'm told."

Toli felt the blood drain from her cheeks.

"Very well, Firstborn. No food. Still, you will return the youngling to me."

Ruby hissed, dropping down onto Toli's shoulder. Toli reached up to stroke the little dragon's head. "I don't think she wants to go." She paused. If Krala *had* taken Ruby's chrysalis—if she did want Ruby dead—would she admit it? "Besides," she added, "there's no need."

Krala rattled a warning. "And why is that, Firstborn? Why is there . . . no need?"

Toli lifted her chin. "Because we're taking her to the Dragon-Mother ourselves."

Krala grew still. "Is that so?" Her nostrils flared. "The puny bite who so bravely hurled ice and insults is your brethren, I think. A sister, perhaps? I wonder—would a secondborn taste different from a first?"

"Leave her alone!"

Krala gave a deep rattle, and though Toli's knees quivered, she stepped forward, looking up into the dragon's face. She lifted one hand for Wix to stay where he was as her damp clothes froze in the wind. A shiver raced over her shoulders.

"Poor things. My little joke made your clothes wet, didn't it? And in this terrible cold." The dragon leaned down. "Shall I . . . warm you?"

Toli cringed as Ruby clutched at her shoulder.

Krala took a deep breath, closing her eyes. She snickered.

"Tell me, Firstborn, did the youngling, by chance, eat any of those beetles that attacked you?"

Ruby tried to rattle, but all that came out was a series of halfhearted clicks.

Toli stilled. "What if she did?"

Krala tipped her face to the sky, bursting into a full-throated laugh. "Oh, very good. Oh, that's perfect. I expect that will be quite . . . surprising for you both."

"What do you mean?" Wix stepped up to Toli's side, casting a worried look at her. Krala's long scaled tail undulated across the ice. "They are poison to us. She will likely die before you reach the Mountain."

"No," Toli whispered.

"Yessss," Krala hissed.

A stab of alarm and adrenaline raced through Toli's veins. She studied Krala's face for any sign that she was lying, but found none—at least no sign Toli could see. Then again, Spar said lying came as easily to dragons as breathing. "You're lying," she ground out. "Dragons lie."

Krala hissed. "I lie, do I? Well, I will not waste my time convincing you of what time itself will teach you. The youngling may be fierce for some few hours yet, but not for long. You should have given me the chrysalis, Firstborn."

"So you could kill her?"

Krala only chuckled. "There will be, as you say, *no need*."

Wix tensed.

"The beetles will take their toll on her," Krala said, flicking her tail toward Ruby. "And really . . . I should thank you."

"Thank us for what?" Wix snarled.

"You've made it so much easier." Krala stretched her neck and peered down at them. "When I gave the firstborn chrysalis to my brother and told him to destroy it, I thought to blame my brethren—those who are the Mother's allies—for the youngling's death. But now I think I have a better way. Once I tell the Mother what *you* have done, when she learns that it was *humans* who took her youngling and poisoned her, the brethren will see how foolish the Mother's idea of consorting with your queen really is." Her eyes lit up.

"But we didn't!" Petal cried from behind the statue. "That's a lie."

Krala continued as if she hadn't heard. "All will know she is not fit to rule, and there will be no more talk in the Mountain of making peace with people—not here, and not in the South. There will be no more of this stubborn resistance to destroying you all."

"But we didn't take her! You did!" Toli shouted.

Krala's pupils dilated and she shot forward with a sneer. She was only twenty yards from them now.

Toli's heart fluttered in her throat. She reached up to touch Ruby, and the little dragon curled her head into Toli's palm.

"Clever child to guess my secret. I am not like this Dragon-Mother. I do not sit idly by and allow a threat to grow. If I were Dragon-Mother, we would take the South and make it ours alone."

Petal moved out from behind the statues to stand behind them, listening. When Wix offered her a knife from the sheath at his ankle, she took it, her face grim.

Krala snapped her teeth. "My brother is weak. He hid the chrysalis away so carefully—expecting to return it and gain us the glory of its finding. Now, destroying the youngling falls to my tooth—and to my claw—as it should have from the start. But you have saved me that trouble too."

The dragon ruffled her feathers and bared her teeth in a savage grin. "Once you and the other bone bags are gone, we can focus on the true threat—the only threat that matters."

"There is no threat," Wix snarled. "We haven't done anything to you."

"The South is always a threat. Our queen believes your mother is the key to making peace with the humans there. Can you imagine it? *Peace.* A true Dragon-Mother would never bend her neck," Krala snarled. "When I am Dragon-Mother, we will have no more of this foolish talk of peace."

Toli froze and Wix gave a too-tight laugh. "What are you even talking about? There are no people to the south. We're alone—the Queendom is alone!"

Krala cocked her head at Wix, her eyes widening for an instant before she burst into a belly laugh that they felt through the soles of their feet.

"Oh, that is rich. That is perfect. You didn't know." She snorted and coughed a burst of flame next to them that slicked the surface of the ice. "Of course you didn't. How could you, so puny, and wingless as you are? Ah-ha-ha." She leaned forward. "Yes, little bone bags. There are many more of you. Many upon many puny bites, where the ice becomes the sea."

Petal covered a gasp. "The old stories," Petal breathed. "The people went south!"

Where the ice becomes the sea. Toli thought of Petal's Memory of the Sea and couldn't catch her breath. Gall was alone. Had been alone since the beginning—hadn't it?

She heard Wix asking her if it was true, but the frozen air stiffened in her lungs and she couldn't answer. At last, she forced words out, as if they were shards of ice.

"I don't believe you." The dragon was just trying to distract them. Right now, they had more important things to do than sift through a dragon's lies. Krala thought she was going to get away with it too. "Does the Dragon-Mother know you're a traitor?"

Krala laughed. "The Mother grows timid. My brethren are fools to remain loyal to her when she falls into the shadow of another—a stronger born."

"Why take Ruby?" Wix called. "She's just a baby."

Krala hissed, crouching low. "She is young and weak. The time is right. She is a Frost."

"Like you," Toli ground out.

Krala stretched her wings. "Not like me. *I* am wise. I am strong."

"But the Dragon-Mother is your sister," Petal began, her voice catching as she tried to look Krala in the eye. "Why not let her rule—any of the first three can take power."

"Can. *CAN!*" Krala roared, shaking the ground. "But they do not. They do not *DARE*. Until this Mother it has been the firstborn. A Frost had ruled across our living memory." Her eyes were lit with fury. "It should have been me."

Wix gave a tight smirk. "You didn't just let her become the Dragon-Mother, did you? If your thirdborn sister became the Dragon-Mother instead of you, then she must have beaten y—"

"Wix, shut up." Toli hissed as a flood of alarm heated her veins.

Krala peeled her lips back, baring her teeth. "We were younger then. I am wiser now. And stronger. She will not beat me again." The dragon's smile widened.

Toli sensed a shift, felt Krala's focus change. The dragon had made a decision, and it wasn't in their favor.

Toli's hands twitched for the bow hanging from her shoulder. "Petal, get behind the statues," she said through clenched teeth.

Petal looked at the short hunting knife in her hand and swallowed, edging backward. Krala watched her go, amusement in her gaze. Wix must have felt it too. He moved to stand shoulder to shoulder with Toli in front of the dragon.

Krala leaned closer. The dragon's hot breath smelled of blood. "Brave little bone bags. My brother is loyal to me, but he is weak. When I have killed the youngling, I will be the only Frost of age to rule. Once she is dead, there will be no other firstborn threat. There will be no more talk of peace. When I tell my brethren that your people took her—and poisoned her—all will turn against *your* queen . . . and mine."

Toli rested her palm on Ruby's tail. "She's not dead yet."

"Toli," Wix whispered. "Are you sure about this?"

Krala's low rattle rolled across the ice.

Toli gave an imperceptible nod. Krala didn't plan to let them leave. Toli saw it in the dragon's eyes. But maybe she could gain some advantage—goad Krala into making a mistake.

She drew her bow. "You took her," Toli sneered. "And you could have killed her, but you were a coward. A *weak* coward."

Krala's eyes narrowed to slits.

Wix huffed his breath and nocked an arrow.

Smoke surged from Krala's nostrils, and Ruby rose into the air above Toli with a sharp cry. Krala lashed the ice with her tail and lurched forward, snapping at Toli.

Wix grabbed her arm, yanking her backward out of reach. Both of them fell to the ice.

Krala stalked around the sled as they scuttled to their feet. Ruby shot a plume of fire that burst over Krala's eyes, and the larger dragon let out a roar of outrage.

Toli rose from the ice and took up her bow again, planting her feet next to Wix.

Krala rattled and lunged, forcing them farther back. She aimed a blast of fire at Ruby, but she aimed too high.

She fixed her gaze on Toli.

Toli heard Wix's breath catch.

Krala grinned. "I will kill you both where you stand. After I kill you, I will kill the youngling. Then I will hunt your sister among your frozen dead. *That* will make a pleasant day."

Toli remembered Spar's lessons. She took a deep breath, centering herself. Then she fired.

Beside her, Wix's bow twanged.

Both arrows soared, straight and true, piercing Krala's shoulder and chest, one just behind the other. Ten times as many arrows would still be unlikely to kill her, but perhaps they would slow her down—make her think twice.

The dragon roared in pain, shaking the ice under their feet.

Toli's throat went dry, but though she braced herself, the dragon didn't attack. Instead, Krala fell back—considering.

Blood trickled down Krala's shoulder. Toli reached for a second arrow, and Wix shifted his grip on his bow, but they didn't look away.

The dragon shook out her wings. "I have bigger battles ahead of me than this one—battles of importance. I should not waste my might on such puny bites. Your lives will come to a close faster than a snap of my teeth once I tell the Dragon-Mother you took her firstborn. While you are breaking your bodies against the sheer cliffs of our mountain, I will be whispering in her ear." Krala chuckled, snapping both arrows out of her body with yanks of her teeth. Drops of blood, black as old ice, fell to the ground.

"I will show her my wounds and she will believe me. So I thank you again, Firstborn. While the youngling dies, this nonsense of yours will serve me well. It will distract the Mother until I can challenge her, with all my brethren behind me."

"We won't let you," Toli said with a calm she didn't feel. She drew her bow. "We'll tell your queen the truth about you."

Krala grinned. "Try, little bone bag! How will you climb the Mountain, wingless as you are? What route will you choose? You can go around to the west. It will take you a week at least. Climb the sheer cliffs of the western slope? The sheer cliffs to the south? Climb it! I insist! With a sick dragon on your back and the brethren I have won to my side hunting you—climb it!"

Wix, tense beside her, nocked another arrow. "We'll take the pass."

Toli blanched at Wix's words. The pass was the one place Spar had told her hunters never to set foot. It skirted the sheer rock walls of Dragon Mountain and could save time, Spar had said, if they had wanted to travel so far to hunt. According to Spar, though, the risk of the pass was far too great, especially with only uncertain results on the far side of the Mountain. The hunt master hadn't offered more information, and everyone had known better than to ask.

Krala's eyes dilated, one tearing and raw from Ruby's scorching. "Ahh. You know about the pass. It will take less time—that is true. There are no cliffs. But there are . . . other things." She let out a low rattle. "Go, then," she said with a snarl. "Die in the pass."

Krala beat her wings once. The force of it knocked them all to the ice. On the second beat, she lifted off the ground, dragging her black talons over the surface as she rose. Long gouge marks followed her in the ice. She pulled her claws up, just missing the sled.

Toli watched Krala rise, her head crowded with thoughts of her mother. Even now, as they stood watching, her mother might be facing an entire mountain full of those creatures—alone. And there was no telling how much time Ruby had left. They had to get to the Dragon-Mother. If Krala got what she was after, Toli's mother would be only the first to pay the price. In spite of Spar's warning, they would take the pass.

CHAPTER THIRTEEN

The dragon's black scales gleamed as she turned in the sky and moved away, lifting into the thick blanket of color-streaked clouds. Wisps chased her in vain, like hopeful children.

The hail had stopped. Nya had risen, her light competing with that of Father Moon.

Petal ran back out from the field of statues and threw her arms around Toli's neck. Toli hugged Petal tightly as Wix leaned into them. None of them spoke. They clung together for a breath—then two.

Toli stepped away first. "We're going to do what we have to. That's all." Toli's whole body was shaking as they silently righted the sled. None of them spoke.

Wix did his best to calm the foxes. He climbed in next to Toli as she took the reins.

Toli risked a glance at him. She knew only two things about the pass that led to Dragon Mountain: She knew it was a huge tunnel that passed through the glacier beyond the Necropolis, coming out at the far side of the Mountain, and she knew Spar had told all of her hunters never to set foot in it. Wix's expression reflected the question in hers: *What is in the pass?*

The tunnel cut through a sheer bluff of glacier that rose up from the ice just to the east of the Mountain. Spar had traveled there once to scout for hunting grounds, long before her quarrel with the dragons. Toli remembered the hunt master striding into the Hall where her hunters waited. Toli and her father had been seated by the fire.

The fear written across Spar's as-yet-unscarred face as she passed made her a stranger, and for a moment, Toli hadn't recognized her. The huntress had stormed past, pointed one finger at the pack of hunters where they gathered around another hearth, and uttered only five words. "Stay away from the pass!"

If her father, or anyone else, had ever asked why, no one had shared the answer with her. As far as Toli knew, no one had set foot out there since.

Until now.

The fact that they had no choice didn't do much to ease her mind.

Toli thought of her mother, inside the Mountain. She thought of Ruby, dying without ever meeting her own mother, and her thoughts jumbled. She tried to find words, but they shifted in her mouth like stones.

She closed her eyes and sent a fervent prayer soaring out to the Daughter Moon to keep Ruby alive, and to help them get to the Mountain in time to save her mother and stop Krala.

Petal wrapped Ruby in a small rabbit-fur blanket, tucking her down inside Toli's hood. As her sister stroked Ruby's head and peered closely into the little dragon's face, worry flooded Toli's mind. She didn't want Ruby to die, and not just because she needed her to save her mother.

She cared about a dragon.

She had no energy to wonder how it had happened; she only knew that it had. "Is she okay?"

Petal pressed her lips together and took her seat in the back of the sled. She didn't answer, but her face was as fierce as Toli had ever seen it.

"Let's go," Toli growled as she snapped the reins.

The wind bit at Toli's cheeks and hair. Though it was almost afternoon, Nya's light was dull. Reflections of the aurora lights chased across the ice alongside them, so bright now that there was no horizon—only streaks of color in the mirrored darkness, above and below. They skimmed over the surface like a dragon flying, fearing nothing.

Petal curled into the belly of the sled. Toli could feel Wix watching her, but he didn't say a word. Not about their choice to take the pass, and not about Krala, or her mother, or about Ruby's illness. They all knew what had to be done. There was no time to waste.

The wind wailed across the empty ice.

Wix said, "I've been thinking about Spar. She might be going to the Mountain too."

Toli had been trying hard not to let thoughts of her mentor into her head. It was already so crammed full of worry, she didn't have room for anything else. "Why would she?!" she snapped.

Wix gave her a sidelong look and shrugged. "To get the Queen? To start a fight? I don't know. Maybe she just finally lost her dragon-blasted mind and took off."

"No." Toli's voice was firm.

His gaze sharpened. "No? That's it . . . just, no?"

Petal sat up and picked her way forward, gathering Ruby out of Toli's hood. "She could be out hunting."

Wix scoffed. "Hunting what?"

There was no good answer to that question, and Toli knew it. She gritted her teeth and thumped the sled with her fist. Ruby gave a halfhearted rattle from the belly of the sled, where she had settled into Petal's lap.

Wix sighed. "Listen. You might be right. Maybe she's gone into the forest or . . ."

"Or maybe she really has lost her mind and is on her way to do something stupid." Toli sighed. *Like start a war with the dragons.*

He paled. "That's what I'm afraid of too. You know her best. What do you think she might do?"

She met her friend's honest face. "That's just it, Wix. I have no idea what she's capable of."

Petal cleared her throat. "We know she hates the dragons."

Toli considered. "We know Krala wants to be the Dragon-Mother, even if it means starting a war between the dragons—and another between humans and dragons." It made her heart ache to think that the truth might be that Spar wanted the same thing.

Petal nodded, pressing her lips together in a determined line. "We know the dragons took our mother, and that Krala thinks that makes the Dragon-Mother weak."

Wix shook his head. "It wasn't taking her that makes the Dragon-Mother look weak, it's that she wants her for something—some kind of help. And Krala said she isn't the only dragon that has lost faith in the Dragon-Mother," he added.

Toli chewed the inside of her cheek, the iron tang of blood on her tongue. Somehow she had to fix this. She'd gotten Wix and Petal wedged in the middle of some kind of dragon war. The whole Queendom was counting on her. Even Ruby. "And Ruby's dying," she whispered, her voice catching.

An image of Spar handing Toli her gift with her eyes full of pride flashed in her mind. "You don't give up," she had said.

Toli snapped the reins. "Right now we just have to try to get Ruby back to the Dragon-Mother. We know Krala is planning to blame us for taking her—"

Wix shook his head. "We can't outrun Krala."

"Then at least we can survive! We can keep Ruby alive!"

Petal nodded. "We can explain to the Dragon-Mother."

Wix dropped his face into his hands. "If we can get there alive, we can try. We'll have to warn the Dragon-Mother about Krala too."

"Maybe she'll believe us," Toli said, trying to sound confident.

Petal reached toward Toli and took her hand. "Maybe we can still save Mother."

"And Ruby." Wix sighed.

Toli didn't answer. She wanted to believe it, and not only for her own sake, but her body felt heavy, as if her fears were stores, piling up inside her. Ruby climbed up to her shoulder and rubbed the top of her head against Toli's cheek. "Don't worry," Toli whispered as she stroked the dragon's head. "I'm taking you home. Your mother will know what to do."

"What Krala said . . . about people in the South . . ." Petal began.

Wix shook his head. "That can't be true. Can it?"

"Of course not," Toli snapped. "She's just trying to confuse us. She wants us to doubt ourselves—to doubt everything. She can't be trusted."

"Then why *did* their queen take Mother?"

Toli didn't have an answer.

Just stay alive, she told herself. *That's what Spar would do.* She didn't dare think about what might happen after that. She tucked the hood of her cloak around the little dragon. Ruby lay, still as death, across her shoulders, but though her scales were cold, Toli knew the little dragon hung on to life. She could feel the beating of the Ruby's heart against her skin. Her throat tightened. She couldn't drive the foxes any faster.

The landscape continued as it had begun, ice upon ice, wind following wind. Even the sky varied little, despite the dancing of the lights. It all blurred together, as if the sled were caught on a pin, the foxes running and running, but getting nowhere.

The stars brightened as Nya began to set again. The whole bowl of the sky was filled with streaks of aurora light, all leading toward the wall of glacier, and beside it, the peaked silhouette of Dragon Mountain taking up the sky ahead of them.

Father Moon glowered at her, watching from his resting place on top of the Mountain. At last, in the dim light, a dark spot grew against the wall of ice—the entrance to the pass. As they drew closer and the pass gaped wide ahead of them, the feeling that something was wrong settled in Toli's guts, twisting and growing as they approached.

The foxes slowed, chattering nervously.

"Whoa," Wix said, leaning over the side of the sled. "Stop the sled!"

Toli pulled on the reins until the sled glided to a stop. "What is it?"

Petal peered over Wix's shoulder.

Under the black ice, she could see strange shining orbs. They hung suspended, some small, others almost as large as the sled itself. Farther off she could see stacks of them under the ice, as though they were in a queue, waiting their turn to reach the surface.

Petal frowned. "They look . . . they look like bubbles."

Toli stepped out, walked over to the nearest stack of orbs, and leaned down to peer closer.

Wix shot her a worried look. "Why do you think Spar told everyone to stay away from here?"

The hair on Toli's arms rose. Low mist hurried past, wrapping around her ankles. Rising curls licked at the foxes' bellies. Her fingers slid over the dragon scales along the edge of her cloak. Spar had acted so strange the last time Toli had seen her. The thought made her chest ache. She pushed it out of her head.

"We need to hurry," Toli said. "If Krala has her way, there will be dragons coming for us."

Wix moved to stand by Toli's side. He squinted, pointing out across the ice. "What is that?"

Some kind of large blur moved toward them across the ice. "I—I don't know, but I'm not sure we should wait around to find out."

A roar echoed across the ice, and Toli caught a glimpse of light reflecting off long white fangs. She grabbed Wix's arm, tugging him toward the sled. "Come on!"

"What—"

"Bear-cat. It's a bear-cat. Nya's bear-cat."

She heard Wix's breath catch; then they were running for the sled. "It must have smelled our food," she gasped as they clambered in.

"Hailfire! From that distance?"

Petal stared at them. "What's going on?"

"Go!" Wix shouted. "Go!"

Toli leaped over her sister into the front of the sled and slapped the reins. The foxes, already straining to run, jumped forward. Petal lurched backward, almost toppling off her bench as they shot ahead.

Toli could see the bear-cat behind them now. Huge and white, with gray-white stripes, it had a thick mane and a long tufted tail that whipped back and forth as it raced along the ice, gathering speed. Bear-cats were five feet tall on all fours, with high, muscled shoulders that sloped down to their haunches, and by all accounts were made of nearly equal parts rage and hunger.

It was catching up.

"Toli?" Petal called to her, her voice tight.

"I know!"

Toli dropped the reins and hung on. The foxes could smell the nearness of the predator and were running hard without any encouragement from her. She reached down into the belly of the sled and lifted her bow. Ruby stirred where she slept under the furs.

Wix gave Toli a nod and grabbed his bow too.

The bear-cat tore the ice as it ran, kicking up shards. It was getting closer. Its huge tongue lolled from its muzzle full of sharp teeth.

Carefully, Toli rose to stand.

And then they were in the pass.

Dark blue gloom surrounded them. A roar echoed through the wide tunnel as Toli let the arrow fly. It disappeared into the distance. *Hailfire.*

The bear-cat roared again.

An answering roar echoed from somewhere ahead of them.

Petal screamed as a second bear-cat leaped at Toli from

above, its body skimming past, so close she could smell the thick, musky scent of its fur. It turned, racing alongside the other.

Wix fired. His arrow struck the new attacker's shoulder. It let out a roar and put on a burst of speed. It was only a few feet from the sled.

Ruby climbed onto the bench, launching herself up to Toli's shoulder, as the foxes, screaming now in panic, raced ahead.

Toli widened her stance and grabbed the reins again with one hand, yanking them back to keep the sled from toppling. They surged past a second smaller tunnel, and a third bear-cat charged from within its depths.

Petal cried out as Wix fired again, this time hitting the third one in the chest. It slowed, but the first one let out a roar and surged forward. Its jaws latched on the arching tail of the sled.

They began to careen sideways.

Petal, with a roar of her own, spun and brought down a beater on the bear-cat's head, splintering the pole.

It released them and fell back, shaking its head and stumbling.

"Yes, Petal!" Wix shouted.

"Two down!" Toli barked. It was all she could do to keep the sled upright. In front, the foxes yipped with fear as they knocked together, with several on the outside being lifted off their feet as they rounded another bend.

Toli and Wix toppled sideways. Toli caught the side of the sled and grabbed Wix as he launched toward the edge, dragging him back. Petal slid into the belly of the sled, clinging to the bench.

Ruby shot into the air with a cry of rage.

Toli saw the flash of the bear-cat's black eyes, but if it slowed at all, she couldn't tell.

Ruby swooped toward it, and Toli's heart flew into her throat.

"Ruby!" Petal cried.

The bear-cat slowed to snap its jaws as the dragon dived at it, missing. Ruby came back around, and as she passed, the bear-cat shot straight up into the air in a leap that put it high above the sled—far enough for Toli to see its huge clawed paws.

Ruby veered away at the last moment, slashing with her talons as she passed. The bear-cat's jaws snapped shut and came away with a feather. Its shoulder was bleeding, and the jump had slowed it down, but it was still coming, tearing at the ice as it ran.

Ruby landed next to Toli. Her red scales had dulled and she couldn't seem to catch her breath.

Toli reached out, but with a cry the dragon launched herself up again, this time aiming directly for the bear-cat.

"Ruby!" Toli lifted her bow and fired. The arrow shot forward to meet the one already in the bear-cat's shoulder.

Ruby coughed a swath of flame that singed the bear-cat down one side. It slowed, falling behind.

The foxes began to tire.

The sled slowed too.

Then they were out of the tunnel, back under the dancing

lights. Toli looked up and saw Dragon Mountain looming above them. They were so *close*.

Ruby dived back toward the sled, crashing at Toli's feet and knocking her down. She grabbed the dragon and pulled her close, breathing hard. "You're okay," Toli said. "I've got you." She looked back. "You did it, Ruby. It's falling behind."

"Friend," Ruby rustled.

A loud boom sounded from the ice, echoing through the miles of empty sky. The bear-cat slid to a stop. So did the sled.

Toli stopped breathing.

"Toli," Petal whispered, reaching forward to grasp her hand. "What was that?"

Knocking echoed below them, and the bear-cat began backing up. It lifted its paws as if it were trying not to touch anything, then spun away, slinking back off into the dark tunnel.

Toli and Wix looked at each other. She swallowed. "What—"

He shook his head. "No idea."

She rose to her feet, still cradling Ruby. "Let's get out of here," she said, snapping the reins.

The foxes pulled away. In Nya's dim light the strange orbs under the ice doubled in number. On the horizon, Toli could see dark lines, twisted trees rising from the ice. There, the ground sloped upward. The foothills of Dragon Mountain. They were almost there.

Ruby climbed down and slid to the edge of the sled. Toli watched as the dragon slowly closed her eyes—and vomited black bile onto the ice.

To birth a man or beast from a block of ice is simple.
You only need to know the secret.

Listen closely. The ice is like us. It sings before it breaks.

—Belgar Walerian

CHAPTER FOURTEEN

Toli reached for Ruby and held her close. Her scales were dull and cool to the touch. "Hang on, Ruby," she whispered into her feathers. "You're almost home." She pulled the little dragon closer to the warmth of her body. "Friend," Toli said softy. Had she imagined the flash of a golden eye opening a crack?

Toli startled as Wix yelled for her to stop the sled. Toli shot him a puzzled look and pulled back on the reins. Then she heard it too. A thumping sound—a deep boom echoing from somewhere below the ice had started again. She could feel it vibrating through the bottom of the sled and into her feet. "What is that?" Toli asked as she settled Ruby in some furs and stepped out.

The strange echoing thumps knocked again. Petal rose from her seat, clutching her shell, the Memory of the Sea.

"There's a high sound too," she frowned. "Listen. It's like singing."

Wix nodded. "It reminds me of when the carvers calve off a block of ice." He paused, his eyes widening. "Toli. Get back in the sled."

Petal leaned out. "Look—those orb things are moving."

Toli grinned, her relief over escaping the bear-cats making her giddy. "Really? Where?" She moved toward where Petal was pointing. A glimmering orb lingered just under the surface.

"I think you should come back now, Toli." Wix reached toward Petal. "Hand Ruby to me."

Toli followed the orb as it rolled along, shimmering and shifting beneath her feet as if it were searching for something. She tilted her head. "I hear it too. It's like the ice is talking to us."

The knocking grew stronger.

Petal draped Ruby over Wix's shoulders and started to climb out of the sled. Wix held her back, his voice urgent. "Hurry, Toli. Please! Come back."

"It's fine, Wix. I'll be there in a minute. I just want to figure out where it's going." She had been tired and scared for so long, it was freeing to be confronted with a mystery that wasn't dangerous or deadly. She walked a little farther, past the sled, following the orb as it moved under the ice. "Where is it going?" she asked with a child's small, delighted laugh.

The thumping had stopped, and the chorus of creaking had broken into a strange series of mismatched melodies. She smiled back at her sister.

Wix's jaw was tight as he watched her. "Toli—"

"You're right, Petal. It is like a song."

The ice gave a single, grating creak and split wide, and the world vanished.

Cold water hit Toli like a blow. Her body seized. Her chest squeezed. From within the frigid black, she heard Petal scream.

Seconds passed like lifetimes as Toli struggled toward the surface. It was so dark, she didn't know her eyes were open until she saw Petal's hands reaching for her from the hole she had fallen through.

She grabbed them.

Petal, lying across the surface of the ice on her stomach, hauled her out onto the bright ice, scuttling them backward.

As they lay there panting, bright cracks split the ice beneath them.

Petal cried out and grabbed Toli tighter. Toli, her whole body shaking with cold, noticed the rope around Petal's waist just as her sister began sliding backward with Toli in tow.

Wix was reeling them in to safety. Toli had just enough time to admire their quick thinking before a jagged crack tore across the ice under the sled, and the whole sled vanished in front of her eyes, pulling Wix, Ruby, and four of the foxes down into the black.

"No!" Toli cried.

The lead foxes scrambled to find purchase, screaming in terror.

The world went silent around her. Toli drew her knife and cut the rope that tied her and Petal to the sled; then she was on her feet, diving forward, cutting the line that tied the harnesses to the sled. Half the foxes got their footing and ran across the ice, disappearing into the fog.

Only seconds had passed.

Toli scoured the water where the sled had disappeared for signs of Wix and Ruby. The ice heaved underneath her.

Toli stumbled back as Petal screamed her name. And the sled rose, its dragon figurehead cracking through the ice in front of her. It bobbed upward, spilling water out over the surface of the ice, the water crackling and hissing as it froze.

Wix came up in it, gripping the side of the sled with one arm and a silent Ruby with the other. Toli took her first real breath. The sled floated in dark water surrounded by ice.

The foxes that had fallen through followed, still tied together, clawing at the edges of the ice. Toli threw herself forward, catching hold of the reins as the top half of her body submerged. She hauled the foxes out one at a time, taking huge swallows of air each time she surfaced again. Their claws scratched at her and at the ice in desperate gouges.

Her arms grew heavy and numb with cold. When she'd gotten the last fox up onto the ice, her arms refused to hold her weight. She scrabbled at the edges of the ice, trying to pull herself back up. She slipped forward into the water.

Petal, on still-solid ice behind Toli, wrapped her hands around her sister's ankles with a firm grip and pulled with all her strength until Toli's chest and then head rose slowly out of the water.

Toli struggled to her knees, coughing and shaking, trying

to get her bearings—trying to understand what had just happened. All around her, half-drowned foxes shook and checked one another over. She stared at Petal, her heart beating in dull, painful throbs.

The ice groaned beneath them.

"W-we've got to g-get away from here," Wix stuttered, his eyes wide. "Come on. T-take what we need." He was still in the sled, and he reached under the edge of his tunic to pull a small clay firepot from around his neck. His face was drawn. "I—I had a bad feeling when the ice started groaning, so I tucked a few embers in here while you were looking at those orb things," he chattered.

"Toss me the peat bricks," Petal said, moving quickly to help.

Wix searched the sled. "Gone. But we have whatever's in here," he added, yanking out a large waterproof bag. He threw it to them."

"We'll need fire," Toli slurred through numb lips.

Petal nodded. "What about extra food? And is there anything else we can burn?"

Wix shook his head. "One p-p-problem at a time," he said as he tossed a second bag to Toli and scoured the sled for anything else they could use, shoving items into the last remaining bag. He pulled a small hatchet from the belly of the sled. "This should help."

Toli knew they had to hurry. There was no telling if, or when, the ice would crack again. As if to prove her point, loud creaking echoed through the air around them. "Hurry," she whispered.

Wix grabbed a coil of rope that had been shoved firmly under one of the benches and tied it tightly around the arched neck of the sled before launching himself onto the solid ice next to the girls.

He handed Ruby to Toli, and she curled the little dragon around the back of her neck, pulling her wet hood up to block the wind. Half the foxes had run off, and the other half were in no condition to pull the sled free of the ice. The leatherleaf runners were gone, and they needed to get away as quickly as possible.

"Wait one minute," Wix said, yanking open the first bag. He pulled out the small clay ember bowl, tossing aside wads of singed leatherleaf wrapping. He emptied his small firepot into the bowl. The embers were black, but Wix pulled his knife free and tapped at each of them gently, knocking away the char, then leaned close and blew. A thin glow brightened his face.

Toli exhaled.

"We need to pull the sled free—t-to that line of stonetrees over there," Wix said. He pointed as the ice knocked loudly on the bottoms of their feet.

"Let's get out of here." Petal spun around.

The light had grown, and in the distance, dark lines rose toward the sky. Stonetrees, climbing up the foothills of Dragon Mountain. "How far is it?" Petal asked, gripping the rope next to Wix.

They began to pull.

Toli squinted at the horizon. "H-half an hour's walk," she stuttered. "M-maybe more." She gritted her teeth so they wouldn't chatter. "We m-might make it," she added, too cold to say more. She tried to help Wix and Petal pull the sled over the lip of the ice and toward the tree line, but her fingers were too cold to grasp the rope.

Wix and Petal's progress pulling the sled was slow, even with the ominous groans from the ice spurring them on. Toli's fingers were useless, and though Petal gave everything she had at Wix's side, she didn't have the advantage of long hours of strength training with Spar.

Wix bent toward the ice, tugging the sled over its rough surface with no runners to ease it along. Sometimes the heavy sled dragged behind them like a dead thing; sometimes it hit a bump and careened to the side, dragging them with it. It seemed to take half a lifetime to get it to the edge of the trees.

It was Wix's strength and sheer determination that, at last, helped them pull the sled safely off the deep ice and onto frozen ground. As soon as Petal dropped the rope, she was in front of Toli.

"Come on." Petal grabbed her, rubbing up and down her arms. "Let's get you in dry clothes." Petal helped her get undressed, the wet fur and leatherleaf peeling away from her skin like a crust. Behind their backs, Wix turned away and did the same.

"We n-need a fire," he said. "But there's nothing to burn."

We're going to die here, Toli thought. She could no longer feel her feet. She could feel the weight of Ruby across her shoulders, but there was no warmth to her. She reached up and pulled the dragon down into her shirt, scale to skin. She could just barely feel her heart beating.

Wix stumbled over. "There's got to be something we can burn. I have the hatchet. Maybe I can climb up into the stonetrees and cut a few small branches."

Petal gave him a sympathetic look. "You know that won't work. It takes more than a hatchet to cut stonetree, and it would take hours to set one burning. We don't have time."

Wix had pushed the sled over on its side to block the wind, so at least they had some shelter, but they were still too cold. They needed a fire. Toli stared at the sled. Her great-great-grandmother's sled. She admired the carving of scales along the sides and what was left of the arching dragon tail at the back—splintered from the bear-cat attack. She turned to Wix. "You have your hatchet?"

He cocked his head at her and nodded. "But Petal's right, it's not strong enough to cut through stonetree. Toli, you—"

She shook her head. "The sled," she whispered, dropping her gaze to the ice. "Burn the sled."

She felt rather than heard Petal's dismay. "But that's—"

"I know. We don't . . . we don't have a choice. If we don't get warm, we die. If we die, Ruby dies, and if Ruby dies . . ." Her voice failed her. But Petal understood.

"If Ruby dies, the dragons won't believe us, will they? They'd kill Mother and the rest of the Queendom too."

Wix lifted his hatchet, and to his credit, there was only the slightest pause before he brought it down on the splintered sled's dragon tail. After a minute, it cracked away from the rest.

Toli pulled out the dry furs and blankets, clearing the ground as best she could with her feet. By the time she'd made them a place to settle, Wix had a sizable pile of boards and kindling. Toli slid Ruby down into her arms. The dragon's scales were the color of ash. Toli wrapped her in furs and held her close, cradling her against her heart.

Petal set out the stonetree base and platform as Wix hurried to get the bowl of embers to light the fire.

"NO!" he cried, startling Petal.

Toli tried to stand up to see what was wrong, but she couldn't get up. Her feet were too cold, and he was nothing but a dark shadow standing among the shambles of the sled.

"What's wr-wrong?" Petal called, her teeth chattering.

"The embers are out. They were strong! I thought I'd saved them . . . but they must have gotten wet after all." His shoulders shook. "We don't have a way to start a fire." Wix dropped his face into his palms and wept. "I'm so sorry."

Toli dragged herself to her feet, and she and Petal moved to either side of him. They huddled together, taking comfort in one another. It wasn't much, but it was all they had. There was no hiding the truth, and so they didn't try. They were alone, with no hope of rescue or revival. Krala had been right. They weren't going to survive.

CHAPTER FIFTEEN

Father Moon's green light crept through the trees like ill intent, and all they could do was watch it come. Even the aurora lights, dancing through the starlit sky, were nothing but distant unkept promises. They wouldn't survive without a fire. Toli settled Ruby in her lap. The dragon seemed to be shifting in and out of consciousness, but somehow managed to crack open one eye. "I'm here," Toli whispered as she stroked Ruby's head.

The dragon wouldn't last much longer. Toli took a shuddering breath. She had failed them all—Father, Mother, Spar, Petal, and Wix—even Ruby. To think her mother had wanted to make her queen. It was laughable. She would have done better with Petal, or even Wix for that matter. Anyone but her.

Next to Toli, Petal's whole body shook. She wrapped her

arms around her legs, dropping her chin down to rest on her knees.

Toli stared up at the stars, bright in Nya's setting light. They should never have come. A sudden movement caught her attention and she looked down to see Ruby propelling herself from the furs. She was unsteady and trembling.

"Ruby!"

The dragon coughed a burst of fire at the pile of kindling and it flared into blinding flame. Toli gasped. The heat was like a slap.

She scooped Ruby up and pulled her close. The dragon had gone an even darker gray. "Thank you," she breathed. "Ruby, thank you." Toli nestled her back in the furs near the fire. The dragon cracked open her golden eyes and gave a shiver.

Wix exhaled. "Nya's light, I'm glad you have her, Toli." He met her eyes. "I'm so sorry about your sled. I'll make you a new one myself. I swear it. I know it won't be the same—can't be the same."

"It's okay." She tried to smile, but her face was painful, full of pins and needles as it began to thaw, and she couldn't. "At least it burns. I didn't know if it could."

He nodded and looked down.

The trees' tall silhouettes pleaded with the stars to come down. Toli's stomach growled.

The crackling of the fire echoed through the dense wood behind them as they stared out at the ice they had crossed. Toli sighed as the fire heated her toes and warmed her face. She lifted Ruby, still swathed in furs, and cradled her, hoping the heat of her body would do the dragon good. Some of Ruby's feathers had fallen from the edges of her wings.

Wix dug through the bag of supplies and came up with salted meat, dried mushrooms, and a handful of lichens. The lichens went into a pot with snow and they drank the broth when it was heated through. The taste was bitter, but Toli could feel the strength in it. She tried to give Ruby some, and a little meat too, but the dragon wouldn't even open her eyes anymore.

The foxes reappeared one by one to gather near the fire. Petal dozed on Toli's shoulder. "What do you think Father would be doing right now?" she asked. "If he were alive, I mean."

Toli's heart thunked against her aching ribs. *Father.*

She deserves to know, a voice whispered in the back of her mind. *After everything you've put them through, they both deserve to know what you did.*

She didn't want to tell her little sister—didn't want to see Wix's admiration falter. But her conscience pinched like too-small shoes. *Between the ice beetles, and the bear-cats, and the ice, they almost died three times. They're risking their lives too. They should know about all your mistakes—how your choices led to Father's death.* "Tell them," her heart insisted each time it knocked against her ribs. "Tell them what you did."

She took a deep breath. "Petal?"

"Mm."

"It was my fault." Toli hurried on before she could change her mind. "Father getting killed—it was my fault."

Wix stilled as Petal cocked her head at Toli. "That doesn't

make sense. Everyone knows the dragons killed him. How could it be your fault?"

Toli let the story roll away from her like meltwater. She told them how she'd disobeyed, how she'd gone after their father. She told about the dragons coming down from the skies, swooping low across the ice. How she had run toward the battle with a sword in her hand.

She had to stop and find her breath when she got to the part about her father turning, distracted. Next to her, Petal's face had gone white as the ice, her dark hair like shadows gathering around her.

"I . . . I was so stupid," Toli cried. "I thought I could protect him, but I only made things worse. One of the dragons saw me . . ."

Wix leaned forward, his eyes fierce. Petal stiffened and seemed to grow even paler.

"It came for me . . . smacked me back across the ice with its tail. I . . . I hit the Southern Wall and"—she took a shuddering breath—"and when I woke up, Father was dead."

"You . . . you've kept this a secret—all this time—just held it inside you?" Petal whispered. "So, why are you telling us this? Why bother? Why tell us now?"

Toli hung her head. Tears dropped into her lap. "You're not safe with me. I can't keep you safe! And now it's too late. You could have taken the sled and turned back."

Wix gaped. "And what about you and Ruby?"

Toli shrugged. "We would have done our best."

Silence fell, and only the crackling of the fire and the

whispering of the wind remained. Toli wished the ground would open and swallow her.

It was Wix who broke the thickening stillness after Toli's confession. He rose to pace. "Honestly, Toli. You may be a princess, but sometimes you're dumber than a bag of ice root."

Toli's mouth fell open. "What?"

He stopped walking and turned on her. "Do you think that's the only time you've screwed up? I mean, you do remember who just pulled you from under the ice, don't you?"

"You think I could forget that?"

"And you remember I was there right after the stampede, right?"

"I—"

"Did I—did either of us—ever give you the impression that we blamed you—that we thought less of you?"

"No, but that doesn't mean—"

"You hid this. You hid this from . . . from your own sister. You've just been stewing in it. You didn't even tell me!"

"I was ashamed, Wix! He died because of me."

Wix stopped walking. "You're not that important, Toli."

Her heart gave a painful throb. "I'm not important at all."

"Argh! That's not what I mean. Not everything happens because of something you do—or don't do." He stilled, his shoulders drooping. "Just—forget it. I don't think you'll ever understand."

"But if I'd listened to Father . . ." Toli's stomach rolled. She thought she might be sick, but she managed a glance at Petal.

Her sister was staring at her as if she'd never seen her before. "Say something," Toli whispered.

Petal blinked. She stumbled to her feet. "How could you be so stupid?" She turned and walked into the trees.

"Petal!" Toli cried.

Wix narrowed his eyes at her. "Did it ever occur to you that we're stronger together?" He tore a piece of board from the sled and dropped his gaze, bending to slice away huge splinters with his carving knife.

"Wix, I"—she swallowed—"I should go after Petal."

He held up one hand. "Leave her be. You'll only make it worse. The mistake you made that day—the day your Father died. That isn't the problem."

"I don't understand."

"Yeah," he ground out. "I know. *That's* the problem."

Toli sat watching the fire, too empty to cry. Ten minutes passed. Then twenty. Petal still wasn't back.

Toli couldn't stand it anymore. She picked Ruby up in her arms and wrapped her in furs before tucking her into her hood. Then she followed Petal's trail into the forest. The dragon lifted her head and hissed at the dark trees above them. Their branches clacked and knocked as they swayed, whispering secrets.

Toli bent her head to look for signs of Petal. She could track her, she just had to stay alert and follow the signs. She stepped into the gloom, a thick crust of ice covered the black permafrost under the trees in a patchwork. Short stretches of leaf litter clustered like scales across the ground. The silence of the forest thickened, but her heart was racing.

She wanted to believe that Petal was fine, but the feeling that she needed to hurry grew with every step. Glancing up a small embankment, Toli came to a halt as she caught sight of a boot print, half in ice and half on the brittle remains of crumbled leatherleaves.

"Petal?" she called.

No answer.

Toli's breath caught as she spotted another print just beyond the first. "Found you," she said, just to hear the whisper of her voice. As she moved on through the woods, she caught flashes of white ice. The foxes were following her, moving through the trees like wind. She tracked her sister back among the trees, farther into the forest.

She shouldn't have let her go alone.

Several dragon scales glinted where they had fallen to the ice.

She followed Petal's footsteps farther and farther. Deep under the canopy, where the trees were thick, there was barely enough light to see by, but patches of algae in the ice and on the bark of the stonetrees glowed in clumps of eerie green.

A bad feeling took root—and grew—at the base of Toli's spine. Didn't her sister know better than to wander this far, alone, in a strange place?

As if triggered by the thought, a piercing scream stabbed through the stillness.

Petal.

"Petal!" she yelled. "Petal!"

"I'm here," her sister's voice called from just ahead of her. "Up here."

Toli ran toward the sound of her voice. "Where?"

"Look up."

Toli stretched her neck, staring up into the dark branches. She startled as something dropped to land with a thunk at her feet. She leaned over. A pile of leatherleaf lizards, already dispatched and tied together with a bit of silk, lay neatly in the snow.

"What are you doing? Why did you scream?" Toli snapped, unable to keep the irritation out of her voice.

Grunts and falling bark announced that Petal was coming down. A moment later, her sister landed on her feet next to the lizards. She brushed off her gloved hands. "I slipped. I'm fine though. I *told* you I could hunt."

Toli gaped at her sister. She stared back up into the tree where the trunk grew thinner. The wind at the top pulled the tree one way, then another, howling and tugging at the man-sized leaves so they flapped like wings. They could have yanked Petal right off the trunk.

The lizards clung to the leaves with their sucker feet as they rose and fell in the wind. It had been a long time since she had hunted lizards. She didn't know Petal even knew how.

"You went up there by yourself?"

"Yes, I did."

"What dragon-blasted idea made you do that? Have you lost your mind?"

There was a long pause before Petal snapped, "I thought Ruby might be hungry for something fresh. I know I am."

"You should have told me! You should have waited until I could go with you, at least."

Petal didn't answer.

"What were you thinking?"

Petal crossed her arms. "You've got a lot of nerve, Anatolia Strongarm. What was *I* thinking?" Her voice got louder. "I was *thinking* that there might be lizards to eat, and that I know how to get them. I was thinking that I could. Do. It. Myself."

"Petal—"

"And that you would just say no."

"Of course I would say no!"

"Well, there you go."

"What good are lizards going to do anyone if you get yourself killed getting them?"

"Yeah? Well, you'd be dead twice over if it wasn't for Wix and Ruby and me—and you're so busy trying to get rid of us, to *keep us safe*, that you can't even appreciate it."

Toli held out her hands, palms up. "That's not true! I appreciate it—I do!"

"You don't. *And* you're a hypocrite!"

"What are you talking about?" Toli's voice rose. She gripped the ends of her braids to keep from grabbing Petal and shaking her.

Petal glared. "You say it's a mistake to trust you. That we're not safe with you? But you're here now lecturing me for going without you. So which is it, Toli? Am I safer with you or without you?"

"I—"

"You don't trust Wix and me enough to talk to us." Petal thrust the pile of dead lizards at Toli. "So maybe *we* should be done talking to *you*." She turned on her heel and stomped away through the trees.

Toli had to work to keep breathing. When she had remembered how, she turned to follow Petal's footprints and met the sympathetic yellow eyes of the lead sled fox. A bitter taste filled her mouth. "I messed up again," she whispered.

The fox didn't blink, didn't even move a muscle, until Toli turned away. Then she followed in Toli's wake, padding back toward the edge of the trees as if there was nothing else to be done.

CHAPTER SIXTEEN

Wix roasted the lizards, and they passed the food around in silence, Toli feeding a few pieces to Ruby. Petal sat directly across the fire from Toli, but no matter how many times Toli tried to catch her eye, her sister refused to look at her. Wix too, stared fixedly at the fire.

Once their clothes were finally dry, everyone pitched in to pack up their things. What little was left fit inside leatherleaf bags they could sling onto their backs. Wix handed Toli her bow and a quiver of arrows without comment.

Toli tied the remaining lizards to her bag and made sure Ruby was secure and warm in her hood. Petal looked at Wix. "What about the foxes?"

Toli shifted and waited for him to answer. For a second she wished she could lean on Spar—or her Mother—and tell them what had happened so they could tell her what to do. The wish withered. She had to do this herself.

"They'll be all right," he said at last. "They're smart creatures. I expect they'll follow us. Regardless, we need to press on up the Mountain."

Petal nodded. Wix was already moving up the slope.

Things were different. Now that her secret was out, it was as if a thick layer of frost had crept between them. She could still see Wix and Petal, she could talk to them, but all the warmth was gone. Everything was hollow, brittle, and cold.

They trudged on.

As Father Moon—the Dragon Moon—edged the summit of Dragon Mountain with green light, sleet began to fall.

"How are we going to get inside the Mountain? We're never going to make it," Petal said softly.

Wix caught up to walk beside her. "We'll know it when we see it, I think. Don't worry, Petal. We'll make it! We're in the foothills now. I mean, I can't promise we won't lose some toes to the cold, but—"

Toli pressed her lips together but said nothing. She didn't know if they'd make it or not.

Wix nudged Petal with his elbow. "Of course, we could always turn back. Fancy our chances of crossing broken ice, outrunning the bear-cats, and getting through a swarm of ice beetles?"

Petal narrowed her eyes at him, but Toli was glad to see a smile playing at the corners of her mouth. She started to reach forward to catch Petal's hand, but fought off the urge. Petal wouldn't want to take her hand. Not now.

Toli swallowed. Anyway, Petal was strong enough without her.

Judging by the way both moons moved over the sky, it took two, maybe three hours of walking before the stonetrees opened up in front of them and the ice began to climb. It was a slow rise, strewn with bits of rock, but reaching it felt like a victory.

Here and there, Toli caught a glimpse of one of the foxes through the fog. The wind rose and the aurora brightened, as if the lights were dancers and the wind was their song.

The ice between the stones was black and slick. They struggled to stay on their feet. Exhaustion clouded Toli's vision. One of them would slide backward, then regain their balance and push forward again, grabbing hold of rocks or one another.

Progress wasn't just slow, it was ridiculous. By the time Toli noticed that there were strange straggly saplings dotting the landscape, her skin was damp with sweat and breathing took a sharp, ragged effort. Ruby woke briefly to slip up to Toli's shoulder and be sick again, then leaned back against Toli with an undragonlike whimper.

"Don't worry," Toli whispered. "I'm taking you home." She cradled Ruby's head as she walked.

Toli didn't know how much time had passed. Dragon Mountain loomed above them, its dark crag casting silent judgment on their progress. She looked back. They *had* climbed. But not far.

Father Moon seemed amused as he watched them from his

high perch, and with a shock, Toli realized Nya must have set many hours ago. It would be morning soon. She thought carefully. This was the second night since they had left the Queendom—two full cycles of the Daughter Moon. She tried to remember the girl she had been before she left, but couldn't.

As they crested the second slope, Petal caught up and moved to walk next to Wix. Toli kept her eyes on their backs as they led the way, a sudden burst of gratitude overwhelming her, even though they were both still mad at her.

Warmth flooded her body as she looked at them walking together. "Thank you," she whispered, fixing her gaze on the ice below her feet. They might be angry with her, they might be in terrible danger, but in this moment, Toli was grateful to have them with her.

She didn't expect them to answer, or even hear her, but when she looked up, they were both staring at her.

Toli snorted a laugh. "What? I'm glad you're here." She hid a smile as she moved past them to lead the way.

Far away, at the bottom of the next peak, they saw a wide swath of odd trees leaned against one another like they too were trying to get up the Mountain but couldn't quite find their balance.

Toli had never seen anything like them. She squinted across the icy valley. Some kind of a chasm opened up farther on. They'd have to avoid that. Better to descend a little and go around, through the trees.

She shifted Ruby's weight on her back. The dragon was fading, and all Toli could do was try to keep her warm and hope the Dragon-Mother would know what to do for her. If they could just get there. Toli quickened her stride.

They passed into the woods. The strange trees were packed close together, leafless twists, thin and scraggly, with curled branches full of thin, sharp needles that gathered in blossoms. The woods leaned out above and around them, smooth and soft as fog. If she stood still, Toli could catch glimpses of the foxes. They had stayed close, as Wix had thought they would, but like pale dreams, they were always just out of sight.

Though the trees were small, reaching just a few feet over their heads, they blocked Father Moon's dim light and the shine of the stars well enough. Under their feet, the ice was so smooth and black it reflected everything like a mirror.

"I know we need to hurry," Petal gasped. "But could we rest? Just for a little while?"

Wix nodded. "We won't be much good if we're half dead when we get there."

Toli considered. They hadn't slept since the Necropolis. She sank down, shifting Ruby to her lap. "We can take a little break here. Just for an hour."

Petal threw a fur piece down and dropped to sit. She leaned back against one of the strange trees and looked up the misty slope of ice and stone. "Where do you think Krala is now?"

Toli snapped off a piece of roasted lizard and chewed. "Ahead of us."

Wix scrubbed his hand over his hair. "Way ahead."

There was a hitch in Petal's voice. "What about Spar? Where do you think she is?"

Toli looked down at her hands so Petal wouldn't see how much it hurt her to admit it. "Your guess is as good as mine," she sighed, rubbing at the freckles on her fingers as if they might come off.

"And Mother?"

Toli's voice was barely a whisper. "With the dragons still, I think. I hope. I don't know." She fought a wave of despair, gritting her teeth. It didn't matter. She wouldn't quit now.

Toli's legs felt like separate creatures, her thigh muscles twitching and burning. Petal was struggling to keep her eyes open. They all needed rest, but they couldn't stop long. They had too far to go, and there was no telling how long Ruby could hold on.

They sat shoulder to shoulder, chewing lizard jerky and listening to the sounds of the snow plopping down from the trees. Wix was carving something out of the piece of Toli's sled he'd broken off. Toli threw one arm around a fox that had sidled up to sit next to her, eyeing the dry lizard. She gave him the tail.

The next thing she knew, she was sitting up with a groan. A strange sound had woken her and she strained to find it in the quiet. Maybe she had imagined it. The cold dug its icy teeth down into her bones. Next to her, Petal's breath escaped in a thin cloud every few seconds.

The noise came again—the cry of a fox, but strange and wrong—frightened. She stared into the trees, reaching out to shake Wix awake. "Wake up. Something's wrong."

His hand moved to his bow.

Petal sat straight up, her eyes so blue, they almost glowed. "What is it?" she croaked.

Toli fought gravity and stood, her whole body heavy. "We fell asleep. Something's wrong," she repeated. "I don't know what, but we need to go."

Petal rushed to loop the ropes of her pack over her shoulders. Toli's knees tried to buckle as she hefted Ruby back into her hood.

"Where are the foxes?" Petal asked.

Wix's expression darkened. "Gone."

"What do you mean . . . gone?"

"He means," Toli panted, "whatever's out there, they want no part of it. Hopefully they're okay. They'll catch up."

Petal turned to peer into the woods around them with wide eyes.

Toli reached out to squeeze her sister's hand.

They had to get through the woods to open ground again. At least there, they could see what was coming. Ahead of them, where the mountainside left the trees to climb again, green moonlight spread like a stain. Then, just for a second, something crossed in front of them—something big enough to block the light as it passed.

Toli stopped. "Did you see that?"

Wix gave his head a tiny shake. "See what?"

"I . . . I don't know. It was a shadow, like something just moved up there where the trees open." A jolt of panic shot up Toli's back. She fought it back down and fixed her gaze ahead, unblinking.

Wix moved to stand beside her. "Could it be a dragon?"

"No. I don't think so. Maybe. I don't know."

"What are we going to do? Should we hide?"

"No. There's no point in hiding. Whatever it is, it already knows we're here."

Wix sighed.

"So then . . ."

Toli gave her sister a grim look. She reached down to draw the knife from the straps of her boot and handed it to her sister. "If we get out of this alive, I swear I'm going to show you how to use that—and a bow too."

Petal gave a sharp nod as she took the knife in her shaking grip.

Toli unslung her bow from her shoulder. "Stay behind me," she added, leading the way. "My cloak is good camouflage. It might buy us a few seconds."

They slunk toward the edge of the trees, Toli regretting every tiny crunch of ice under her feet. At the place where the wood opened up, a giant shadow stepped out to block their path.

Wix spun to guard their backs as Toli grabbed Petal's hand, pulling her so they all stood back to back.

Toli looked up and peered into the bright eyes of a huge green dragon. Her breath stopped in her throat. The dragon's green eyes were like jeweled crescents of the Dragon Moon. Vertical pupils lengthened as it considered them. "Where is she?" the dragon hissed. "Where is the youngling?"

"I have her here," Toli managed, turning so the dragon could see Ruby's weight in her hood. "She's safe."

The dragon didn't answer as she slid closer, her talons clicking softly against the ice. She leaned over them and inhaled. Toli's cloak shifted with the pull of the dragon's breath. "I can barely smell her. What is wrong with her? Why did you take her?"

Toli shook her head. "We didn't take her! It was another dragon—two dragons. I swear it!" She took a breath to steady her heart.

The dragon tipped her head, leaning forward so her eye drew even with them. "Which dragons?"

Toli caught the sharp scent of electricity. Petal stepped to Toli's side. "A brother and sister," she said firmly. "Dral and Krala Frost."

"Frossst," the dragon hissed. "Krala Frost, you say. That is interesting." The dragon stared, her forked tongue flicking forward. "I am a Stone—secondborn. I have never liked Krala's ways," she rattled. "To my thinking, firstborns are often shortsighted."

Wix snorted, and Toli shot him a dirty look.

"Krala has always had ambitions, though unfortunately, she is not alone in her foolish desires."

Petal stepped forward. "She tried to kill Ruby!"

"Ruby?"

Toli pulled Petal back. "The . . . the youngling."

The dragon huffed a cloud of steam, leaning through it to look Toli in the eyes. "She would not dare."

All three of them took an involuntary step back as the

enormous green dragon leaned closer, studying them. Toli swallowed, lifting her chin. She wouldn't hide the truth anymore. Not about this. Not about anything.

The dragon's crescent-shaped pupils dilated. "Humph. Is what you say true?"

"It is," Petal said, and the tone of her voice left no room for doubt.

"Krala *has* always resented our queen." The dragon considered them. "I am Bola Stone, secondborn, sister to both Krala and our Dragon-Mother." Another pause. "And you are?"

Toli cleared her throat. "Anatolia Strongarm, firstborn. Petal Strongarm, secondborn, and Wix Walerian, um . . . onlyborn."

Bola blew a breath of steam over them and for a moment Toli couldn't see anything.

When it had cleared, Toli asked, "Did Krala really fight with your thirdborn sister and lose? Is that how this Dragon-Mother came to rule—by challenging Krala?"

A gleam of pride came into Bola's eyes. "Yesss. Our Dragon-Mother had died, and although my sister was a thirdborn Sky, she challenged Krala Frost for the title of Dragon-Mother and won her challenge. We are loyal to her."

The dragon shook her green-feathered wings. "Our queen's might is great. She has won many challenges in her time. Only Krala Firstborn harbors bitter dreams."

So the thirdborn sister *had* defeated Krala to become the Dragon-Mother. No wonder Krala hated her.

Toli nodded. "But she . . . Krala hinted there were other . . . brethren who were on her side too."

"It is true that not all in the Mountain agree with our Dragon-Mother. My sister has made some . . . unusual choices."

"You mean like taking my mother," Toli ground out, letting her bow fall to her side. She cleared her throat. "That's why we're here. To bring my mother home and return Ruby."

Bola leaned closer. "And the youngling is safe?"

"For now." Toli nodded.

The dragon drew back, her words dropping like stones. "You threaten—"

"No! We . . . she was protecting us. She ate something that made her sick. She's—she's dying."

The dragon inhaled again. Toli shivered as her hot exhale whipped her hair back.

"That is why I cannot smell her. She has been poisoned."

"It was an accident."

The dragon pressed her muzzle right up against Toli, where Ruby was huddled close against her skin. Toli turned to ice and tried not to move at all as the dragon's lips parted and drew in a breath. "Beetle," Bola rattled.

"We wanted to take her home. There must be *something* you can do to save her."

"Mmm. Yes. This will not do," the dragon said. Wix coughed as she blew a wave of smoke over them. Next to Toli, Petal shivered under the dragon's gaze.

Wix tightened his grip on his bow. "What are you going to do with us?"

"You came to return our youngling. What should I do with you?"

Petal choked out, "Kill us?"

The dragon drew back. "What a strange little bone bag you are. Why would I kill such a puny bite?"

Toli snarled, "Because you're a dragon! Because we're worth *nothing* to you. Maybe you feel the same way as Krala. Maybe you want us all dead."

The dragon dragged one talon in the snow, tracing a long line between them. "What a strange idea." The dragon turned to Wix. "Tell me, boy. Do you agree? What is your thinking? Why should I wish to kill you?"

Wix glanced at Toli, hesitating. "Just . . . maybe . . . for fun?"

The dragon lashed forward. Her forked tongue tasted the air around Petal's head as she considered their words. "Would killing you be . . . fun?"

Wix grabbed Petal by the arm, tugging her behind him and Toli. "Probably not," he whispered.

"Well, then."

Behind them, Petal nodded vigorously, her eyes squeezed shut.

The dragon laughed through her nose, sending puffs of smoke steaming into the sky. "Funny little bone bags," she chuckled.

Toli swallowed her surprise. Unlike Krala, Bola seemed amused by humans—almost as if she found them endearing instead of infuriating.

"So now what?" Petal whispered.

"Now," the dragon began as she executed a slow turn, her talons leaving deep punctures in the ice, "there is no time to be wasted. I will tell our Dragon-Mother what you have said. She will want to see you. Leave your tasty morsels, and I will take you to her."

"Tasty morsels?" A rush of dizziness washed over Toli as she let out her breath.

The dragon extended a long, clawed finger and pointed toward a small hill of snow several feet away. "These tasty morsels," she growled, reaching out and flicking her talon. The hill scattered into whimpering foxes. They scurried into the trees to hide in their shadowed edges.

"Will they be all right?" Petal asked.

The dragon sighed. "You worry for nothing. They will find their way home, as all wise creatures do." Petal's face cracked into a wide grin, but Toli wasn't sure this whole thing was such a good idea. Wix gave her what she was sure was supposed to be a reassuring smile.

A rush of pride and fear swamped her heart as Petal met her gaze—the same little sister who had just crossed the ice with her and who had helped her best friend pull her from the grip of the long-gone sea, the same sister who had collected lizards to feed them and stitched her friend's wound. It seemed like forever ago.

"You know the Dragon-Mother might not listen?" Toli whispered to Petal and Wix.

Wix nodded. "Doesn't matter."

"We're going." Petal scowled.

The dragon snickered and opened her taloned hand with a sigh. "I do not know what our Mother will make of your arrival. Shall we find out?"

CHAPTER SEVENTEEN

Toli watched the blood drain from Petal's face and knew her own face looked the same. Though Toli had always wondered what it would be like to fly like the dragons, she had never imagined she would have a chance to do it. Her spine tingled.

Bola Stone flexed her three huge black talons. The fourth, smaller talon opened like a thumb. "Coming?" She snickered at the looks on their faces.

With a sick feeling in her stomach, Toli asked, "You want us to ride . . . in your talons? I was wondering if we could . . . um . . . Is there anywhere else to ride?"

Petal cast her a grateful glance as Bola Stone considered her request. "On my back is tolerable—if you can find something to hold on to." She eyed Toli doubtfully. "I fly high. You may freeze—if that sort of thing is bothersome to bone bags?"

Wix's brow furrowed. "We have extra furs, clothes, in our packs. Maybe we could tie some of those around us."

Toli held a hopeful breath as she and Wix stepped closer to look at the dragon's back. The surface between her wings was nothing but a wide expanse of smooth, interlocked scales. Toli's heart sank. Trying to ride that would be like clinging to a wall of ice. Petal had already read the answer on Wix's face.

"Come," said Bola Stone, leaning down. "If you are coming, come. I have no care about how. You will come with me now, or I will take you. Or perhaps I will take the youngling and leave the rest of you to die. In any case, I am done with waiting."

Toli nodded. Talons it would be. She should go first. She steeled her nerves as her stomach churned. The dragon's scales were warm against her palms as she took hold of one finger and stepped into Bola's palm.

Petal climbed in next to her. Toli could feel her struggle not to panic. Wix clambered in on the other side of Toli. Toli's pulse hammered so loud it drowned out every thought. She shifted to hold Ruby at her front, quickly looping a sling of rope around her. The little dragon's soft scales were cold, and Toli fastened her cloak around them both. At her back, through a thick layer of scale, Bola Stone's pulse beat a steady rhythm.

The dragon's voice rumbled against her. "When we arrive in the Mountain," she said, "keep the youngling hidden. Her illness will keep any brethren from finding her scent. If what you say about Krala is true, we will take no chances. Our Dragon-Mother will know what to do."

Bola beat her wings once, twice, and they lifted from the

ground, lurching upward into the air with such force that all three children fell to their knees in Bola's palm. Above them she laughed.

Her talons were crisscrossed above them, but the cracks between her fingers were big enough to fall through. Each of them clung to a black talon.

Toli couldn't hold back a laugh as she stared out at the ground blurring past. The thin black lines of the trees looked like the tangled nests of serpents as they rose higher. The wind rushed past them—threatening to topple them out.

Toli caught the electric scent of dragon as Bola banked to the left. The dragon let her forearm skim the craggy rocks, chuckling as Petal yelped.

A blast of cold wind took Toli's breath away, but as she peered down at the dark rising surface of the Mountain, her heart sang. The crags and trees of Dragon Mountain blurred beneath them as they flew.

Wix held tight to Bola's talon and leaned forward, laughing. Toli reached out and got a firm hold on his tunic. Through the space between Bola's fingers she could see the sky, streaked with lights. They seemed just as far away as ever. She stared out past the foothills to where Nya rose, her warm light stretching toward them like the promise of a friend.

"Look!" Petal cried over the roaring of the wind. "I can see the Queendom!"

Toli squinted into the distance and could see, just beyond the wide expanse of ice, the spark and gleam of the statues on the Southern Wall, and rising above it, the dark shadow of stone and forest.

Wix laughed loud and long.

After a moment, Toli laughed too. The cold burned her ears, but she couldn't bring herself to lean back. There was too much to see. Minutes passed, but it was as if, after years of starvation, she had sat down before a feast. All of Ire stretched out in front of her. She couldn't bear to turn away. Her eyes teared in the wind.

Bola turned to rise up the steep edge of the Mountain, and for a moment, a bright gleam of light caught Toli's eyes. She pointed. "Look!"

"Is that water?" Petal gasped, jumping up. "Toli, it's the sea!" She stumbled forward.

"Petal!" Toli cried out, hauling her back.

Petal dropped back down and shivered. "I forgot. For a second, I forgot."

Toli nodded and forced herself to let go of her sister's arm. The side of the Mountain now blocked their view. Wix still leaned as far as he could, craning to see more.

So Krala was right, after all. The sea did exist. Toli had the uncomfortable thought that maybe she had been telling the truth about the people in the South too.

It was Petal's turn to let loose a laugh as they dived lower, veering toward a huge black cavern that gaped open, seemingly from nowhere. As they turned, low over scraggly patches of trees, Toli saw something that made her breath catch.

She elbowed Wix. "I think I just saw a sled down there under the trees."

Her sister stopped smiling. "Where?"

Wix leaned forward until Toli couldn't keep herself from grabbing the back of his tunic again. "I didn't see anything," he said. "Are you sure?"

Toli didn't answer, and they were quiet as the ground got closer, none of them willing to speak their thoughts.

At last, Toli shook her head. "Why?" she wondered out loud. "Why would Spar come here? Could she be here to rescue Mother?"

"By herself?" Wix shook his head." And how would she get in?"

Petal knit her fingers together. "Maybe she climbed the cliffs. Anyway, we don't know it's her. Not for sure."

"It's her," Wix said. "Who else could it be?"

The thought itched under Toli's skin as Bola Stone landed, her claws touching stone with the gentleness of an old friend.

Wix tumbled out as Toli launched to the ground like a spring, brushing herself off. They waited as Petal climbed out with her usual slow precision.

Toli had been too busy worrying to think much about what the inside of the dragons' mountain home might be like, but as she stood up and adjusted Ruby inside her tunic, the sight of it drove away any thought at all.

She stood in a massive cavern, at the toppling edge of a deep pit. From the basalt ledge, she looked down into a seethe of young dragons. She would have guessed it was some kind of punishment—a crushing mass of bodies—except for the way the dragons swam over and under one another. They wove through tangled knots in a leisurely dance, a rush of scales crossing scales. The dim light ran along their bodies, first one, and then the next, with dizzying speed.

Their wings lay folded tightly against their bodies as they moved, feathers like foam trailing behind and across the surface of the seethe. Several of the dragons had long, iridescent quills tipped with feather. The quills lifted now and again along their backs, flickering and shaking as the dragons glided among one another.

Bola appeared next to Toli, startling her. How something as big a Bola could move so quietly was a mystery. "This is the rest of the youngling's seethe," the dragon breathed, indicating the dragons below. "These will see Ruby rise or fall."

Every year, Toli watched from within the safety of Gall's walls when the dragons left their mountain with the aurora lights. Everyone in the Queendom did. It was spectacular, even from a great distance.

This was different.

This was up close—and there were so many! She'd never dreamed there were so many.

"There are many," Bola said, as if she could read Toli's mind. "But new seethes are cause for celebration. They do not happen often—sometimes not for centuries."

Toli dragged her eyes away from the writhing mass and turned to Bola. "Can you take us to my mother now? Please?" Now that her feet were on the ground inside the Mountain, not even the heat and color of the dragon stronghold were enough to distract her. She needed to know her mother was okay—that there was hope to bring her home. Had Krala already spread her lies? "Krala—" she began.

"Mmm," Bola rattled. "All will be up to the Mother."

Toli tried to calm the fluttering inside her chest by looking around at the rest of the cavern. Bola was the closest thing to an ally she had—and the dragon might make the difference between success and failure. This was the time to move slowly—breathe slowly—just as Spar had taught her to do on any hunt.

Bola looked over her shoulder as Wix and Petal gawked at everything around them. "Gather," she whispered. Wix and Petal moved closer. Massive dragons lumbered past them on the smooth black basalt, slipping by without a sound, or even a glance. "Now, little bites," Bola said. "Follow me and be quiet. Dragons do not like disruption."

Sweat beaded on Toli's forehead and ran down her back in warm rivulets. It was hotter in here than in the Hall with all its fires blazing. Thin, fiery cracks branched out along the surface of the walls, reaching away into dark tunnels that stretched into the distance. "It's just like the Telling says," Petal whispered, shaking Toli's arm. "The dragons heat the world."

"Stay close," Toli whispered as they followed Bola along the basalt path. Above them, dragons clung to enormous mineral stalactites that hung from the ceiling high above, or slept on ledges along the walls. Their tails dangled, flashing in the dim light as they spread wide their bright, feathered wings.

The quiet was disturbing. The only sound was the soft rush of scales slipping together or sliding along rock. None of the dragons spoke—not to her, and not to one another.

"Stay close," Toli said again, shifting the sling that held Ruby so that the little dragon lay against her back, farther out of sight.

"Boiled," Wix said with a grimace as a few of the dragons cast curious glances at them. He turned his head, nodding toward another group of dragons looking their way with narrowed eyes. "Fried."

Toli squinted. "What are you talking about?"

He made a slow turn as Petal followed his gaze to more dragons on their other side. "Raw."

The dragons hissed and whispered to one another. Most looked away. Petal leaned toward Toli. "He's listing how he thinks they'll eat us," she muttered.

Toli studied her friend. "Well, he doesn't seem too put out about it."

Wix snorted as Toli tamped down her rising anxiety. Soon she would know if her mother was alive or dead. Soon they would know if the Dragon-Mother would thank them for returning her young—or kill them for their transgressions. Soon they would find out if Ruby would live long enough to singe any more of Petal's dresses.

The heat of the cavern scorched the inside of her nose and throat as she breathed. The silence grew heavy, as though everyone was anticipating a spark that would ignite a blaze. The air was filled with the sparkle and shifting of the dragons' movements and a dark, earthy heat—like a stone waiting to melt and become something new.

Toli's thoughts turned back to her mother. Where was she—alive? The question was a thorn under her skin, prodding until she thought she might start to bleed. She was so distracted, she almost missed the small yellow dragon that sidled toward them with narrowed silver-gray eyes. Wix bumped her to attention.

Bola rattled. "Ah, Cata! I need brethren I can trust with these while I speak with the Mother."

The yellow dragon ducked her head with a rattle. "I will help you with your task, Bola Stone. You may rely upon me."

Toli shook her head. "But—you were taking us to the Dragon-Mother."

Bola rattled. "It is better that I speak with her first. She does not like to be disturbed. I think it would not be . . . healthy for you."

The yellow dragon—Cata—seemed to consider Bola's words. "It sounds like a wise choice. I will watch them. But you must hurry. I have duties of my own."

Bola Stone cast a glance at them over her shoulder and, without another word, moved off down the winding basalt ledge that seemed to serve as a main road.

The yellow dragon watched as Bola disappeared into the darkness. A bead of sweat ran into Toli's eyes as Cata turned to face her.

"I am Cata," the dragon hissed, her neck moving like a serpent. "You will follow me now."

"Bola told us to wait here," Petal said.

"Bola!" the yellow dragon hissed, and Toli caught a glimpse of fire in her throat.

"I don't think she's giving us a choice, Petal," Toli said, tasting salt on her lips. "Where are you taking us?"

Cata showed her teeth. "To see an old friend."

Toli paused. Was the dragon talking about her mother? She looked around, but the few adult dragons in the cavern were either sleeping or preening. Not one spared her a glance.

Wix caught her eye and tightened his fingers on his bow as they turned to follow Cata down a narrow alley of basalt that ran along the back of the chamber. As they came to the far side of the cavern, it opened out into other spaces. Smaller caverns, like rooms, branched off everywhere from a lacework of black paths. Cata slipped into the dark. The path led downward, the fiery cracks in the walls providing the only light.

Toli could feel Petal close behind her, could just make out the movement of the yellow dragon ahead of her in the darkness. Cata took a path that moved to the left, then another sharp right, and two more lefts. Toli tried to keep track as they zigged and zagged down into the Mountain, but the darkness pressed in, leaving little room for thought.

A glow ahead of them brightened, and Cata turned toward it, leading them into a smaller chamber of gleaming black. A fissure in the middle glowed, lighting up the cavern like a sky without stars.

It was full of heat—and dragons—but Toli hardly noticed them. All her attention was focused on the tall figure in front of them, her burns shining like the molten rock that ran through the walls.

"Spar," she whispered.

Spar smiled and stepped forward, clasping her in a tight hug. "I wondered what was keeping you, Princess."

CHAPTER EIGHTEEN

Toli's thoughts spun as she stared at her mentor's face. In the heat and dim light, her burns almost seemed to glitter. "What are you doing here?"

Her focus broadened as she took in the dragons that stood leering down at them. She scuttled backward, dragging Wix and Petal with her. The other dragons pressed close, and Toli counted six of them as Cata moved to join them.

A black dragon shifted her weight to push forward, and Toli recognized Krala. The dragon's eyes widened, but the shock of seeing them alive passed quickly. She sneered. "The pass did not kill you. Well, I think you will find no better end here. You see that Spar is with us now. She has had her calling."

"What's that supposed to mean?" Toli's eyes slid back to her mentor "Spar! Where's my mother?"

Spar gave a small sigh. "Still no patience."

"What? I don't—"

"Traitor," Wix spit out.

Petal cried out as Spar lurched forward and grasped Toli's forearms, yanking her close. Though the grip made her cringe, Toli lifted her face, meeting her mentor's eyes with a defiant glare. "What does she mean, you've had your calling?"

"It's not what you think. Listen to me. I can't escape it now," the hunt master hissed, tapping her forehead. "Their Dragon-Mother is always . . . whispering." She leaned closer. "Ever since I was burned, there has been a . . . connection." She tapped her temple. "I hear her voice. Telling lies."

Toli's stomach flipped. Was Spar here because the Dragon-Mother wanted her here? "What do you mean, a connection? Between you and the Dragon-Mother?"

"Yes," Spar snarled, spittle flying. "A bond."

"I don't understand," Petal said.

"You cannot understand our justice," said a large blue dragon, her scales sparking like light on water. "This Mother's time is over. No more soft talk of friendship with your kind. We are dragons. We will *take* what we like, from you—or from the South. And I, Ata Sky, will—"

Krala let out a roar that shook the chamber, forcing Toli to cover her ears. "*I* will lead them, Ata Sky. *I* will lead the seethes. *I*—and no other."

Ata Sky blew steam. "You do not lead yet."

But she scuttled back nonetheless as Krala leaned forward into Toli's face. "Give me the youngling."

Spar shoved Toli back, out of Krala's reach. Toli stumbled toward Petal, and her sister caught hold of her.

Ruby lay pressed against her back, unmoving. Toli prayed the folds of her cape would hide the dragon's lithe form, and that Bola Stone was right about Ruby's sickness covering her scent. "She . . . she died!"

"Lies. Why would Bola Stone bring you into the Mountain if you do not have the youngling?"

Petal shrugged, but Toli could see the tension in her shoulders.

"Ask her yourselves," Wix snarled. "Ruby died before we came up the Mountain."

"It was the pass," Petal added with a sidelong look at Krala. "We came through the pass and—and were attacked by bearcats. They . . . your youngling was killed."

"Fooliiiish girl," Krala hissed. "We will find her body and owe you nothing. You three," she added to the dragons standing behind her, "go find the youngling's bones, and bring them here. Now the Mother will *have* to give me audience—she will have to gather *all* the brethren to hear my words. We will prove the treachery of the bone bags to all at once! All will see the truth of my position. Then I will issue my challenge."

Toli was surprised to see sorrow in the dragons' faces as they slipped past to look for Ruby's body. Only Krala's eyes held a gleam of triumph. Spar lifted her gaze to meet Toli's.

"Where's the queen of Gall?" Toli asked. "Where's my mother—*your* queen?"

Spar frowned. "I'll do what I can for her. For all of you. But you must understand, there can be no more avoiding the truth. The dragons must be destroyed."

Wix scratched his head. "You . . . you realize you're *with* the dragons."

Ata Sky chuckled. "It is a temporary alliance. A common goal." The dragons shifted, a red one bumping a smaller turquoise dragon, who reacted by blowing fire at the chamber wall, lighting up the small space like a sun. It grew harder to breathe in the stifling heat.

Toli glared at Spar. "You said they couldn't be trusted."

"They can't be trusted. But they want what I want: to get rid of the Dragon-Mother. I'm already lost," Spar pleaded, holding up her hands. "I was lost the day that dragon burned me. But if I'm going to die, at least I can take her with me. Don't you see? Everything will be different . . . better, when their Queen is gone." She was leaning forward as if she were telling Toli a secret. "Without her, they'll be at one another's throats. They'll fall apart."

Toli shook her head. Behind Spar, Krala heard every word. Her eyes gleamed, as though she found some kind of sick humor in the hunt master's whispers.

Spar's dark eyes softened. "Help me, Anatolia. With you and your sister at my side, we can convince your mother too. When their Queen is dead, my burns will heal. They've told me so. Then we can go home again and prepare for war while they fight among themselves—while they destroy one another."

Petal had crept to Toli's side, listening. "And what about Ire? Without the dragons, the world will freeze for good. Even Nya won't be able to save us."

Spar narrowed her eyes at Petal. "You always were a gullible child. That is only a story—no doubt started by the dragons themselves to get our food."

"The tithe is our way of thanking them for the heat," Petal whispered before her expression hardened. "It doesn't matter. You're insane if you think they'll let you leave the Mountain alive."

Krala hissed. "Do not listen to the fears of children, my sister. You are one of us now. We are united in our purpose."

Spar smiled, cringing, the skin around her eyes shiny and tight. "Your concern is touching, Petal. I will take each challenge as it arrives, as I always have. I assure you that they hate their Dragon-Mother too," Spar explained. "It seems she has more than her fair share of enemies."

But she also has her fair share of allies. Toli thought of Bola Stone and all the other dragons she had seen on the Mountain.

Ata Sky began to laugh, and Krala lashed out with her tail, slapping her back toward the fissure. "She denies us all our true power! As if I am not frostborn! The South should be ours—it should belong to Frost, and Stone, and Sky—as should this frozen land. We should not have to share it with your kind."

"She has slighted us all," said the small yellow dragon.

Krala snarled. "I am a *Frost*. You are not as insulted as I."

"Take care *you* do not insult us, Krala," a dark-blue dragon called from the back, long spines raised along her back. "I am Turu, fourthborn. I have turned my ear to you, but though I have no second name—no rank among the brethren—I swear that if you lead us astray, I will gnaw away your heart. Then you will not misunderstand our intent." The room filled with hisses and snarls.

"See," said Spar, her eyes black in the dim light. "They will destroy one another." A shiver passed over her and she clutched her own head. "Shhh—she'll hear. She'll hear."

Krala snapped her jaws disdainfully. "She will not. She hears nothing that happens in the obsidian chambers."

"She wants me at her side," Spar whimpered, falling to one knee.

Dismay rolled over Toli like fire. To see her mentor brought so low. If she were well, Spar would choose death before she would kneel to dragons. Toli wanted to reach out and lift Spar up again, to help her remember herself—anything that would restore her, whole and unbroken. But Spar had betrayed her. She had betrayed all of them, so instead of helping her mentor, Toli bit her lip and squeezed her hands tightly behind her.

Krala Frost loomed over Spar, her eyes glittering. "Take this one out. The Mother does not like being unable to reach her." She leaned down, her voice a thin shadow of a whisper. "Do not fret, little sister. Soon your pain will end and you will grow into your inheritance."

"I am not your sister," Spar hissed back. "I am your ally. Your ally for now—just until the life leaves her eyes."

The huge blue dragon, Ata Sky, laughed, like a rumbling of stones. "We shall see, *little cousin*."

Spar rose and allowed herself to be led out by one of the dragons, turning back a moment before she would disappear into the dark. Toli stared at Spar's fever-bright eyes.

Petal crossed her arms. "You've betrayed us all—the entire Queendom, Spar."

"No," Spar hissed. "No, I did that a long time ago. Now I'm saving us."

Krala moved toward them, her scales silent on the glassy floor. "Spar's time has come. She understands that there is only one way to break the bond of burning."

"I must kill the Mother with my own hands." Spar smiled as the darkness swallowed her.

For a long pause the chamber was silent. Ata Sky stared out the door to where Spar had disappeared and huffed smoke from her nose. "She will fail and die, of course. But she will provide a good distraction."

Krala leaned down to narrow her eyes at Toli and Petal. "And then we will put these bone bags to good use at last, along with all the others of their kind."

"What does that mean?" Wix asked.

"We can eat them now," the dark blue dragon simpered, shifting closer to the front of the cavern. Toli took a step back, tightening her grip on her bow.

Ata laughed, and even Krala looked impressed. "Your appetite knows no bounds, Alto Sky, but I think they may yet be useful alive. Ata—contain these bites."

"Do not order me, Frostborn! Your plans for our rise have been tenuous at best. You will have my loyalty when you have secured your place as our Mother. That time has not yet arrived."

A drip of liquid fire fell from Ata's mouth to the floor of the cavern. "You told us the Mother would easily believe our brethren stole the chrysalis, and that she would leave the heart of the Mountain to hunt for it. That did not come to pass. Then you told us she would end this repulsive exchange with their queen—that when she heard their firstborn had poisoned her child—"

"Quiet, thirdborn! You are a Sky like the Mother—unworthy of my explanations."

Ata snarled. "The Mother would have been easier to kill, but she remains. She has not even granted you an audience. Now the youngling is lost to us, too. You said the chrysalis would be returned, but you let these bone bags gets the better of you."

Hope lanced through Toli and she fought the urge to look at Wix and Petal to see if they had heard it too. Krala had not been granted an audience yet. And, Toli thought, if she had understood Ata, it was Krala alone who wanted Ruby dead. For the rest of them, stealing the chrysalis was just a means to an end, a chance to get rid of the Dragon-Mother.

Krala snarled and drew herself up. "It would have worked if the human queen hadn't calmed her."

"You should have killed these bites at the first chance." Ata's slit pupils dilated as she fixed her gaze on Petal. "We could kill them now."

Toli's hand tightened on her bow. From the corner of her

eye she saw Petal move her hand toward the handle of Wix's knife where it still hung at her waist.

"I thought that once," Krala sneered. "But now I see the truth. It is better if the Mother declares the human queen an enemy and strikes the first blow. These bites are braver than I expected. We can use them. The more enemies the Mother and her loyal brethren have, the better."

"No! Now!" Ata threw herself at Krala with a hiss, but Krala knocked the blue dragon away, dropping low. Wix scuttled backward, pulling Petal and Toli with him as Ata Sky closed in on them.

"You are a fool, Ata." Krala unfolded one wing and knocked Wix and Petal to the ground, sweeping them up into one taloned hand, and Toli into the other. "I will do it myself."

Toli's arms were pinned tightly to her sides. Wix and Petal also struggled in Krala's grip as she pushed through the wall of dragons the back of the small cavern. A massive geode, its inside covered in pointed indigo crystals, stuck out from the back wall as if it floated in a sea of black. She dropped them into it, chuckling as Toli tripped over the crystals and toppled to her knees. Wix and Petal fell on her in a pile.

"When we come back," Krala hissed. "The battle will be won." She lowered her head to peer at them. "Perhaps I will eat Spar and let the three of you live." Her eyes narrowed thoughtfully. "It would please me to be served by royalty."

The dragons filed out behind her.

Toli struggled to her feet and peered over the edge of the geode, Petal right behind her.

Wix blew out his cheeks. "Now what?"

"We've got to get to the Dragon-Mother before Krala does."

"How?"

Petal peered at the ground. They were at least fifty feet up. "Too far to jump," she said.

"Children," came a rattle from the shadows of the cavern.

Toli and Wix lifted their bows.

Dral shifted out of the darkness, his ruff of green feathers shifting as he stalked forward.

Petal fumbled for her knife.

"Don't take another step," Toli shouted.

Dral paused, his eyes widening. "I have no interest in puny bites," he began. "I simply did not wish to be seen by my sister and her followers. Now that they are gone, I thought I . . . might be of some assistance."

Wix lowered his bow. "Why would you help us? What about Krala?"

"I do not approve of our Mother. She has made mistakes—important ones. But sacrificing any youngling, much less a firstborn, is a line I will not cross. It brings me shame that Krala wished the chrysalis to be truly lost to us."

Dral brought his head up, peering into the geode. "Is the youngling really dead?"

Toli thought about lying again, but they were running out of time. Ruby was running out of time. She shook her head. "No. She's here, with me. But I . . . I don't think she's doing very well."

"We must get her to the Mother."

Toli turned and looked out across the obsidian cavern. "Can you get us down?"

"Not all." He cocked his head at them. "Two must stay—in case my brethren return. They may not notice one is missing. They will notice three."

Toli studied the glint of crystal at her feet.

"Which one?" Dral whispered, suddenly so close that Toli stumbled backward into Petal.

She glanced at Wix. His eyes were fierce as he gave her a nod.

Petal's hand clasped her shoulders. "You go, Toli. We'll be okay."

She pressed her lips together. "I'm so sorry, Petal—about father and about dragging both of you into this."

"The way I remember it," Wix said, "we dragged ourselves into it."

Toli laughed despite the sudden tightness in her chest. "And I'm sorry for not telling you. I should have trusted you."

Petal took her hand. "Did you mean what you said?"

Toli shook her head. "When? What did I say?"

"Before Bola found us—in the wood, you said that if we make it out of this alive, you will show me how to use a knife properly . . . and a bow too. Did you mean that?"

Toli considered Petal. Her sister was strong—willful, independent, and brave. Did she really believe Petal couldn't learn to defend herself? She lifted her chin. "Of course I meant it. I know you can do anything you set your mind to."

Petal's chin quivered. "Thank you," she whispered, reaching out to take Toli's other hand. "It's not your fault, you know."

Toli blinked. "What?"

A small, sad smile settled on her sister's face. "I've been thinking about it, and what happened to Father was not your fault. You made a mistake. And—you told us in your own time. I . . . I wish you had told me—us—sooner, but . . . I understand."

"But if I had just listened, he wouldn't have turned his back on the dragons. He wouldn't . . ."

Petal sniffed, and letting go of Toli's hands, she shook her head.

"You're wrong," Wix said, picking his way across the crystals to stand next to them. "Listen. You haven't thought this through. What do you think would have happened if you'd listened to your father?"

"I think he'd still be alive, that's what I think."

"I'm not sure that's true, Toli."

Toli opened and closed her mouth as if she'd forgotten how to form words. "Well. We'll never know."

"Wix is right. You couldn't have saved him," Petal insisted. "Even if you hadn't been there, Toli. Even if you'd listened to him and stayed in the Hall, you still couldn't have changed what happened."

Despite the darkness under the Mountain, and the hollow feeling in her chest, Toli felt a weight lift. She let her eyes drift shut. "I'm sorry," she said again. Petal didn't say anything, but after a long moment, she wrapped her arms around Toli with a sigh.

Toli met Wix's eyes as she held Petal close. "Thank you for coming with me. Both of you."

Dral cleared his throat. Toli was surprised to see the dragon had stepped back, giving them a moment to say good-bye. "We must hurry," he growled.

"There's no one I'd rather have a death-defying journey with, Princess," Wix squeezed her tightly enough to make her back crack. "I'll give you some advice for free, though," he added, tipping his chin at her bow. "If you decide to shoot something . . . don't miss."

Petal rolled her eyes. "Just find Mother, and stay safe."

"What about you?"

"What about me? We're the princesses of Ire, and we're in this together. I'll trust you to stop this. And you—you have to trust Wix and me to take care of ourselves in the meantime. Okay?"

Toli pulled Ruby into her arms, cradling her close. The dragon was gray. Only the scales around her mouth and at the crest of her head still held their fire. Goose bumps ran down her back. What if she didn't make it?

Her sister wasn't a child anymore. She could take care of herself. "At least take my cloak." She slipped it off, the soft fur caressing her hand as she gave it to her sister. "It may come in handy and . . . be careful! You too," she snapped at Wix, forcing a laugh. "Stay alive, or I may kill you myself."

He gave her a mock salute. They watched, holding tightly to the crystals along the edge of the open geode, as Dral plucked Toli up and set her down on the cavern floor.

"Find your queen. When you do, you will find mine. They will be down—near the heart of the Mountain. Return the youngling and warn her," he said. "Tell her that Dral has given this gift freely."

Toli nodded and ran from the chamber. She couldn't help but wonder if Dral's words would help her earn the Mother's trust—or if they would only make things worse.

CHAPTER NINETEEN

With careful steps, Toli followed the path back out to the main cavern, staying as close to the walls as she could. Her fingers hovered over the curve of her bow. She wasn't sorry she'd left Spar's gift with Petal. She had no need for it in the heat of the Mountain, but she missed the comfort of it all the same. The thought made her heart hurt.

She passed several dragons dozing or grooming. At first she thought they didn't notice her, but as she passed by, a blue dragon near the edge of a wide crevasse cracked open an eye to follow her progress. A huge yellow one huffed steam as she passed, but none moved to question or stop her. They must have seen her with Bola or with Cata.

A narrow entrance at the far side of the cavern coiled down into the Mountain. It got darker the farther she went. Every inhalation scorched her throat. She followed the path down and down into the darkness. The heart of the Mountain, Dral had said. The Dragon-Mother was near the heart of the Mountain. She prayed to Nya that her own mother might be there too.

With every step, Toli agonized over what words she should say. She imagined trying to convince the Queen of dragons. "I'm sorry we nearly killed your child. Yes, she's here. Yes, still alive. We didn't realize Spar hated you so much, and by the way, you're about to be betrayed by the dragon who took Ruby in the first place. Please don't hurt my mother. Please don't hurt me. Please don't destroy us all."

Toli took a gulp of air. She fought the urge to yell her mother's name—to call out and listen for her answer. The longing to run ahead and search gathered in the muscles of her legs like an ache, but they were heavy with the heat, and ahead of her, more darkness awaited.

She started to feel light-headed, her vision narrowing as she took one step and then another. *I'm going to pass out*, she thought.

A cool gust of fresh air brushed across her like a beacon.

One shuddering breath, and Toli couldn't wait a second longer. She pushed forward into a chamber off to the left, where the air was coming from. A wide shaft in the vaulted ceiling stretched up, open to the sky. Moments passed as she stood gasping. The weaving aurora, visible through the hole and so very far away, told her she was much deeper inside the Mountain than she had realized. She'd never been happier to see the Father's stingy green light.

It wasn't until she had stood for some time, gulping air like some kind of dying beast, that she was able to lower her gaze from the sky and really look around the chamber.

It was huge, and the walls and the arching ceiling—even the floor—were covered in glittering gems. Purples and reds and blues competed for her attention as she turned around to take it in.

A soft rushing sound caught her ear. A sinuous white dragon curled around an enormous crystal. There was only *one* white dragon. The Dragon-Mother's eyes watched Toli as she slid closer. Her head was massive, encircled by a mane of what looked like long white quills, each tipped with iridescent feathers. They quivered and waved in the air as though there was a breeze.

Her eyes were the same silver hue as Nya's light when it shone against the frost. The Dragon-Mother shifted forward until the quills danced over Toli's head. They shook in the air around the Mother's long scaled muzzle when she spoke, as mesmerizing as the aurora. Her voice was like the last breath of a storm—so quiet, Toli had to lean closer to catch her words.

"So. You are one of hers."

Toli answered with her own voice pitched low, hesitant to disturb the peace. "If by 'hers' you mean Queen Una's, then yes. I'm Anatolia Strongarm—firstborn. I think you know my mother."

The Dragon-Mother's quills waved and shook. "I am aware."

Toli paused. That could mean anything.

"So, Princess. My sister Krala has told me that it was not my brethren, but you and your people who took my child. Tell me, have you come to return my youngling?" A deep rattle filled the room as she slid around Toli.

"That's a lie!" Toli said, forcing herself to stay calm. "Krala lied to you. We didn't take her . . . but, yes . . . I do have her with me now." She loosened the rope around her waist and reached into her tunic to gather Ruby into her arms. "We named her Ruby," she whispered, a surge of pride echoing in her voice. "Will she be okay?"

The Dragon-Queen hesitated, a split-second pause before she finished shifting around Toli, and lowered her head. She placed her muzzle over the young dragon, inhaling deeply. "What you say about Krala interests me. You will explain. *Ruby.* You have named her in the way of your people."

Words stuck in Toli's throat, and she nodded.

"I see." The Dragon-Mother inhaled, pressing her nostrils close again. Toli shivered, despite the heat.

"Is my mother safe? Is she—alive?"

"Did you steal my child?"

"We didn't steal her. I swear! It was Krala Frost—"

The Dragon-Mother hissed a laugh. "So you say."

"But it's true!"

"Shhh. You want answers. So do I. But first there must be trust between us. You have brought her home. That speaks of your wisdom, child, but not of your intent." The mother's head lifted high above Toli. "I have my own questions about my sister Krala. So I will have the truth of you, though we have no Seer as they do in the South."

Toli swallowed.

"Follow me."

The Mother led her to the back of the cavern. There, a large geode, neatly sliced in half, rose from the floor. It was about two feet across and filled within a few inches of its crystalline edge with thick silver liquid. Toli reached out to touch it.

"Do not," the mother hissed. "It is sacred. And," she added, lowering her head to peer at Toli, "it is poison."

Toli snatched her hand back.

"Look inside, and tell me what you see."

"But—" Toli stilled as the Dragon-Mother's gaze narrowed.

"There will be something between us, Firstborn. It will be trust, or it will be death. You will choose."

Toli's throat tightened. She set Ruby down gently, and bent to peer into the silver liquid as it lapped at the crystals inside the geode. At first she saw nothing. Then images began to roll like fog over the surface. She saw the shapes of people. Lots of people. They were in a place Toli had never seen before.

Something wide and dark rolled over the landscape. Toli remembered Petal's story of the long-ago sea. "Waves," she whispered. Sleds scattered over the surface. Hundreds of sleds like hers—like the one they had burned. Her breath caught. "It's true!" A chill shook her body. "There are people in the South."

She saw dragons filling the sky, their feathers and scales flashing reflections on the water. She gasped when they began to fall. One by one the sky emptied as they lost control and plunged, disappearing under the dark water.

The scene changed as the sea rose and fell in waves, and she could see that there were things below the water—huge forms that shifted with bright flashes of light. Were they *dragons*? If so, they were like no dragons Toli had ever seen before. She leaned closer, struggling to see more as they undulated through the water.

The sea in the South.

The *people* in the South.

"Who are they?" she cried as the scene changed again and she watched people along the shore drag nets from under the surface. The nets appeared out of the dark waves as though they were being conjured from nothing, and they were full of fish— more than Toli had ever seen in her life.

The faces of the people turned toward her. She caught glimpses of luminescent skin—amber eyes. Did they know about Toli and the people of Gall? Had they always been there? The dragons were back in the sky—all around, but how could that be? Questions piled up in Toli's head, all clamoring for answers.

Toli shuddered. This was all wrong. There were no people in the South. Her mother would have known. Wouldn't she? *Someone* would have known!

She leaned closer to the surface of the silver liquid, and as if it somehow sensed her need to understand, her view shifted closer. Their faces were strange—yes, but certainly human. A girl Toli's age spun to stare up at the sky as if she could feel Toli watching.

Dread shifted in Toli's gut like a living thing, cold and squirming. "It can't be true," she whispered, her thoughts rolling like the waves in the liquid silver beneath her. "I don't understand."

The rush of the Dragon-Mother's breath echoed around her. A cloud of steam rolled across her vision. "Your understanding can wait. Tell me what you see. Tell me the truth."

Could the Dragon-Mother not see the truth for herself? Toli wondered. Or was it a test? She considered lying. She could share a vision of her mother, walking free—of all of them, leaving the Mountain together, safe and sound.

The Dragon-Mother rattled. "What . . . do . . . you . . . see?"

The pool of silver showed her something else.

Toli leaned closer, her nose almost touching the surface. It smelled of salt, and metal, and heat.

Something huge fell from the sky, sending up a giant wave.

Toli jerked back.

"What is it? What do you see?"

"Wait. Just a minute." Toli took a breath and leaned in again. A dragon rose, struggling out of the surface of the sea.

She leaned closer as it turned.

"Tell me, Firstborn!"

Toli gasped. It was the Dragon-Mother. It was the Dragon-

Mother sinking again below the surface of the dark water. This time, she didn't come back up.

The truth spilled from Toli's lips, her voice cracking like ice. "You can't win," she said, and scuttled back as the enormous head of a strange dragon, more spines than scales, rose from the pool of silver. It crackled with electricity as its mouth gaped wide. Toli stumbled, falling against the Dragon-Mother as the strange dragon withdrew into the silver sea.

The Dragon-Mother turned away. "What else?"

"I . . . I saw people. People everywhere—but they don't look like us! They were on the land and . . . and in the sea, on sleds. They have nets full of fish. And I think there were other dragons too, below the water. They lit up under the water. And I . . . I saw your dragons falling from the sky, disappearing into the sea."

The Dragon-Mother spun with a hiss.

Toli raised her eyes to meet the Dragon-Mother's gaze. "And I saw you fall too."

The dragon's muzzle wrinkled into a sneer, as though the thought carried a bad smell. "Just so, Firstborn." She slipped around Toli, circling her and the silver pool with a rasping of scale on stone.

"Who are they? All those people?"

The Mother rattled. "They are humans—like you."

"But they look so different. Where did they come from?"

Dry laughter rustled through the cavern. "Perhaps your Daughter Moon made them. They have been there as long as I."

"And the dragons in the South? They aren't like you, are they."

"No. Not like my brethren."

A growing sense of foreboding made Toli pause. Was there a connection between her vision and what was happening now? "Is that . . . is that why you took my mother? Is it something to do with them?"

"If I am to have allies of your kind, only the mightiest will do. Your mother is a queen. I need a queen's might. I must have the strongest weapons at my side. Now it is my turn, little Firstborn. Give me my child. I'll send for one I trust to take her to the center," the Mother hissed. "The Mountain will heal her."

"Will I . . . will I see her again?"

The dragon's eyes widened. "Do you wish to?"

Toli swallowed. "Yes," she whispered. "And . . . what about my mother and my sister—and my friend?"

The dragon rattled, lifting one pale talon. It came to rest on Toli's chest, gentle as a kiss. "Now. You will tell me everything. You will tell me which of my seethe you believe has become unfaithful, and I will judge your words. You will tell me how my young came to be poisoned in your care. You will tell me what you know," she said, her silver pupils narrowing. "And you will be precise."

Toli wanted answers—about her family, about Ruby, and about what she'd seen in the sacred pool. But one look at the Dragon-Mother's silver eyes told her she would have to be patient. She swallowed, and began to talk. She didn't hold back. Every instinct told her that if she wanted to save her mother, she should tell all, and that if she lied to the Dragon-Mother, or left things out, the dragon would know—so she told her everything. She started with the day her father died, the same day Spar got her burns.

Toli was telling how Ruby had saved them by starting the pieces of the sled blazing when a small red dragon entered the cavern to take Ruby to the heart of the Mountain. Toli's heart sank as they vanished down a winding black path into the dark. She hadn't even had a chance to say goodbye.

A bitter taste rose in her throat as she hurried to tell the rest, and when she was done, the Dragon-Mother coiled around her. She lowered her head so that it hung even with Toli's. Her silver eyes held golden flecks that sparked in the light. Like Ruby's, Toli thought.

"So, Dral is true." The Dragon-Mother rose, lifting her ample, sinuous body to tower over Toli. "You were wise to tell me all." Her tongue flicked the air near Toli's head. "I would taste human lies." A smug look settled on her face. "Krala Frost has forgotten how to scent a lie—or perhaps she never knew. She was always less than I. Tell me, girl. Will they be here soon—my treacherous brood?"

As the Dragon-Mother spoke, she coiled around Toli, not quite touching Toli's body, the rush of scales like a rising wind. "Are they on their way now—my unfaithful aunts? My false uncles? My faithless daughters? Are they coming to free the blood from my veins?"

"Yes." Toli forced the word through her stiff lips. "I don't know when. I don't think Dral will come. I . . . I'm telling the truth."

The Dragon-Mother's head dropped. "Dral mourns for his sister. He knows Krala is mine to punish. I am the Mother," she said, her body rising higher. Her eyes gleamed down at Toli. "There is nothing in this mountain that is not mine."

Like prey, Toli froze, fighting the urge to run—to try to run. "What can I do?" The words, dry with fear, stuck at the back of her throat.

The Dragon-Mother's quills stiffened, the shining feather-tips shivering around her face like leaves on a tree. "You cannot help me, Gall's firstborn. I will have help enough."

"Then please. Please tell me if my mother is okay? Is she alive?"

The Dragon-Mother uncoiled, spinning away as if she were going to leave. Toli opened her mouth to protest, then caught a glimpse of something beneath the dragon's scales. Her mother's face, peering up at her from under a layer of crystal, and smiling.

Toli fell to her knees, peering down through the floor. There was a small cave below this one, sealed with crystal. Her mother was there, one palm pressed upward to meet Toli's own. She could see her mother's mouth moving, but the crystal was too thick to hear her.

"She asks if you are hurt," the Dragon-Mother whispered, coiling back to hang over Toli's shoulder. "You may reassure her."

Toli shook her head, then pointed at her mother. The queen

shook her head too, and Toli exhaled a sigh. Her mother glanced over Toli's shoulder, and the flash of alarm that flew over her face tipped Toli off. She dived away, rolling to a crouch as the Dragon-Mother's teeth snapped behind her. "What are you doing? I thought you believed me! I brought Ruby back to you!"

The dragon's quills quivered. "I do believe you! That is why you are alive. But you are a queen's firstborn! All firstborns must endure testing. I wish to know your mettle. You wish me to trust you—therefore you must be tested. Did you think there would be only one test?"

The Dragon-Mother huffed a breath of steam. A slow rattle filled the room. Toli raised her bow and drew the arrow back. As she looked the Dragon-Mother in the eyes, Spar's words came back to her. *A child of Gall is a child of the ice. You must be centered and certain before taking any action—even a breath.*

"You're fast. That is good. So is your mother."

Toli took a deep breath, and her mind cleared. She lowered her bow. *I'm not here to kill an enemy*, she thought. *And I'm not here to make one either. If it is a test of trust, then my only task is to survive.*

"A wise choice," the Dragon-Mother rattled. "But the test is not over." She shot forward, her mouth gaping, fire bursting in her throat. The flames raced toward Toli as she launched herself backward over the dragon's tail. A tall, transparent crystal clipped her shoulder, but protected her from the blast. She could see the fire on the other side of her. The crystal grew hot.

"Why is my mother in there?" she called, running for

another gem—a wide red stone. She felt, rather than saw, the Dragon-Mother behind her and turned, throwing herself behind a cluster of obsidian.

"For her own safety."

"Why are you doing this?" A rush of scales sounded against the floor of the cavern as the Mother came slowly around to face Toli.

"Might," she hissed, "isss right."

Sweat dripped down Toli's face and into her eyes. She wiped it away, trying to will her heart to stop racing. She caught a glimpse of the Dragon-Mother's quills dancing above her.

"My children are full of pride," the dragon hissed. "As is right. In the South, there are many upon many of your people. They aid our foe—you glimpsed them in the silver—dragons of the sea." She slipped forward, her scales gleaming. "I do not wish to have any more of my children taken from me."

"The dragons falling—" Toli began.

The Dragon-Mother shook her head, sending her mane of quills waving like a forest in the wind. The quills clacked like trees shivering together, echoes ricocheting off the cavern walls. "I hoped what I saw was a mistake. But you saw the same—saw us fall. The visions are signs, I believe. A sign of failure if we do not find a different way."

She turned away from Toli, her slow hiss echoing as she rose to survey the cavern. "There will be time enough for this chatter later," she whispered. "You will do."

"I will?"

A cloud of steam. "You have earned my trust. For now. Let us wait."

Toli gave her head a shake. Talking to the Dragon-Mother, it was hard to know which way was up. Was she safe—or not? Her mind had to run just to keep up. "What are we waiting for?"

"I will settle with Krala, and with all my disloyal brethren. Your mother has explained that your people will worry. I see she was correct. If I survive the battle, I will send Bola Stone to your home. She will assure them."

Toli had the fleeting thought that she would be sorry to miss that—the look on Pendar's face when Bola Stone *assured* him. "And if . . . if you . . ."

The Dragon-Mother began to move away.

"Wait! What happens if you lose to Krala?"

"I will not lose."

The sweat on Toli's skin was cold. "But . . . but if you do?"

The dragon paused. "If Krala becomes our Mother, I die. And you die. Your mother dies. Your sister dies, and your friend."

The breath stopped in Toli's throat, but the Dragon-Mother wasn't finished. Every word was like a blow. "If Krala rules, there will be no peace for my children, nor, I think, for your people. Does that answer your question, Firstborn?"

Toli's mouth opened and closed, but her mind was blank. There were no words.

At that moment, a rattle filled the chamber. Krala Frost slipped in, trailed by dragons.

"I have heard that you call me faithless. But you are no Mother of mine."

"Will *you* be our queen, then, Sister?" The Dragon-Mother lifted herself, opening her wings in a display of white feathers and rainbow scales. "I would like to see you bring a seethe into battle. I would like to see you fail."

Krala Frost hissed and reared up, opening her blue-black wings as more dragons flanked her on either side. "You were great once. I do not doubt your greatness, but your time has come. Your time has passed."

"You have spoken your challenge," the Dragon-Mother snarled at Krala. "We will not settle this dispute in the sacred chamber. We will gather on the scorched lands."

Between them, Toli sank to the ground. She pressed her hand to the crystal pane that separated her from her mother. Below her, the queen pounded on it, yelling words Toli couldn't hear.

Krala grinned and shot up, flying out of the Mountain through the wide opening far above. The other dragons followed like arrows.

The Dragon-Mother turned to Toli, considering. "It seems to me I would be wise to test you further."

"What do you mean?"

"You are firstborn, yet I cannot tell if you are worthy to be a queen. You show great might in coming here to me. You have beaten death more than once, I think. And yet, I have not seen you tested in battle. That must change. Your mother will remain. She is safe here."

Before Toli could reply, the Dragon-Mother grasped her in a cool grip, spread her wide white wings, and rose like wind.

"I'll come back for you," Toli called out to her mother as the cavern fell away. Above them, the vast sky opened.

CHAPTER TWENTY

On the far side of Dragon Mountain stretched a charred black landscape, wide and dotted with melted stone. The air was fresh and cold. The afternoon sky was laced with aurora light and stars, and both moons were clear, on opposite sides of the sky, as if they too were about to do battle.

Toli shivered as the smell of charred ground and dragon drifted over her.

The Dragon-Mother touched down, setting Toli on a rise of black stone, like polished glass. "Now we will see what you are made of," the Dragon-Mother whispered as Toli fell to her knees.

Get up, Toli told herself, leaning into the rock. She didn't know what to expect in this battle, but as dragons began dropping out of the sky like a rain of jewels, she knew it couldn't be good news for her. She crouched low. *Just survive,* she told herself as her heart threatened to throw itself out of her chest. *You can figure out what comes next later.*

The Scorch Lands, as the Dragon-Mother had called them, reached far into the distance. They crept from the lip of the Mountain down across a wide plain. Toli could just see the outer edge, where it met forest again. Dragons lined either side in wave upon wave of glittering scales and teeth.

Toli's heart pounded. She scrambled up on the rock to get a better vantage point. Her stomach sank. It was the highest point for miles. There was nowhere to run to—and nowhere to hide.

I'm going to die here. The thought ran through her head on a loop as she watched Krala and the Mother circle each other.

At one side of the Scorch Lands, Ata crouched, with waves of gleaming dragons behind her. At the other side of the charred arena, Toli spotted Bola, with the Mother's loyal brethren gathered behind her. And still more dragons flew in, picking their sides.

Toli dropped to the ground with a cry as one passing over her got jostled and shot flames. The heat roared over her head. Her stomach convulsed as the Dragon-Mother's roar filled the sky.

Toli pressed herself to the smooth surface of the outcrop and tried not to scream as Krala Frost and the Dragon-Mother crashed to the ground together in front of her, knocking bits of scale from each other's wings.

The scales rained down on her like light.

Along the edges, dragons snarled and snapped.

With dragons on either side of the Scorch, the only place out of the way of the battle was behind her, toward the Mountain.

She could stay near the rock, but she was right in the middle of everything. Toli was almost ready to make a run for it, away of the center of the expansive battleground, when a movement caught her eye. Something small moved closer through the jostling legs and wings. She paused, squinting to see around the twisting, howling fight. Krala drew back for a moment, and Toli lost sight of it.

Blood coursed down Krala's side as a cry echoed through the mass of dragons behind Ata. "First blood!" someone roared.

The two ranks of dragons attacked from opposite ends of the Scorch in a mass of boiling flame and claw.

Toli stood next to the only rock in the Scorch Lands, precisely between them.

First blood, she realized too late, must be the signal for both forces to battle in earnest. Heart pounding, she looked back toward the Mountain. The edge of the battlefield looked to be a ten-minute run. She'd never make it.

She spun, balling herself up in the lee of the stone as flames shot back and forth above her. The ground shook with the impacts of dragons meeting in the sky and on the ground around her.

Her mind went back to the bison stampede. She'd had Spar with her then. Everything was different now. The air was rife with growls and the sound of tearing flesh. *I have to get out of here*, she thought as a huge blast of flame rolled just inches above her, its heat filling her lungs. Scorched feathers drifted down like ash, bringing with them the scent of burning.

Toli crouched low and watched the ground between her

and the Mountain. She just needed the right time to make a break for safer ground.

Two dragons battled in her path—a huge red one with a riot of feathers and a small, fierce green one with almost no feathers at all. Toli took a deep breath. If she moved fast, she might be able to slip around them.

She took another deep breath and steadied her will. She tried to imagine herself standing on the far side of the battle, out of harm's way.

Then she ran.

She passed the two dragons just as the green one took hold of one of the red one's wings. The red stumbled back, forcing Toli to dodge left.

Behind her the red dragon crashed to the ground, its wing feathers burned away. A foul smell drifted through the air. Toli started coughing.

A black blur dived past her in a flurry of feathers, a wing whipping across her. She shot backward—straight into the middle of the battle, her ears ringing.

Toli rose from the ground and stumbled sideways. She caught herself on the charred ground, crying out as a long slice opened across her palm.

There were dragons everywhere, filling Toli's view in every direction. It was impossible to see for more than a few feet, much less guess who was winning the battle.

Blue forelegs touched down over her, one to either side, narrowly missing her as talons gouged the earth. Toli had time to gasp, reeling back, before a huge yellow dragon descended and used its tail to smack the blue dragon across the Scorch Lands. The sounds of talons grasping and clawing at the burned ground echoed in her ears. The air filled with deafening roars and a constant, shifting hiss. Toli shook her head, trying to get her bearings.

Which way is back toward the Mountain? The yellow dragon shifted and she spotted the sloping ground beyond the Scorch just as the dragon turned and met her eyes.

Toli turned and ran.

Blood stained the ground. The yellow dragon lurched forward, snapping its jaws as Toli switched directions and somersaulted forward, just out of its reach. Dragons filled the space between her and safety.

Sweat ran into her eyes, blurring her vision. Where could she go?

She spun.

The stone where the Dragon-Mother had set her down was just a hundred yards away.

In a heartbeat, Toli made her choice. Her ears rang as flame heated the air behind her, instinct driving her forward. She half ran, half stumbled her way back toward the rock. There was no time for thought. No time for breath.

A deep-purple dragon dropped to a crouch in front of her, a long bloody tear marring her left eye. She came at Toli, low to the ground and roaring. Toli sprinted out of the dragon's reach, pulling an arrow from the quiver on her back and lifting her bow. The dragon advanced and Toli put on a burst of speed, hoping it would give her the distance she needed to aim true. The chances of hitting anyplace that would cause damage were almost none, but it might distract the dragon long enough for Toli to reach the shelter offered by the stone.

She spun to shoot as the purple dragon inhaled to blast her with fire.

Her arrow flew, but never landed. A green dragon shot past, grabbing the purple dragon's neck and rolling.

Toli reached the rock and leaned forward, dragging air into her lungs. Then she pressed her back against the stone and looked up.

A loud rattle echoed across the battlefield like a handful of rocks dropping down the walls of a chasm. Toli lifted herself far enough to peer over the far side of the stone, just in time to see the Dragon-Mother shoot a wave of barbs from her ruff of quills. They lodged themselves in three dragons, who cried out together. The Dragon-Mother rose, her gleaming white teeth stretched wide toward Ata Sky as she swooped down to attack. Her jaws closed on Ata's neck.

Moments later, Ata Sky fell to the ground next to Toli, her once-bright eyes dull and fixed in death. Krala dropped to the ground just to Toli's left and rose up on her hind legs. She opened her wings and roared. The Dragon-Mother stalked toward her.

Behind her, Krala's faction of traitorous dragons began to scatter, rising into the sky. Some of the Dragon-Mother's brethren gave chase, but the attention of most was riveted on the Dragon-Mother as she faced down her challenger. Toli tried to figure out what was happening. The air around her was tense—waiting. It didn't feel over, but most of the dragons were as still as statues. It was as though the death of Ata had stopped them in their tracks.

"You are losing, Sister," the Mother said with bloodstained teeth as her talons gouged the earth. "Look around. Mine have won their battles, and Ata has taken the fate meant for you. Will you stop the fight now, or will you join her in the other lands?"

Toli let out a breath she hadn't realized she'd been holding. Was it over?

Krala dropped to the ground and let out a roar that shook the surface under Toli's feet.

Spar's tight voice echoed from behind Krala. "I'm glad you live," she called.

Toli saw a sudden flash of movement, and an arrow soared toward the Mother. It bounced off the Dragon-Mother's scales. *A distraction*, Toli's instincts told her as she scoured the Scorch for signs of Spar. Her mentor would be looking for a way to get closer—to find the Mother's weak spot.

Bruised and dizzy, Toli wiped her hands over her face. Her vision was blurry, but even so, Spar was nowhere to be seen. *How did she just disappear?*

From the corner of her eye, Toli caught sight of Krala. The dragon was looking around the field, assessing her losses. She turned to narrow her eyes at Toli and fled, launching herself into the sky. Several other dragons followed.

The Dragon-Mother inhaled, then made her deep rattle, rising up to look across the charred ground, searching for Spar. Another mantle of barbs were shaken forward from underneath her quills. *If I can stop Spar before she causes damage*, Toli thought, *maybe the Dragon-Mother will let her live.* Maybe the Mother would spare her mentor if Toli could end this madness.

A flash of black as Spar moved, and Toli realized what she had done. Spar had covered herself in ash from the ground, hiding herself in plain sight.

Toli's grip tightened on her bow. Another flash of Spar—this time right behind a coil of the Dragon-Mother's tail. Toli had one arrow left. She took careful aim at her mentor's leg. If she could just stop her . . . but Spar was already moving again.

Spar launched herself through the air, a blade held high.

The Mother took two running steps to meet her attacker. Barbed quills flew like arrows. One caught Spar in the shoulder and she fell to the ground, sending up a plume of fine gray dust.

Without thinking, Toli rushed to Spar's side, lifting her head and clutching the barb. Spar cried out, putting her hands over Toli's to stop her.

Spar's face was sad. "Leave it."

The Dragon-Mother crouched low, waiting. Spar's eyes slid from Toli's to focus on the Mother again. She reached up to Toli with one arm and for a single wild moment, Toli thought her mentor might be drawing her down to say goodbye. Her heart turned over. Then she felt the sharp cold of Spar's blade at her throat.

For a moment, Toli couldn't breathe. A flash of anger freed her words. "What are you doing?" she asked between clenched teeth.

The dragon's pale barb glowed where it stood out from Spar's shoulder. "Look what they have brought us to," Spar hissed. "Look what you've done!" she shouted at the Mother. "Help me up. Slowly," Spar said to Toli. Toli helped her mentor rise to her feet. Nausea rolled over her. What could she say to get through to Spar?

"Spar, please stop this. You're going to get killed," Toli whispered as her gaze flew to the white dragon's bristled face.

Hundreds of dragons stood still around them—witnesses to this last battle rage. Many were bleeding. Some had flown in pursuit of Krala's traitors, but among those who were left, tooth and scale gleamed in the dim light as they waited for the Dragon-Mother's judgment.

"Shhhhh," Spar hushed as Toli met the dragon's wide, fathomless eyes, her expression pleading with the Mother not to kill them both out of sheer frustration. There was nothing to stop the dragon from eating them in one open maw-ful.

"Don't move, Toli," Spar hissed in her ear. "Don't struggle."

The Dragon-Mother's head hovered above them. Twin flames lit her nostrils. What was she waiting for?

Hissing surrounded them as the Dragon-Mother addressed Spar. "Your burns . . . do they pain you still?"

Spar's body went rigid. Toli's blood ran cold.

"Always. Every moment," Spar said.

"It is hard—to be a child," the Dragon-Mother said. "It is hard to lose—and to be punished." She slid behind them, her head weaving back and forth.

The hair rose on the back of Toli's neck as all the dragons

rattled around them in an eerie chorus of support for the Mother. None spoke or dared to interject.

Spar spun. Her arm wrapped around Toli's neck from behind, and the blade of her knife pressed tightly against Toli's skin. "Stop moving. Stop moving, or I'll kill her."

Toli opened her mouth to plead with Spar, but no words would come out. It was as if Spar had already stabbed her in the chest, and all her air had drifted away until she was empty inside.

"You won't," the Dragon-Mother hissed. "I hear your heart."

Toli could see Spar's pulse beating in her neck. It was the same profile she had always admired. The same strength. She couldn't look away.

"I will." Spar grimaced. "Believe me."

Toli wanted to pretend this wasn't happening—that her mentor wasn't threatening her life, but she couldn't. It wasn't a bad dream. Spar had made her choice.

The Dragon-Mother let out a dry chuckle. "I see it in your eyes. Her heart beats fast. Yours races too—like prey." She paused. "Do you hear it?"

Spar's face contorted. "You know nothing about me. Nothing!" Spittle flew. "You have ruined me!"

Toli's chest flooded with rage and sorrow as she edged her fingers down to wrap them around her last arrow.

"You are fire kissed. Honored above all others," the Mother hissed at Spar. "You will never be a dragon, but you will be special. Soon we will see your scales. Rejoice in it."

A cry ripped from Spar's throat. "What have you done to me?" she wailed. "What have you done?"

"This is the right question at last, my youngling," the Dragon-Mother rattled as if she were scolding a child.

"I'm not yours," Spar cried, letting go of Toli and diving at the Dragon-Mother with a roar, her blade raised high. Toli stumbled and fell to the ground.

The dragon's head lashed out fast and low, grabbing one of Spar's legs and whipping her to the ground. Toli heard a sickening thud and saw the knife drop from Spar's hand.

Toli watched, as if from a great distance, as the Dragon-Mother enclosed her mentor in one taloned hand. "I will *discuss* Spar's transgressions with her when she wakes," the Dragon-Mother said.

There was a hollow ringing in Toli's ears. "She . . . She's not dead, is she?"

"No. She lives." The dragon lowered her head until one silver eye was even with Toli's. "But she is mine."

Despite all that Spar had done, Toli shuddered at the thought of her fate.

Two dragons appeared—one was blue, and Toli recognized the other. Bola Stone. The green dragon shifted forward. She rumbled a greeting. "The battle is won, Great Mother."

Bola moved to her other side and the Dragon-Mother hummed a purr. "Traitors who return to the Mountain will be judged," the Mother said. "After your judgment, they will swear an oath of loyalty in the heart of the Mountain. Those who leave will be tracked and killed." Her pupils dilated. "Where is Krala?"

Bola cringed. "Fled, when Spar attacked, along with several others. We will find her."

The blue dragon lifted her snout, inhaling inches from the Dragon-Mother's face. "Are you well?"

The Dragon-Mother rattled. "The battle is ended. Now we can have quiet."

Goose bumps raced up Toli's spine. "Are you going to kill them? Krala? And Spar?"

The Dragon-Mother lifted a single claw, pressing it gently against Toli's chin to lift her face. "So you have survived the challenge. You are strong, little truth-teller . . . What do you think we will do, little warrior?" The Mother paused. "I am curious. What would you do with such broken and inconstant things?"

Moments passed as Toli tried to find an answer through the sound of her pulse pounding in her ears. The blue dragon gave a loud cough of laughter.

The Mother coiled with an agitated shiver. "Well?"

Her father's gentle smile flashed through Toli's head, and she remembered something he had told her late one night by the fire. "We . . . we don't have much in Gall," she began. "And what we do have is far too precious to waste." She lifted her gaze to the Mother's. "Even the most broken things can be made into something new."

The Dragon-Mother gave her a considering look. "Hm. Well, it does not matter now, firstborn daughter of Ire. The Spar child is ours."

Toli knew truth when she heard it.

"I need to see my mother." Toli was surprised by the strength in her own voice.

"You have earned your freedom, Anatolia Strongarm, and your family's, but you will not return home yet. We have things to discuss."

The dragons returned to the Mountain, some returning along the route they had taken while others took a longer route back to the wider entry. Bola carried Toli out of the Scorch Lands. When they got to the crystal chamber, the Dragon-Mother, silent as the dark itself, moved beyond the cavern, deeper into the Mountain. Toli followed, the heat closing around her in thick waves.

The path turned, winding downward. She hadn't thought it was possible for the air to get hotter. She imagined she could hear the walls sizzling. That couldn't be right though—no drop of moisture could have made it this far. Her skin, which had been prickly with sweat in the crystal chamber, was now parched dry enough to crack.

Ahead, the tunnel opened into a small, low chamber. Still shaking, her thoughts spinning, Toli moved toward the small piles of glowing crystals that were parceled out around the cave. Though the light from them was dim, she blinked in the sudden brightness after the long dark tunnel. The Dragon-Mother rose up to survey the room from above, then sank back down. "You asked of your mother."

"Yes, I'd like to see her, please."

Before the Dragon-Mother could respond, Toli's mother

appeared from behind a pile of gems. She froze as she saw Toli, joy radiating over her face.

A moment later, she had Toli wrapped in a hug that stole Toli's breath away. "Thank Nya's light, you're all right! What are you doing here? Where's your sister? Is everyone all right?"

As the questions tumbled out, her mother turned to look at the Dragon-Mother and her voice faltered. "You swore you wouldn't hurt them."

"Nor have I, little queen. We will meet your other child, and their friend, in the large cavern soon. Bola told me they were being held in the obsidian. She will fetch them now."

Her mother pulled her close, and Toli felt her sigh. Toli glanced at the dragon. It was hard to be certain—her eyes were so painfully dry that it was hard to see clearly—but she thought she saw a flicker of amusement in the Dragon-Mother's eyes.

Ignoring the heat, and the watchful stare of the Dragon-Mother, the queen held her tightly, as if she were afraid to let go. Toli pressed her cheek into her mother's shoulder. She would tell her everything—everything that had happened and everything she had learned—but later.

"I'm so glad to see you," she mumbled.

"Your people bond well," the Dragon-Mother said in her voice like the wind.

"Our bonds are everything to us," her mother answered with a hitch in her voice.

The dragon paused, lowering her head level with theirs. "This is something we have in common." The force of her breathing tugged at Toli's clothes. "So, little truth-teller. Here is your mother—your reward for returning our youngling to us and bringing us the tale of my betrayal, and yours."

The queen's grip tightened on Toli's arms as she pushed her away. "'Yours.' What does she mean, 'yours'?"

"Spar betrayed us." Toli's chest burned with tears she couldn't cry. "She threatened to kill me and tried to kill the Dragon-Mother, to be free of their bond. And she wanted the Queendom and the dragons to go to war." Toli hurried to get the words out as shock etched lines across her mother's forehead. "She's okay though . . . sort of . . . she's . . . the Dragon-Mother claimed her."

"Claimed her? I don't understand," the queen said.

The Dragon-Mother hummed. "Nonetheless, it is so. Spar is fire kissed. Her connection to me is unbreakable—she is now one of us."

The Dragon-Mother led them into the dark tunnel took them farther from the chamber. Toli heard her inhale, and in a whisper that seemed, in the darkness, to come from everywhere, she said, "I have been generous to spare your life. I have brought you far into the Mountain. You, of all your kind, have approached the heart, where one day, a new seethe will come into being. Now, little warrior, you must give something in return. You must tell me something."

The darkness crowded around Toli, her words sinking into the heat. "What do you want me to tell you?"

Her mother felt for her hand, clasping it tightly.

The Dragon-Mother gave one of her strange rattles, a dry

chuckle that ricocheted from the walls. "A truth. You will offer me a sacrifice of truth in repayment."

"But I told you the truth. When I looked into the silver, I—"

The silence thickened.

Toli paused in midstep, one foot not quite touching the ground. She thought of Petal and Wix waiting in the geode. "Okay," she said.

The Dragon-Mother huffed out her breath. "You know— we killed your father."

Next to her, the queen stilled, and for several long moments, Toli couldn't speak. "Yes," she said at last, "I know."

The darkness grew heavy with a weight of its own. She sensed, more than saw, when the dragon moved forward again, and the tunnel opened into another cavern. Ahead, she heard the slip of scales as the Dragon-Mother coiled, turning to face them.

"Where is your anger, then, little bag of bones—little child? I have seen none of it. I have come to understand your mother in our time together, but where is *your* rage? I scent it in you. Do not lie to me. I will taste it."

Toli's stomach turned. Her consciousness shrank. Had the dragon brought her all the way into the heart of the Mountain, into the dark, to kill her—or only to torture her?

"Well? I've asked for your truth. So, tell me, what truth will you give me, for these honors that I share with you?"

"Honors?" Toli repeated dumbly.

"Life! You live! Your sister, and your mother, your friend—all live! Perhaps I am too generous," she hissed.

Her mother gasped as the Dragon-Mother shifted, knocking Toli off-balance so she stumbled and almost fell. "Tell me. Where is your anger?" the Dragon-Queen asked. "Will you threaten my seethe with it? Do you come here to learn our secrets?"

Toli's throat tightened around the words as if her body wanted to hold tightly to them, but she forced them forward. "You're right. I am angry." The Dragon-Mother's chuckle drove away Toli's pride. She closed her eyes. It made no difference. She inhaled, scorching the back of her parched throat, and croaked, "I'm angry, but not just at you."

"Don't," her mother said. "Don't make her talk about it." She moved close in the dark, her shoulder pressing into Toli's, one hand gripping tightly to hers.

"Be still, little queen. I am not speaking to you now." In the darkness, Toli could hear the Dragon-Mother draw back. Scales slipped along the rock as the dragon circled them. Toli could feel the heat of the dragon's breath on her skin. "Who else could you blame? Your Daughter Moon? Your father? Is it he?"

Toli's voice caught as the words pushed from her center. "No. I blame . . . myself."

"Toli—" Her mother's voice was thick.

The Dragon-Mother's warning rattle filled the darkness, and her mother fell silent.

"Explain."

Seconds passed, each sharper than the last, as Toli fought the desire to keep her guilt to herself. She had been pretending it was better that way for so long, believing that if she didn't tell, she'd never have to see the disappointment and betrayal in her mother's eyes.

Now it wasn't that Toli had stopped being afraid, but telling Petal and Wix had made her ready to sacrifice her fear. She would let it burn in the heart of Dragon Mountain, and she would trust her mother with her story.

You want to find happiness? Do what I tell you.
Learn patience.

Let go of things that don't belong to you. Speak your truth.

—Rasca

CHAPTER TWENTY-ONE

Words caught on the edges of Toli's thoughts. By telling Wix and her sister, she'd given her secret a way to the surface, and it had been waiting there ever since for a chance to escape. Her sister had forgiven her, but she knew that didn't mean her mother would. Part of her still wanted to bury it all here, in the dark.

But her mother deserved more. Wix and Petal had taught her that. And she deserved to be free of the secret.

Toli pressed her lips together but then let the words claw their way out. "I should have done what I was told. I should have stayed inside," she said. "When I charged the . . . When I charged the dragon, it distracted him. It distracted Father." It was too hot for tears, and Toli rubbed at the salt gathered on her lashes. "He died because of me."

Silence filled the space. All she could hear were her mother's shallow breaths. The queen's hand tightened over hers.

Toli felt the soft rush of the Dragon-Mother's scales as she gathered her coils, her whole body blocking the path forward. Her hot breath stirred the air without cooling it at all. "*You* were the child who charged." The Dragon-Mother rustled. Toli nodded, and somehow the Dragon-Mother knew it. "I thought so. We have spoken of your courage here in the Mountain. Were you not injured?"

Toli's shoulders sagged. She almost wished the Dragon-Mother *would* eat her. "I was. One of them hit me with its tail. I . . . I was unconscious for the rest. I'm sorry." Her shoulders began to shake as she sobbed without tears. "I'm sorry, Mother."

Her mother didn't answer, just pulled Toli into a crushing embrace. "It isn't your fault, Anatolia."

"How can you say that?"

Her mother's arms tightened, but as she took a breath to speak, the dragon rattled. "Shush. Do not answer her. They are so foolish, these children. I have been a mother much longer than you. I will speak to her. Shush now." The dragon huffed a burst of steam that scorched Toli's face. "You are strange creatures—so filled with bile and bite—but I think your people cannot see very far."

Toli, staring into the shadows, couldn't think of anything to say. The Dragon-Mother continued. "You cannot see what you gave your father that day."

Toli stopped breathing. "Gave him? What do you mean?"

"My young brought me the story," the dragon whispered. "The one who returned told me of your father's bravery in battle." The Dragon-Mother paused. "You did not see it while you slept in the snow. His death is not on your hands. My young would have attacked your Queendom in their haste. Your father saved your people, and had you not been there, he would not have had the weapon you handed him."

"I didn't give him a weapon."

"Oh, but you did. Without you, your father would not have had his *anger*, and my children would have killed many upon many. His love and fear for you became his anger. That is what caused him to lead the charge. That is what fueled him—that is why he was able to injure both of my children—and save your people."

Next to her, Toli could feel her mother listening in the darkness.

"It is hard to be a child," the dragon whispered. "You have carried this sacrifice to me over a long path of time, so I will give another gift of truth. Your anger should be elsewhere. With us— perhaps. Or heaped upon my Spar's brittle spirit. Perhaps you do not realize—it was Spar's actions that brought the strike on your father. It is the barb under her skin."

"Spar? What do you mean?"

"She did not keep to your ways. She wished to take back the tithe and see what we would do. She and your father had almost come to blows when my young arrived."

Next to Toli, her mother's breath caught. "But—"

"That is the story my young returned to me. She wanted to keep it, against your father's wishes. They were nearly at each other's throats when my brethren came to them. Once my children believed that Spar would win the fight and keep the tithe, they attacked. They were right to take offense, but it was impetuous of them to attack. They should have come to me. It was my judgment to make."

The Dragon-Mother blew steam. "They underestimated your people," she added with a long, knowing pause that said she didn't plan to make the same mistake. "Spar should have protected your father, but in her anger, she let him fall. Your father was fierce. My youngling's blood had already been spilled across the ice. He was already dying when Spar delivered her final blow."

"What are you saying?" her mother asked.

"It is as you say, little mother. Your firstborn bears no fault. No, if you wish to find blame with one of your own people, you must look to my Spar."

At first, all the words spun through Toli's mind like a wind, carving away everything they touched. She remembered what Spar had told her in the obsidian chamber after Petal had accused her of betraying the Queendom. *I did that a long time ago*, she had said.

Toli had been too distracted to think about it then, but now understanding clicked into place. The dragons hadn't just been hungry. Spar had provoked them. She had betrayed the Queendom a long time ago, and it wasn't just her burns, but the guilt of that treachery, that made her hate the dragons so much.

How long had the hunt master dreamed of revenge and self-destruction?

Her mother's voice was soft and thick. "I should have been there to fight at his side."

Toli leaned into her mother. "But if you had been there—you'd be dead too."

She sighed. "My head knows it, but my heart won't listen."

Toli understood all too well. A sliver of gratitude pierced through the haze clouding her head. Spar had betrayed them all, and her father had fought well after her reckless mistake. Maybe it was foolish for her to blame herself. She could never truly know what would have happened that day had she not gone out on the ice. The past was like the ice—it would never bend, but it would also never forget.

"You must be very grateful," said the Dragon-Mother. "I think I have given you another gift. You will return this debt when I request it."

The Dragon-Mother's silhouette lurched close to the queen. "You will tell her of your choice now. You will tell her, Ire's queen—what you have chosen."

Toli focused on the dim impression of her mother's face. What did the Dragon-Mother mean? "What did you choose?"

Her mother didn't answer at first, shifting in the dim light cast by one of the fissures in the wall. Then she sighed. "I'm not going back with you," she said.

"*What?* What do you mean, you're not going back?"

"The Dragon-Mother wants . . . It's complicated, but she's asked me—"

"Tell me!"

The Dragon-Mother rattled a warning.

"Shhh, Toli. Listen. I'm going *with* them," she explained, her eyes begging Toli to understand. "When they fly. The Dragon-Mother said she has need for one of our people to travel with them. She wants it to be a queen."

Toli recalled the images in the silver pool. "To the south? No. You can't."

"The Dragon-Mother wishes to create some kind of understanding with the people to the south. We need to go as allies to make them listen. If we're successful, there might be trade between us—and more food for everyone. They'll bring me back when they return, assuming . . . assuming everything goes well." Her mother's hand brushed her cheek. "I never even dreamed that there are more of us in the South. It will be lovely to see it."

Toli heard the sadness in her mother's voice and studied her feet, trying to clear her head, to hear her own thoughts over the pounding of her heart. "No," she said. "Let me go."

"What? No!"

"Please, Mother. Listen. I'm not ready to rule our people, but I'm ready for this. This is how I want to serve Gall." She paused. How could she explain? She took her mother's hands in her own. "Do you know why I love hunting?"

"Because of your father."

"Yes, because of Father, but also because of the way I feel when I'm on the ice, with Nya shining and the wind at my back. And when I saw the dragons in the South, and—and the people in the Dragon-Mother's crystal chamber? It was like that. Like being out on a hunt. You should see the people there, Mother! They're like us—but they're different too. And the sleds! There were sleds riding the waves of the sea. I've never seen anything like it. I want to know what Ire is like without the ice holding her back."

"But, Toli—"

Toli gripped her mother's arms. "And this way, maybe I can see Ruby again too."

"Ruby?"

Toli smiled. "She's a dragon. It's a long story."

"Your firstborn will suffice," the Dragon-Mother hissed over her shoulder as she turned to go. "There is a trust between us, and she has been tested. Your queen-to-be will go in your place—she has proven herself. I have decided." She paused. "And did you not tell me that a queen's place is with her people?"

Toli could almost feel her mother glare into the dim tunnel where the Dragon-Mother lingered. Her grip tightened on Toli's arms, and she dropped her voice to a hiss. "Anatolia. You know . . . you know how fickle they are." She lowered her voice. "They can't be trusted. Not fully. You do know that."

Toli considered it. She thought of Ruby saving them from the bear-cat, sacrificing her strength for their warmth. Maybe not all dragons could be trusted, but some could. Just like people. They were predators, it was true, and there was no telling what they might do—or what they might expect. But Toli would not follow Spar's path of hatred.

Gently she peeled her mother's hands away, and stood as tall as she could in the dark. "Let me try—please! The Queendom has to know what's really in the South. *I* have to know who the people there are—and if Ruby is with me, she and I will learn more about dragons together. Trust me," Toli said, imagining her mother's worried face. "I can do this. I know I can."

A pause. "You're sure?"

Toli had never been so certain of anything in her life. "Yes."

Her mother shifted, stepping closer. "I told you there was more to being a queen than just hunting. It seems to me you've learned that." Her voice broke. "I'm proud to call you my heir, Anatolia."

"Thank you," Toli wrapped her arms around her mother's shoulders.

Her mother's fingers tightened into fists at her back as she bent her mouth to Toli's ear. "But if anything happens to you . . . make no mistake. There will be war."

Toli swallowed, her heart skipping a beat. She wondered whether her mother knew the Dragon-Queen could hear them.

"Tell me you understand," the queen of Gall said.

"I understand, Mother."

"Good." After a moment, she let go. "Let's go find your sister," she whispered.

The Dragon-Mother hummed a purr. "I will return to the heart of the Mountain to see to who you call Ruby. You will follow this path up. Bola has the others." She slipped past them with a rush of scales and was gone.

Toli and her mother walked shoulder to shoulder, and as the path rose closer and closer to the main cavern, the air got cooler and brighter. When the huge chamber opened up in front of them, her mother's breath hitched.

At the edge of the seethe pit, Petal and Wix stood waiting for them, watching the young dragons writhing in their own light. Petal ran to throw her arms around Toli and the queen.

"I knew you could do it," Wix said, thumping her on the back.

Petal grinned. "Hello, Mother."

The queen tugged Petal close, her knuckles white as she kissed the top of Petal's head. "My girls," she said, and Toli's heart lifted.

Bola Stone brought them water in a grade while they sat together at the edge of the seethe pit, and Toli told them what had happened. When her throat was parched again with talking, she turned to Petal. "What about you? I mean, I see you're okay, but what happened? Where's Dral?"

"Bola got us down," Petal answered. "I think Dral is gone. He left us there not long after you had gone." She paused. "Where do you think he went?"

They sat, considering this for a few long moments before Wix tipped his head back, staring fixedly at the ceiling. "When will you be back?" he asked.

Toli bumped him with her shoulder. "When molting season begins—with the dragons."

"That's months away."

Toli grinned. "Guess I'll have a lot to tell you."

Petal leaned her head against Toli. "When are you leaving?"

"In a few weeks."

"Are you sure you can't come home first? Not even to say goodbye?"

"You heard what Bola said. I have a lot to do here to prepare. Maybe I'll figure out a way to ride on Bola's back without falling to my death."

Wix nudged her with his elbow. "If I know you, you'll be riding on the back of the Dragon-Mother herself."

Toli's mother rolled her eyes. "Regardless. I must agree that whichever dragon you ride with, you had best avoid falling to your death." She ran her palm along Toli's braid.

Wix met Toli's eyes. "And what about Ruby? Will she be all right?"

Toli fiddled with her fingers. "I don't know. The Dragon-Mother took her to the heart of the Mountain. She said it was the only thing that could heal her."

Petal stared toward the tunnel that led down into the heart. "What it's like down there?"

"Hot," Toli and the Queen said together, then laughed.

Wix rolled his eyes.

Petal wrapped her hair up into a tight bun like the queen's. "Maybe if she's well enough when it's time to fly, they'll let her ride with you."

Toli cracked a smile. "If Ruby is as much of a pest to the Dragon-Mother as she is to us, they'll probably beg me to take her." She turned to her sister. "I know you'll be busy—and in high demand. You won't even have time to miss me."

Petal gave her a sideways smile. "I'll have time to miss

you—but yes, I will be busy. I've got to help Rasca organize the stores, and I'm hoping to help judge the carving work this year."

"Any favorites?"

Petal blinked. "I've always loved Yassa Rall's work. I'll be interested to see what she carves."

Toli scuffed her toe against the cavern floor. "I'm sorry I won't be able to teach you how to use your knife—or the bow."

"Actually, I thought maybe I'd ask Wix to teach me to hunt. We'll be shorthanded until you get back, after all." She paused, uncertainty filling her eyes as she met Toli's gaze. "Do you think I can learn?"

Toli laughed. "I think you can do anything." She pressed the tip of one finger to her lips and gave Wix a sideways look. "In fact," she said, "if he teaches you to hunt bison—successfully, mind you—maybe we can set up a little competition when I get back."

Petal snorted. "That ought to do it." She broke into a laugh. "That's going to make Pendar and Rasca crazy."

Toli bit her lip. "Hug the old bat for me—but don't tell her I called her that. Pendar too."

The queen chuckled. "This is a great honor, Anatolia. Remember that, and remember to remain cautious. Guard yourself well, and you'll learn more about them, even as they learn more about us. It's a big step forward." She paused. "I'm very proud of you."

Toli's eyes prickled. She looked up. Above them, crystal stalactites sparkled and gleamed, but in that moment, all Toli could think about was how she wasn't going to see her family for months—and that was if everything went well.

Light from the jewels bounced off Petal's dark hair as dragons slipped past, ignoring them. Petal cleared her throat. "What do you think they're like—the people down there? Do you think they know about us?"

Toli hesitated. "I guess I'll find out soon enough."

Her sister nodded and gave a delicate snort. "Promise to tell me everything?"

Toli noticed how young Petal looked, and she gave her a soft smile. Her sister would be fine. "I promise," she said.

Wix nudged her. "Here," he said. "For luck."

She met his hazel eyes as he handed her a cunningly carved dragon.

"It's from your sled," he explained. "I . . . I thought you might want something to remember it by."

Toli wrapped her arms around him, squeezing until he burst into a laugh. "Okay, okay. I'm glad you like it."

They sat watching the dragons, talking until they ran out of things to say. Toli racked her brain for more—more questions to ask or things she'd left out—anything to make the time with them last a little longer.

Hot breath at their backs nearly startled Wix into the seethe pit with the young dragons. Toli looked up, and Bola chuckled.

"Yes?" Toli's mother asked, standing. Bola stepped back.

"Our Dragon-Mother sends me to take you and the others home. She's tired of your yammering. She says enough is enough—you're too loud."

Petal swallowed. "She . . . she can hear us . . . all the way up here?"

"Come on, love," her mother whispered, pulling Petal to her feet. Toli and Wix stood too.

Toli wondered where Spar was now and what she was doing. Did her former mentor regret what she'd done—and did she think of Toli at all? "Do you think they'll kill Spar?" she asked her mother at last.

The queen's face fell. "It's possible. I don't know," she said. "But the Dragon-Mother has claimed her, for better or worse, and I don't envy Spar right now. That's certain."

Petal cast her eyes down. "She would have gotten us all killed."

"I wish I'd seen what was happening to her sooner," Toli whispered.

Queen Una put one arm around each of her daughters. "Never be ashamed of trusting another person." Her mother pressed her lips together. "And don't worry. Instinct is a muscle. It will get stronger the more you use it." She turned Toli to face her. "We'll see you in a season's time, Anatolia, under Nya's promised light."

Toli's throat tightened. "Tell everyone I'm okay, and that . . . and that I'll be back."

Wix and Petal hugged her tightly.

When they pulled away, Wix's expression was fierce. "Don't die," he said, then spun away, hurrying toward Bola. A lump rose in Toli's throat as he walked away. She bumped Petal with her elbow. "Thank you, Petal."

Petal's eyebrows rose. "For what?"

"For stowing away in my sled. For . . . following me onto the deep ice even though you knew it was likely to kill us both. For saving me." She paused. "For being my sister."

Petal turned a shade of red that Toli had never seen on her before. She opened her mouth, and for a moment Toli thought her sister's throat might have closed. She was about to whack Petal on the back, when she choked out, "You're welcome."

They hugged each other once more, and then it was her mother's turn. "I'm proud of you, Toli," she said.

An ache filled her chest, but she nodded against her mother's soft shoulder, then turned to Bola. "Now what?"

"Now we get on with it." The dragon unfurled her taloned fingers, and Petal stepped up into her palm, holding out a hand for their mother to climb on.

Wix jumped in with a laugh, and Toli watched as Bola's wings beat the air, carrying her family into the aurora-streaked sky.

EPILOGUE

Eight weeks had passed since they left Toli behind in the caverns of Dragon Mountain. It wasn't that everything had changed, Petal thought as she moved her dragon piece five squares east. It was just that, with Toli gone, nothing was the same. Given how often her sister had been out hunting or training even when she was here, Petal was a little surprised by how much she missed her.

Wix frowned, studying her move on the board. He toyed with his own carved dragon piece. As long as he didn't remember that she'd moved more ice in from the west, her plan would work and she would trounce him again.

The fires in the Great Hall burned bright and merry. Petal brushed fritter crumbs off her soft blue dress. It was her favorite because it was pretty and practical. She could wear it whether she was working with Rasca in the storerooms or practicing knife work with Wix.

Wix looked up and brushed an unruly curl out of his eyes. "Tell me again about Pendar's face."

Petal lifted an eyebrow. "You're not trying to distract me, are you? You know that won't work."

His chin dropped into his hand. "'Course not. Why would I do that?"

"Because I'm winning again. Anyway, you were there."

He placed a settlement wall. "Yes, Petal. I know I was there. I just like the way you tell the story."

Her dragon soared seven squares north, toppling two more of his hard-won settlement markers. "Oh, all right," she sighed, grinning at the dismay on his face. "But it's the last time. For real this time."

Wix shifted, stretching toward the rafters. "If you say so."

Rasca dropped a bowl of eggs next to the game board. She nudged him with her knuckles. "Gotta keep your eye on the dragon, boyo, or she'll knock you back every time."

"Thanks," Wix muttered as the old woman shuffled away chuckling.

Petal's voice was warm and quiet. "When Bola landed with us in her talons, everyone came running."

"Tell about Luca."

Petal rolled her eyes. "Luca crouched so low to the ice, I thought she had fallen through."

Wix let out a bark of laughter.

"Pendar came forward and asked Mother where Toli was."

Wix's grin widened.

"She told him that Toli was to be an emissary to the drag-ons. She said her firstborn daughter would travel to the South to aid them if she could, and to learn more about the people of the Dragon Sea. Then Pendar said, 'Who?' And Mother explained there was a whole other Queendom in the South."

"And . . ." Wix giggled.

"And then Pendar opened his mouth."

"Like a—"

"Like a fish gasping."

"And—"

Petal sighed. "And he kind of choked a bit."

"And—"

"And then he passed out."

Wix let out a howl of laughter. "Tell the next part! Tell the next part!"

"And then Rasca nudged him with her foot—more of a kick, really—and asked Bola if she liked deerberry sauce."

Wix was just winding himself up for another round of howls when Pendar burst through the doors, his cheeks red, breathing hard. "They're coming," he said.

Petal and Wix hurried out to join the rest of the Queendom. People had clustered around the Southern Gate, some even spilling outside. Many more filled the narrow streets stretch-ing in both directions. They stood shoulder to shoulder as they waited, gazing up. Everyone was out, even the children, gathered in the streets, necks strained to watch the sky.

Petal's heart skipped a beat when she thought of her sister

passing by on a dragon's back—so high up and vulnerable. She wondered if Toli was happy with the choice she'd made, or if she was scared about leaving to go so far away with no one but dragons for company.

Wix glanced at Petal and cleared his throat, his voice a soft rasp. "Remember last week when the Dragon-Mother sent that red dragon . . . What was his name?"

"Rannu."

"Rannu, right. Remember what he told your mother?"

Petal nodded. "I guess so."

Wix tapped her foot with his. "He said they would be passing by today, and that Toli was well. He said Ruby would be riding with her. And he said they would all do their best to keep them both safe. And, yes, to answer your question, it does."

Petal scowled at him. "What question? Does what?"

Wix smirked. "Yes, it does make me feel better to hear it too—a little."

Petal rolled her eyes, but some of the tightness in her chest loosened. "Do you really think they'll fly right over the Queendom this year? They've never done that before."

Wix pressed his lips together. "Well, it's way out of their way, so it's either they're doing it as a gesture—for Toli, or for their Queen, or your sister made them mad and they're planning to eat us all."

Petal couldn't help the laugh that bubbled up. Wix grinned and gave a stiff nod as they both lifted their faces back toward the broad expanse of sky. Soon Nya's rise would drive away the Father's thick green light for the rest of the year. They would say goodbye to the wending streaks of color in the sky until next year too. But this time, the lights weren't the only thing they'd miss.

Petal looked up at the queen, atop the Southern Wall, standing next to her own statue as she scanned the distance. "Do you think we'll be able to see Toli—or Ruby?" she whispered, shifting her weight for the eighth or ninth time in as many seconds.

Wix frowned. "I hope so. Didn't your mother say they would pass over from the north, after they checked the forest bluff for prey?"

Petal nodded.

"I mean, I don't really get that, to be honest. There's no prey up there. Not at this time of year."

Petal rubbed her nose. "It's like you said. They're going way out of their way. I—I think they just said that about looking for prey because they needed a reason, you know? I mean, they needed a better reason than doing something nice for us—and for Toli." She paused, shooting him a teasing look. "Or maybe we *are* the prey."

Wix snorted, and off to his left, someone's breath caught.

"There they are," Rasca called from just behind them. Pendar's belly laugh echoed from somewhere in the crowd.

Skimming the ridge, the dragons soared over the Queendom. They had never been so close. Before this, they'd always flown high, circling the mountain before they left. They could almost have been brightly colored birds in the distance.

Not this time.

"Look," Petal breathed as a huge turquoise dragon passed.

More came, and more again. People spoke in hushed voices all around Petal and Wix. They had never seen so many—hadn't realized their full might. The dragons passed low over the ice, moving off into the distant sky like a tribute to the aurora itself.

"Told you they'd fly close." Wix laughed under his breath.

Petal grinned back at him. "Don't be smug. Maybe *that's* why the Dragon-Mother brought them all this way. Not to be nice, but so we wouldn't forget our place. Look! Is that—"

"There she is," the queen cried.

The Dragon-Mother soared over them, the pale glow of her scales so low that the rush of her wings blew Petal's hair forward across her face. Iridescent feathers brushed the tops of the statues on the Southern Wall as she passed, but few people noticed. Most of them were staring up at the small figure that lay prone against the ice-white dragon's back. Some even glimpsed the flash of Ruby's red scales where she curled across Toli's neck. As they watched, Princess Anatolia turned her head to look back at them—and lifted her hand to wave goodbye.

Acknowledgments

When a book enters the world, it gets there because of the many wonderful and talented people who loved it and worked to make it better. These folks didn't just believe in this story, they believed in me. This is EVERYTHING. This sentiment is all the more true with a debut, so I have many people to thank. While the journey required patience, practice, and persistence from me, I also want to acknowledge my luck and my privilege. They are real. I was bolstered by many other authors, aspiring authors, professionals, and "regular" people. I could not have done this without their support, seen or unseen.

I want to thank my parents, George Kirouac and Sally W. Kirouac. I don't have the words to thank them for the way they always encouraged me, regardless of what strange paths I picked or how often I changed my mind. I want to thank my mother in particular. She showed me what it means to be a loving force in the world, for which I am forever grateful.

Thank you to my husband and best friend, Daeg, who never doubted, and almost always said yes to making dinner. I am so proud to walk through this life with you.

Thank you to my agent, Catherine Drayton, for believing in my work and for her persistence. My characters and I are lucky to have you as our champion. Thanks also to the fabulous Claire Friedman—you do so much.

An endless murmuration of thank-yous to Nicole Otto and Rhoda Belleza, who loved and understood Toli from the get-go, and wanted her to be in the world. I am so very lucky to travel this path with you.

Thank you to Erin Stein, Raymond Ernesto Colón, Dawn Ryan, John Morgan, Natalie Sousa, Jessica Chung, Madison Furr, Katie Halata, and *the rest of the amazing staff at Macmillan Children's*! You all make me wish I lived in the city so I could soak up all your fun vibes and brilliance in person. Thanks to Ellen Duda and Kelley McMorris for my absolutely stunning cover!

I want to thank Lynne Schmidt. She was my very first critique partner, and I learned a lot from her. I hope you'll see more of her soon. I also want to thank Hilary Harwell, Laura Bartha, Gita Trelease, Julie Artz, and Kristi Wientge. It wouldn't be the same book without you ladies. Thank you to the inestimable Matt Bird. Long may you edit. Thank you to the excellent writers of the Fellowship of the Winged Pen but especially to Jessica Vitalis, Jennifer Park, and Mark Holtzen for your support and feedback. Thank you also to Carissa Taylor and Megan Reyes.

Thank you to Brenda Drake, and to all the #PitchWars mentors for their love and support, and to Steph Funk for her excellent editorial advice back when I was her mentee. Extra special thanks to the PitchWars PNW mentors (Rebecca Skye, Rebecca Schaffer, Joy McCullough, Heather Ezell, Rachel Griffin, Shari Green, Julia Nobel, Cass Newbould, Rachel Solomon, Julie Artz). Your friendship and support matter so much to me. *Grazie molto* to Joy for being there when I needed a shoulder to cry on. Thanks also to the Novel 19s group for their love and support and to Heidi Heilig and the KidLit Alliance. It's a privilege to listen and learn with you all. Special thanks to Karen Foxlee and to Martha Brockenbrough for their support. Thank you to Melissa Marr for her kind DM all those years ago. It came at a much needed time. Also, big thanks to Lia Keys. When I was first peeking through the crack in the door into the world of writing, I had questions. You gave me patient, compassionate answers. It mattered. Thank you, readers. Thank you, universe. Keep going. I love you.